This ... ore

Portrait of Emily Dickinson

Portrait of Emily Dickinson

The Poet and Her Prose

by David Higgins

RUTGERS UNIVERSITY PRESS
New Brunswick, New Jersey

ISBN: 0–8135–0542–9 Cloth
0–8135–0798–7 Paper

Copyright © 1967 by Rutgers, The State University
Library of Congress Catalogue Card Number: 67-28132
Manufactured in the United States of America.

To the memory of
Christopher James O'Connor
1929–1963

Acknowledgments

I am grateful to a number of people for their help in the making of this book. These include Lewis Leary, Theodora Ward, Dennis Byron, the late Christopher O'Connor, and several others. The greatest help has come from Millicent Todd Bingham, whom Emily Dickinson knew, who has given many days and much wise advice to me throughout the six years it took to create this book.

D. H.

Contents

Introduction: Emily Dickinson's Prose » 3

1 Home and Family » 25

2 Growth » 51

3 Preceptors and Poetry » 77

4 Crisis » 101

5 Royalty » 129

6 The Queen Recluse » 158

7 Sacred Friendships » 183

8 The Weight of Grief » 214

Notes » 246

Index » 261

An earnest letter is or should be a life-
warrant or death-warrant, for what is each
instant but a gun, harmless because
"unloaded," but that touched "goes off?"
—*Emily Dickinson*

Introduction:
Emily Dickinson's Prose

"Last night the Warings had their novel wedding fes-
tival," T. W. Higginson wrote to his sister in 1876. "The
Woolseys were bright as usual & wrote some funny things
for different guests—one imaginary letter to me from my
partially cracked poetess at Amherst, who writes letters to
me & signs 'Your scholar' " [II, 570].[1]

His partially cracked poetess, Emily Dickinson, had no
idea her letters were shown to strangers or parodied, but
she knew they were unusual. A few days before Higginson enjoyed the Woolseys' imitation of her style, Emily
had sent his wife Emerson's *Representative Men* as "a
little Granite Book you can lean upon." In lieu of a signature she had written, "I am whom you infer –" [II,
569].

Mrs. Higginson had no trouble inferring. The prose of
Emily Dickinson was as unmistakable as her poetry. In

both she tried to condense thought to its essence in epigram, trusting her reader to solve the puzzling paradoxes
and puns and ambiguities along the way. While her contemporaries gushed pages of nature description, Emily
achieved single sentences like "The lawn is full of south
and the odors tangle, and I hear today for the first the
river in the tree" [II, 452]. Such impressionism, for all its
economy and beauty, must have sounded strange to mid-
Victorian ears. Prose, especially in letters, was supposed
to be prosaic. Emily was aware of this: about 1865 she
parodied the flatness of most correspondence by writing
a poem in the form of a letter:

> Bee! I'm expecting you!
> Was saying Yesterday
> To Somebody you know
> That you were due –
>
> The Frogs got Home last Week –
> Are settled, and at work –
> Birds, mostly back –
> The Clover warm and thick –
>
> You'll get my Letter by
> The seventeenth; Reply
> Or better, be with me –
> Yours, Fly.[2]

If Emily Dickinson's letters did not sound like Fly's, it was
because the subtlety and surprise of her thoughts required
subtle and surprising words.

A biographical portrait of Emily Dickinson is neces-
sarily the portrait of a letter writer. Emily's physical existence in the Dickinson homestead was merely a round of
household chores, aside from her writing. Her poems, except for those sent to friends as messages, are doubtful

sources of fact. There are few accounts of her conversation because she preferred to write to her friends rather than see them. Indeed, some of her most intimate friendships were conducted almost entirely by mail. When, in her early thirties, she decided against publishing her poems, letters became the sole vehicles for her poetry. Her eventual publication and her present rank as a world poet depend to a great extent on the letters she wrote to Colonel Higginson and Mabel Loomis Todd, her posthumous editors. Higginson visited Emily only twice; Mrs. Todd talked with her between rooms and around corners but never met her face to face.

It is not a great exaggeration, then, to say that Emily Dickinson lived through the mail. Such a life is a hindrance to biography: the usual travels, public appearances, meetings with other poets, criticism by contemporaries, and so on, all are lacking. On the other hand, her very remoteness from her neighbors gives her posthumous audience an advantage. Today's reader of Emily's letters can know her almost as well as the friends who received the letters nearly a century ago. In fact, the modern reader may know her better than the correspondents who neither met her nor had access to her letters to others. For Emily Dickinson was audience conscious; she carefully adapted each correspondence to her estimate of the reader's capacities. Today it is possible to compare letters and to see that Emily sent her most prosaic messages to dull friends, her most striking, oblique flashes of thought to those who would grasp them.

Sometimes she misjudged. She thought Helen Hunt Jackson, for instance, acute enough to understand the most esoteric letters. Though Mrs. Jackson was the only contemporary to call Emily Dickinson a great poet, she could not measure up to Emily's pronouncement, "Helen of Troy will die, but Helen of Colorado, never" [III,

889]. In October 1875 Emily sent the following wedding congratulation to Helen Jackson:

> Have I a word but Joy?
>
> > E. Dickinson
> > Who fleeing from the Spring
> > The Spring avenging fling
> > To Dooms of Balm —

> [II, 544]

Mrs. Jackson returned the note, asking for an explanation. Emily did not reply, of course. To do so would have been like explaining a joke.

Whatever the disadvantages of society-by-mail, there were rewards as well. Emily Dickinson lived deliberately and preferred to present herself to the world only by deliberate art. On the rare occasions when Emily met her friends, she made almost theatrical entrances, dressed completely in white and carrying flowers. Her conversations at such times are said to have been brilliant, but a conversation can have no second draft. Letters, however, can be deliberate creations from salutation to signature, and the letters of Emily Dickinson show a great deal of "stage presence."

Emily's creation of a letter might begin years before she mailed the final draft. Among her papers at the time of her death were hundreds of scraps and drafts of her writing. Some were torn corners of envelopes or backs of grocery lists; others were fair copies ready for mailing, or letters marred by corrections. The collection included poetry and prose in all stages of composition. It was the scrap basket of Emily's workshop and she kept it as other New England women saved string and wrapping paper and ribbon, against a future need.

The greater part of the scrap-basket collection is poetry, but there is much prose, almost entirely in the handwriting of Emily's last ten years, 1876–86. Certainly she made earlier collections: phrases and whole sentences were repeated in letters written years apart. Probably she systematically destroyed all but the last group.

Emily jotted sentences as they occurred to her while she worked in the kitchen or garden. The roughest of the scraps were penciled scrawls, almost illegible, on any handy bit of paper. Later, in her room, she added them to her workshop collection. When she wrote letters she chose appropriate fragments and worked them into her prose. Sometimes the letter as a whole would pass through two or more drafts before it satisfied her. Meantime she would have chosen poems from the scrap basket or from her "packets" [3] and fitted them also into her letter. The final writing—the letter her correspondent actually received—might look spontaneous, but it was the last of several creative stages.

An illustration of Emily's method of composition is a letter of 1885 to Helen Hunt Jackson. The message Emily mailed is missing, but all the preliminary drafts remain. On February 3, 1885, Mrs. Jackson wrote to Emily from California. She described her convalescence from a badly broken leg, and the natural beauty of Santa Monica:

> —As I write—(in bed, before breakfast,) I am looking straight off toward Japan—over a silver sea my foreground is a strip of high grass, and mallows, with a row of Eucalyptus trees sixty or seventy feet high:—and there is a positive cackle of linnets.
>
> Searching, here, for Indian relics, especially the mortars or bowls hollowed out of stone, . . . I have found two Mexican women called *Ramona*, from whom I have bought the Indian mortars.—
>
> I hope you are well—and at work—I wish I knew what your portfolios, by this time, hold.
>
> [III, 869]

The "portfolios" Mrs. Jackson wondered about contained, among other things, the following prose fragments: "Strength to perish is sometimes withheld" and "Afternoon and the West and the gorgeous nothings which compose the sunset keep their high Appointment Clogged only with Music like the Wheels of Birds" [III, 868]. The final phrase appeared in another fragment somewhat altered: "It is very still in the world now – Thronged only with Music like the Decks of Birds and the Seasons take their hushed places like figures in a Dream – " [III, 868].

Early in March, Emily composed her reply to Mrs. Jackson. Her first draft included the two fragments, as well as a poem which Emily had used in a letter to Eben J. Loomis the previous January:

> Dear friend –
> To reproach my own Foot in behalf of your's, is involuntary, and finding myself, no solace in "whom he loveth he chasteneth" your Valor astounds me. It was only a small Wasp, said the French physician, repairing the sting, but the strength to perish is sometimes withheld, though who but you could tell a Foot,
>
>> Take all away from me, but leave me Ecstasy
>> And I am richer then, than all my Fellow Men.
>>
>> Is it becoming me to dwell so wealthily
>> When at my very Door are those possessing more,
>> In abject poverty?
>
> That you compass "Japan" before you breakfast, not in the least surprises me, clogged only with the Music, like the Wheels of Birds.
> Thank you for hoping I am well. Who could be ill in March, that Month of proclamation? Sleigh Bells and Jays contend in my Matinee, and the North surrenders, instead of the South, a reverse of Bugles.

Pity me, however, I have finished Ramona.
Would that like Shakespere, it were just published!
Knew I how to pray, to intercede for your Foot were
intuitive—but I am but a Pagan.

> Of God we ask one favor,
> That we may be forgiven —

[III, 866]

At this point the draft ends. The second draft continues
to the end of the poem, adding, "May I know once more,
and that you are saved?" It is signed, "Your Dickinson."

The greater part of the letter, answering Mrs. Jackson's,
occurred to Emily as she wrote her first draft. The changes
from one draft to the next are minor, but they are an
artist's changes. The separate origin of the prose fragments seems to have caused the most difficulty. Emily was
dissatisfied with the words which introduced "Take all
away from me. . . ." She cut out portions of the second
draft and rearranged them, in effect creating a third draft.
"But the strength to perish is sometimes withheld" finally
became a separate sentence at the end of the poem. The
second fragment was replaced by the third, its alternate
form: "That you glance at Japan as you breakfast, not in
the least surprises me, thronged only with Music, like the
Decks of Birds" [III, 867].

Emily's fragmentary prose could serve more than one
purpose. Another 1885 letter adapts the last quoted scrap
to the memory of Judge Otis Lord: "He did not tell me he
'sang' to you, though to sing in his presence was involun-
tary, thronged only with Music, like the Decks of Birds"
[III, 861].

The exact point at which Emily Dickinson became conscious of prose style remains obscure, but it certainly was
early. In the first months of 1850, when she was nineteen,

she wrote several letters in an exaggerated rhetoric which was nearly metrical. To her storekeeper uncle Joel Norcross, who had failed to write her after promising to do so, Emily depicted a lighthearted apocalyptic vision:

> And I dreamed – and beheld a company whom no man may number – all men in their youth – all strong and stouthearted – nor feeling their burdens for strength – nor waxing faint – nor weary. Some tended their flocks – and some sailed on the sea – and yet others kept gay stores, and deceived the foolish who came to buy. They made life one summer day – they danced to the sound of the lute – they sang old snatches of song – and they quaffed the rosy wine – One promised to love his friend and one vowed to defraud no poor – and *one* man told a lie to his niece – they all did sinfully – and their lives were not yet taken.

The letter went on to picture the forgetful uncle in hell and to deliver a series of curses: "You villain without rival – unparraleled [sic] doer of crimes – scoundrel unheard of before – disturber of public peace – 'creation's blot and blank' – state's prison filler – *magnum bonum* promise maker – harum scarum promise breaker – " [I, 78]. The final rhyme undoubtedly was intentional. A valentine letter of the following month, published in the Amherst College *Indicator* (and incidentally the only prose of Emily Dickinson known to have been published in her lifetime) contains three pieces of verse written as prose. The longest, with its typically Dickinsonian off-rhymes, can be read as four long lines or eight short ones: "Our friendship sir, shall endure till sun and moon shall wane no more, till stars shall set, and victims rise to grace the final sacrifice" [I, 92].

The first hints of Emily's later prose came in letters of 1854 to an Amherst College student, Henry Vaughan

Emmons. Among the long-winded sentimental letters Emily was writing to others appear messages like this:

> Friend.
> I look in my casket and miss a pearl – I fear you intend to defraud me.
> Please not forget your promise to pay "mine own, with usury."
> I thank you for Hypatia, and ask you what it means?
> [I, 294]

Emily exchanged poems with Emmons and they discussed books. The tone of her letters to him became the one she adopted when writing to men of letters—especially Thomas Wentworth Higginson—a few years later. Eventually it spread to almost all her correspondence.

Letters of the mid-fifties suggest the existence of a prose scrap basket. In January 1855 Emily wrote to her brother's fiancée Susan Gilbert, "I fall asleep in tears, for your dear face, yet not one word comes back to me from that silent West. If it is finished, tell me, and I will raise the lid to my box of Phantoms, and lay one more love in . . ." [II, 315]. The next year Emily used the final sentence again, altering it to fit the departure of her cousin John Graves: "Ah John – *Gone*? Then I lift the lid to my box of Phantoms, and lay another in, unto the Resurrection –" [II, 330]. In 1859 she wrote to Mrs. Joseph Haven, "Thank you for recollecting me in the sweet moss—which with your memory, I have lain in a little box, unto the Resurrection" [II, 357].

During the eighteen sixties Emily seems to have repeated herself very little. Perhaps she was more inventive than before or after; more likely, though, she was conducting her correspondences so individually that few sentences appropriate to one could be used in another. The letters to Colonel Higginson, for example, were far more mannered than those to her cousins Louisa [4] and Frances Norcross or her friend Mrs. J. G. Holland, far less ardent and frightened than those to Samuel Bowles. It was only after her father's death in 1874 that the several variant styles began to approach a single manner. In her last years only a few of her most intimate correspondents—the Norcrosses, Judge Lord, and Mrs. Holland—received letters distinctly separate from a general style.

The legendary Emily Dickinson—the one about whom a number of novels and plays and pseudo-biographies have been written—is a romantic figure. She is imagined as completely remote from the life of her generation, a classic artist-in-a-garret (in all but the standard poverty), unknown, unrecognized by her contemporaries. She writes because of a hopeless love and for the same reason becomes a total recluse at an early age.

The real Emily was just enough like the mythical to keep the legend alive. In the last fifteen years of her life (she was fifty-five when she died) she secluded herself from all but children, servants, doctors, immediate family, and a few friends. But her way of life was as deliberate as her poems and letters. Though she avoided direct contact with most of her friends, they remained vivid envoys of the daily world, and, more important, of the world of arts.

For a shy spinster in a small town, Emily Dickinson knew a surprising number of notable contemporaries. Her regular correspondents, all but a few, were known to the public of the day. Among her closest friends were the Reverend Charles Wadsworth, sometimes considered second only to Henry Ward Beecher (himself a friend of the family) as a pulpit orator; Samuel Bowles, whose *Springfield Republican* had gained a national reputation; T. W. Higginson, a leading man of letters and reformer; Helen Hunt Jackson, author of *Ramona* and (in Emerson's opinion) the best poet of her time; and Josiah G. Holland, editor of *Scribner's Monthly Magazine* and best-selling novelist. The one man who indisputably returned Emily's love was Judge Otis P. Lord of the Massachusetts Supreme Court.

Many of Emily's friendships came about through the social standing of her father and brother in Amherst and the Connecticut Valley. Emily, as her sister Vinnie said, "was always watching for the rewarding person to come." [5] When one did, famous or obscure, Emily began another correspondence.

At a certain level of New England society everyone knew everyone else, or so it seems, at least, to the modern student of nineteenth century New England writers. Among Samuel Bowles's writings one finds mention of almost all of Emily's close friends. Helen Hunt Jackson, whom Emily had first known as a child, was a protégée of Higginson, a regular writer for Holland's magazine, and a friend of Bowles.

Those correspondents who were not well known themselves were usually close to the New England Olympus. Maria Whitney, who was in love with Samuel Bowles and a relative of his wife, was the sister of three notable men—one of them the Yale philologist William Dwight Whitney, another the geologist for whom Mount Whitney, California's highest mountain, was named. Emily's aunt Catharine Sweetser had received love letters from Beecher.[6] Franklin B. Sanborn was a friend and biographer of Thoreau. Higginson's first wife was closely related to Ellery and William Ellery Channing. Mrs. Lucius Boltwood was a cousin of Emerson. Mabel Loomis Todd corresponded with Howells and the Thoreau family; her father, Eben J. Loomis (to whom Emily wrote several notes), had been a companion of Thoreau and Whitman. Emily's girlhood friend Emily Fowler was a granddaughter of Noah Webster. Even the thoroughly commonplace cousins Fanny and Louisa Norcross were friends of the sculptor Daniel Chester French, whom Emily had known slightly when he lived in Amherst and to whom she wrote at least one letter.

The foregoing list (by no means complete) suggests how close even a recluse might be to the intellectual currents of her time. It explains how she could write to Higginson, "You ask me if I see any one – Judge Lord was with me a week in October, and I talked . . . once with Mr. Bowles" [II, 548]. There was no need to tell which Judge Lord, which Mr. Bowles she meant. Higginson would know.

Emily Dickinson's correspondents were the only readers of the poetry she refused to publish, but she could hardly have found a more perceptive audience. Higginson and Helen Jackson shared with each other the poems and letters Emily sent them. In 1875 Higginson read and discussed some of Emily's poems in a Boston lecture on unknown poets. Mrs. Jackson memorized poems and copied them into a commonplace book. She even mentioned them to her publisher, Thomas Niles of Roberts Brothers, who wrote to Emily in 1882, " 'H. H.' once told me that she wished you could be induced to publish a volume of poems. I should not want to say how highly she praised them, but to such an extent that I wish also that you could" [III, 726].

The survival of a handful of letters written to Emily Dickinson by Niles, Higginson and Mrs. Jackson—most of them praising her poetry and asking her to publish—is still a mystery. In 1872 Emily told Louisa Norcross how she disposed of such requests: "Of Miss P [perhaps Elizabeth Stuart Phelps, an editor of *The Woman's Journal*] I know but this, dear. She wrote me in October, requesting me to aid the world by my chirrup more. Perhaps she stated it as my duty, I don't distinctly remember, and always burn such letters, so I cannot obtain now. I replied declining" [II, 500]. Just before she died, Emily asked Lavinia to burn all correspondence. Vinnie, when she carried out her sister's wish, did not read or set aside any of the letters Emily had received.[7] But on March 3, 1891, Mabel Loomis Todd wrote in her diary that Vinnie had found "a lot of letters from Col. Higginson and Helen Hunt to Emily—thank Heaven!" [8]

Probably Emily herself separated these letters from the others she had received. Since she did not order Vinnie to destroy her poems, she may have hoped that letters praising them would aid in their eventual publication. Posthumous publicity would not compromise her objection to it during her lifetime. "If fame belonged to me, I could not escape her," Emily wrote to Higginson in 1862 [II, 408]. Publication then was out of the question. Editors, Emily had found, tried to smooth her off-rhymes and variable metres. She even declined to answer Helen Hunt Jackson's request to be her literary executor. That request, however, was among the letters Vinnie discovered in 1891. Perhaps, at the last, Emily tried to make sure that fame would not escape her.

In a way, her own letters were guarantees of recognition. Emily often wrote in aphorisms which transcended the daily events she was describing. The sense of royalty which she cultivated in her poems was frequent in her prose. These timeless elements have helped to keep the letters from oblivion. Even when Emily's inward royalty carried her to the brink of rudeness, her phrasing redeemed her. Mrs. Holland once made the mistake of addressing a letter to both Emily and Vinnie, and received this reply:

> A mutual plum is not a plum. I was too respectful to take the pulp and do not like a stone.

> Send no union letters. The soul must go by Death
> alone, so, it must by life, if it is a soul.
> If a committee – no matter.
>
> [II, 455]

The overstatement, understatement, and paradox which
characterized Emily's poetry became part of her prose.
Sometimes wit, sometimes pathos was conveyed by turning a thought inside out. In December 1881, two months
after J. G. Holland died, his daughter Annie was married.
Emily wrote to Mrs. Holland with paradoxical optimism,
"Few daughters have the immortality of a Father for a
bridal gift" [III, 720]. A distraught 1861 letter to the man
Emily called "Master"—probably Samuel Bowles—was an
attempt to convince him of her love and pain. She began,

> Master –
> If you saw a bullet hit a Bird – and he told you he
> wasn't shot – you might weep at his courtesy, but you
> would certainly doubt his word.
> One more drop from the gash that stains your Daisy's
> bosom – then would you *believe?* Thomas' faith in anat-
> omy was stronger than his faith in faith.
>
> [II, 373]

Emily's anguish was genuine, but she could not resist a
bon mot.

One of her favorite devices was the inclusion of poetry
in the body of a letter, either in stanza form or disguised
as prose. Not that all poems sent to her correspondents
were made parts of the letters: the greater number of
poems she gave to Higginson and to her sister-in-law Sue
were enclosures on separate sheets of paper. Often,
though, Emily led up to a stanza or a complete poem with
a prose introduction. A love poem could become a praise
of spring, for instance, by a sentence or two of preface:

Infinite March is here, and I "hered" a bluebird! Of course I am standing on my head!

> Go slow, my soul, to feed thyself
> Upon his rare approach.
> Go rapid, lest competing death
> Prevail upon the coach.
> Go timid, should his testing eye
> Determine thee amiss,
> Go boldly, for thou paidst the price,
> Redemption for a kiss.

[ɪɪ, 523]

The final stanza of another love poem, "There came a day at summer's full," took on a new meaning when adapted to the memory of a friend, Mrs. Edward Dwight, whose picture Emily had just received from the bereaved husband:

Again – thank you for the face – her memory did not need –

> Sufficient troth – that she will rise –
> Deposed – at last – the Grave –
> To that new fondness – Justified
> by Calvaries of love –

[ɪɪ, 389–90]

Sometimes the prose of a letter becomes merely a setting for poetry. The rough draft of an October 1870 letter to Colonel Higginson shows how much verse Emily could crowd into a single letter:

> The Riddle that we guess
> We speedily despise –
> Not anything is stale so long
> As Yesterday's Surprise –

The risks of Immortality are perhaps its' charm –
A secure Delight suffers in enchantment –
The larger Haunted House it seems, of maturer
Childhood – distant, an alarm – entered intimate at last
as a neighbor's Cottage –

> The Spirit said unto the Dust
> Old Friend, thou knewest me
> And Time went out to tell the news
> Unto Eternity –

Those of that renown personally precious harrow
like a Sunset, proved but not obtained—
Tennyson knew this, "Ah Christ—if it be possible"
and even in Our Lord's "that they be with me where
I am," I taste interrogation.

> Experiment escorts us last—
> His pungent company
> Will not allow an Axiom
> An Opportunity –

You speak of "tameless tastes" – A Beggar came last
week – I gave him Food and Fire and as he went,
"Where do you go,"
"In all the directions" –
That was what you meant

> Too happy Time dissolves itself
> And leaves no remnant by –
> 'Tis Anguish not a Feather hath
> Or too much weight to fly –

[II, 480–81]

Emily's handwriting, in her last years, was childlike and
resembled widely-spaced printing rather than longhand.
She wrote only two or three words to a line, so the poems
she put into her letters were difficult to distinguish from

her prose. Realizing this, she wrote messages which might be either. The following note, sent to Mary Warner Crowell in March 1885 as a *bon voyage* message, is a four-line stanza plus a line of prose, but the first line of the poem is separated from the others to seem a prose introduction:

Is it too late to touch you, Dear?

We this moment knew –
Love Marine and Love terrene –
Love celestial too –

I gave his Angels charge – Emily –

[III, 865]

George F. Whicher described such letters as Emily's game of "Guess what I am thinking." [9] There can be no doubt that she liked to mystify her correspondents. The number of puzzles depended upon the abilities of the recipient, as Emily judged them. There are few enigmas in the letters to Loo and Fanny Norcross, but a great many in messages to Higginson and Samuel Bowles.

One of Emily's strangest patterns of speech, her use of personal pronouns, seems less intentional. "Would it teach me now?" she asked Higginson in 1867 as if the Colonel were inanimate. There is the remote chance that this was the effect she intended, in order to show respect for her "preceptor," but more probably she began to write "it" or "they" instead of "you" and "he" for the sake of privacy. The first friend so impersonalized was "Master." Emily's use of this name, coupled with "Daisy" (herself), appears in the 1859 poems of Packet 1. In the same booklet is this poem:

My friend must be a Bird –
Because it flies!

> Mortal, my friend must be,
> Because it dies!
> Barbs has it, like a Bee!
> Ah, curious friend!
> Thou puzzlest me! [10]

Not a good poem, but well enough disguised. If someone in the Dickinson household had come upon the poems of Packet 1 he would have found nothing that clearly specified a man who interested Emily.

The last of the three surviving letter-drafts to "Master" (with deleted words and phrases in brackets) begins, "Oh, did I offend it – [Didn't it want me to tell it the truth] Daisy – Daisy – offend it – who bends her smaller life to his (it's) meeker every day – who only asks – a task – [who] something to do for love of it – some little way she cannot guess to make that master glad – " [II, 391]. The letter dates from about 1862, and 1862 poems also make the master impersonal. But in both poetry and prose, Emily usually slipped back into the personal before she was finished. A letter-poem to Samuel Bowles, written in 1863 or 1864, begins,

> If it had no pencil
> Would it try mine –
> Worn – now – and *dull* – sweet,
> Writing much to thee.[11]

Another poem (of about 1862) is an enigmatic mixture of personal and impersonal pronouns:

> Why make it doubt – it hurts it so –
> So sick – to guess –
> So strong – to know –
> So brave – upon it's little Bed
> To tell the very last They said
> Unto Itself – and smile – and shake –

For that dear – distant – dangerous – Sake –
But – the Instead – the Pinching fear
That Something – it did do – or dare –
Offend the Vision – and it flee
And They no more remember me –
Nor ever turn to tell me why –
Oh, Master, This is Misery – [12]

In this case Emily is "it," the master "They." A substitution of pronouns makes the meaning clear:

Why make me doubt? It hurts me so –
So sick to guess –
So strong to know –
So brave, upon my little bed,
To tell the very last you said
Unto myself, and smile and shake
For that dear, distant, dangerous sake.
But the Instead – the pinching fear
That something I did do or dare
Offend the vision, and it flee
And you no more remember me,
Nor ever turn to tell why –
Oh, Master, this is misery!

Emily was aware of the strange effect she was creating in such poems. An 1862 poem begins, in its draft form,

While "it" is alive –
Until Death – touches it –
While "it" and I – lap one – Air – [13]

as if the poet could not decide whether to set off the unusual pronoun by quotation marks. In the final copy of the poem there are none.

Many of Emily Dickinson's 1862–64 poems employ "it" or "this" to refer to death, perhaps as an extension of the theme of death which runs through so many poems about the dangerously ill "Master." After 1864 the peculiar pronouns diminished. Emily called Colonel Higginson "it" in 1867, but she did not repeat the word in a personal sense until December 1878, when she congratulated him on his engagement to Mary P. Thacher: "Till it has loved – no man or woman can become itself – " [II, 628]. Here the problem seems to be grammatical. The construction demanded the singular pronoun, but "her" or "she," "himself" or "herself" would have been inappropriate.

Meanwhile another circumlocution had appeared in Emily's letters. She was peculiarly sensitive to the words "wife" and "husband," and she often found ways to avoid them. The series of marriage poems she wrote between 1860 and 1863 establish the special meaning of the words:

> I'm "wife" – I've finished that –
> That other state –
> I'm Czar – I'm "Woman" now – . . .[14]

> "My Husband" – women say –
> Stroking the melody – . . .

> [II, 758]

Emily began to avoid the words when she spoke of others' marriages. Like her impersonal pronouns, her oblique references to marriage were sporadic. When she spoke of the first Mrs. Higginson in the letters of 1876–78 she sometimes wrote "Mrs. Higginson," sometimes "your friend." In November 1878 she was able to write, "I had a sweet Forenoon with Mrs. Jackson recently, who brought her Husband to me for the first time – . . ." [II, 627], but Mr. Jackson was not always so described. Helen Hunt Jackson quoted one of the circumlocutions in an 1879 letter to Emily: " 'The man I live with' (I suppose you recall designating my husband by that curiously direct phrase) is in New York— . . ." [II, 639].

Colonel Higginson and Mrs. Jackson were amused by such oddities of speech. Yet obliquities also occur in Lavinia Dickinson's letters. When Mabel Loomis Todd was away from Amherst in the spring of 1883, Vinnie wrote to her about Professor Todd: "I've seen your companion once. I should be glad to lessen his loneliness in any way in my power." [15] Either the sisters habitually avoided speaking directly of marriage, or Emily's substitute words crept into Vinnie's vocabulary.

Other oddities of the Dickinson prose style include archaisms and localisms. Emily's capitalization of words within the sentence may be called archaic, but it is not a problem of style, nor (usually) are the short dashes she used as a rhythmic device or in lieu of punctuation. More fundamental are her Elizabethan turns of speech, probably gained through her intimate knowledge of the King James Bible and Shakespeare. When Emily writes "What Miracles the News is!" [II, 483] one is reminded of Shakespearean constructions like "All is but toys." [16] There is the flavor of Shakespeare, too, in a comment on a dead child: "The little Furniture of Loss has Lips of Dirks to stab us" [III, 679].

Emily's subjunctive was another archaism. Coupled with the New England colloquial substitution of "be" for "is," it appeared often in her poetry, occasionally in her prose. When the old-fashioned form appears in a letter, there is a good chance that a poem is present, disguised as prose. "That you be with me annuls fear" [II, 482] is strictly prose, but the following sentences make a poem: "Too few the mornings be, too scant the nights. No lodging can be had for the delights that come to earth to stay, but no apartment find and ride away" [II, 488].

Regionalisms are most frequent in Emily's girlhood

letters,[17] though she wrote "a'nt" (for "isn't"), "he don't" and "eno'" when she was mature. Like her subjunctives, most of her localisms made her writing terser. One of the few exceptions is the added "that" in "because that you were coming" [II, 402] or "because that he would die" [II, 431]. Occasionally Emily's expressions may mislead the modern reader. For instance, a poem sent to the Bowleses after the birth of a son in 1861 hopes that when the baby begins to talk, his scriptural "Forbid us not –" will sound "Some like 'Emily'": *somewhat* like "Emily." [18] The conditional "did you not" for "if you did not" has misled many editors of "The Snake."

The uniqueness of Emily Dickinson's prose style does not depend on these minor oddities of diction. Rather, it lies in her originality of thought and her ability to set down her ideas in prose almost as compact and dramatic as her poetry. Emily pared all that seemed superfluous, even usual connectives, from the essence of her thought.

The letters Emily wrote were part of her art, but the life she chose made them also her conversation and autobiography. Her prose tells a great deal about her poetry, simply because the same mind conceived both in much the same way. The letters point the way toward art before Emily wrote a line of passable verse, and the last words she wrote were those of a letter. Now that more than a thousand of her letters are in print it is possible to follow with some accuracy the course of Emily's life in her prose expressions of it, and in the letter-poems she sent to friends. There are still gaps—some as long as a year—but the real Emily Dickinson, far more interesting than the legendary one, has begun to emerge from generations of myth and misconception.

And first of all, we should render devout
thanks to Almighty God, for our ancestry;
that the kingdoms of the Old World were
sifted to procure the seed to plant this
continent; that the purest of that seed was
sown in this beautiful valley; that the blood
of the Puritans flows in our veins.
                    —*Edward Dickinson* [1]

1
Home and Family

Emily Dickinson was born on December 10, 1830. Her
first known letter is dated April 18, 1842. The years between the two dates shaped the mind which would in
turn shape poetry, but few traces of them remain. Emily's
own accounts of "childhood" cannot always be taken literally. For instance, she called the Reverend Charles
Wadsworth "my Shepherd from 'Little Girl' hood"; she
was in her mid-twenties when she first heard him preach.
The stories she told Colonel Higginson in 1870 do not
agree with her early letters, as the Colonel himself discovered in 1894. "But how is it possible," he wrote to
Mabel Loomis Todd, "to reconcile her accounts of early
book-reading . . . with the yarns (O! irreverence) she
told me about their first books, concealed from her father
in the great bush at the door, or under the piano cover?" [2]
Emily's few trustworthy reminiscences, like the following

prose fragment written late in her life, are vague enough
to be any country child's memories: "Two things I have
lost with Childhood – the rapture of losing my shoe in the
Mud and going Home barefoot, wading for Cardinal
flowers and the mothers reproof which was more for
my sake than her weary own for she frowned with a
smile . . ." [III, 928–29].

Evidence from others is likewise indistinct. At two-
and-a-half, Emily was "a very good child" who called the
piano "the *moosic*," her Aunt Lavinia reported (I, 33). A
stylized portrait of the Dickinson children, painted when
Emily was about ten, shows a wide-eyed child with short
hair, holding a rose and a book. The family did not consider it a good likeness. Emily's earliest letters, therefore,
remain the only intimate view of her childhood.

The Emily of 1842 is far more alive than a second-hand
account of her words or even her portrait. The reader finds
himself caught up in the breathless detail of her daily life.
Emily at eleven is not, of course, the poet Emily Dickinson. But she has a keen eye for detail already, and a pre-
cocious wit to match. She writes to her thirteen-year-old
brother Austin,

> Aunt Elisabeth is afraid to sleep alone and Vinnie has
> to sleep with her but I have the privilege of looking
> under the bed every night which I improve as you may
> suppose the Hens get along very nicely the chickens
> grow very fast I am afraid they will be so large that
> you cannot perceive them with the naked Eye when you
> get home . . . the temperance dinner went off very
> well the other day all the Folks Except Lavinia and I
> were there over a Hundred there the students thought
> the dinner too cheap the tickets were half a dollar a
> piece and so they are going to have a supper tomorrow
> Evening which I suppose will be very genteel Mr Jones
> has found in looking at his policy that his insurance

is 8 thousand dollars instead of 6 which makes him feel a great deal better than he did at first. . . .

[1, 3]

Three years later, writing to her friend Abiah Root, Emily was a little more sophisticated. The formal phrasing she was learning at Amherst Academy sometimes hid the sound of her own voice, only to give way suddenly to a colloquialism:

> What delightful weather we have had for a week! It seems more like smiling May crowned with flowers than cold, arctic February wading through snowdrifts. . . . My plants look beautifully. Old King Frost has not had the pleasure of snatching any of them in his cold embrace as yet, and I hope will not. Our little pussy has made out to live. I believe you know what a fatality attends our little kitties, all of them, having had six die one right after the other. Do you love your little niece J. as well as ever?
>
> [1, 9]

The trouble with Emily's early letters is that they are so long, so full of domestic detail. Only at rare moments are there glimpses of the poet-to-be. The "stale inflations of the minor news," as Emily later described gossip, have little to do with the artist who wrote,

> The only news I know
> Is bulletins all day
> From immortality.

On the other hand, the Dickinson family, in all its moods and doings, was Emily's lifelong context. The letters of 1842–56 delineate the family and so established the atmosphere in which Emily lived and wrote.

Aside from Aunt Elisabeth, who lived with various relatives until her marriage in 1866, the household in 1842 consisted of Mr. and Mrs. Edward Dickinson and their three children, Austin, Emily, and Lavinia. The family lived in a house some distance from the Dickinson homestead, which had been sold in 1833 and would not be repurchased until 1855.[3]

The members of the family require only brief introduction. Millicent Todd Bingham has published a detailed picture of their lives in *Emily Dickinson's Home*. Emily's view of herself depends a great deal upon which correspondent she was writing to. She was most informal when she wrote to Austin, though she sometimes mocked highflown language. For instance, she wrote to him in 1848 about receiving one of his letters at pious Mount Holyoke Female Seminary:

> I deliberated for a few moments after it's reception on the propriety of carrying it to Miss. Whitman, your friend. The result of my deliberation was a conclusion to open it with moderation, peruse it's contents with sobriety becoming my station, & if after a close investigation of it's contents I found nothing which savored of rebellion or an unsubdued will, I would lay it away in my folio & forget I had ever received it. Are you not gratified that I am so rapidly gaining correct ideas of female propriety & sedate deportment?
>
> [1, 62]

Emily's distaste for "female propriety" appears in her letters as early as May 1845—she was fourteen then—when she wrote to Abiah Root, "How do you enjoy your school this term? . . . I expect you have a great many prim, starched up young ladies there, who, I doubt not, are perfect models of propriety and good behavior. If they are, don't let your free spirit be chained by them." In the same letter Emily told Abiah about her own ambitions, which were not especially prim. "I am growing handsome very fast indeed! I expect to be the belle of Amherst when I reach my 17th year. I don't doubt that I shall have perfect crowds of admirers at that age. Then how I shall delight to make them await my bidding, and with what delight shall I witness their suspense while I make my final decision" [I, 13].

In an 1845 silhouette [4] Emily was not yet handsome, with long upper lip and weak chin, and had the profile of a much younger child. The single daguerreotype of her,[5] taken two or three years later, shows that she was no "belle of Amherst" at seventeen, though her eyes are striking. Her pale skin freckled easily, and freckles were not in fashion. Her friend Emily Fowler Ford recalled, "Emily was not beautiful, yet she had great beauties. Her eyes were lovely auburn, soft and warm, her hair lay in rings of the same color all over her head, and her skin and teeth were good." [6] Emily Dickinson never had crowds of admirers, but her intellect and humor guaranteed her a small circle of them.

Austin and Vinnie, as Emily's letters and their own reveal them, had strong personalities. Both expressed themselves with clarity and wit. Austin, with his strong face and mane of auburn hair, seems to have been Emily's equal in intelligence; had it not been for his unfortunate marriage and his reluctance to disobey his father, he might have become illustrious in national affairs rather than simply a leading citizen of Amherst. Vinnie, less bright though rather pretty, spent her wit in neighborhood feuding, and her love in devotion to the family and several generations of cats.

Emily, Austin and Vinnie never lost their deep childhood affection for one another. In 1853 Emily wrote to Austin, "I think we miss each other more every day as we grow older, for we're all unlike most everyone, and are

therefore dependent on each other for delight" [I, 239].
Thirty years later she described her household as "Vinnie
and I, and two servants, . . . though my brother is with
us so often each Day, we almost forget that he ever passed
to a wedded Home" [III, 765]. A few hours before Emily
died, Vinnie asked Mrs. John Jameson, "How can I live
without her? Ever since we were little girls we have been
wonderfully dear to each other—and many times when
desirable offers of marriage have been made to Emily she
has said, 'I have never seen anyone that I cared for as
much as you Vinnie.' " [7]

Brother and sisters were almost always united with their
parents for the two great holidays in Amherst: Thanksgiving and Commencement. The role of Thanksgiving in
their lives can be summed up in the words Austin wrote
to Susan Gilbert in 1851: "I love this Thanksgiving day—
Sue—it is so truly New England in its spirit—I love New
England & New England customs & New England insti-
tutions for I remember our fathers loved them and that it
was they who founded & gave them to us—" [8] Years after
her husband's death, Emily's mother always cried on
Thanksgiving Day, so strong a reminder was it of Edward
Dickinson and a unified family. At Commencement time
each summer, the whole family helped as their father held
his customary reception at the Dickinson home. As years
passed and Emily gradually became a recluse, she still
made her one annual public appearance as her father's
Commencement hostess.

Emily's mother was a background figure in the life of
the family. Quiet, dutiful, and pious, she became the subject of Emily's letters chiefly when her illnesses disturbed
household routines. She had little interest in either the
political concerns of her husband or the intellectual activities of her children. In February 1852 Emily wrote to
Austin that Professor Fowler had lectured on Adam

Smith: "mother went out with Father, but thought the lecture too high for her unobtrusive faculties" [I, 180]. Ten years later Emily said simply, "My Mother does not care for thought" [II, 404]. The kind of woman she was is evident in the quiet, patient letter she wrote her husband while he was serving in the Massachusetts legislature in 1838:

> I realize your absence deeply, and sometimes feel that I cannot wait, the appointed time for your return, but I endeavor to disipate such feelings as much as possible, knowing that it is not right to indulge them as I have evry thing provided for my comfort and I know my dear husband does not leave me except from a sense of duty. . . .[9]

Mrs. Dickinson was wholly accessible, completely predictable, and therefore of little interest to her brilliant daughter. By contrast, Edward Dickinson was remote; "his heart was pure and terrible"; he did not unbend easily, even at home. Emily loved him and was in constant awe of him. As long as he lived he kept a distance from his children which drew them to him. As Vinnie remarked, "he never kissed us goodnight in his life—He would have died for us, but he would have died before he would have let us know it!" [10] A few days before his death, Emily found herself almost embarrassed when he said he was pleased with her companionship. On the day of his funeral, Austin kissed his forehead, saying, "There, father, I never dared to do that while you were living." [11]

Stern as he seemed, Edward Dickinson was not the stereotyped Victorian paterfamilias. He expected a great deal of his children, especially Austin, but he allowed Emily to develop her unusual pattern of life, demanding only that she greet his guests at his annual Commencement Week reception. He had a sense of humor much like hers, though he rarely let it show. One of the great projects of his life was the extension of a railroad to Amherst. When the goal was accomplished, however, he wrote to Austin, "We have no r.r. jubilee till we see whether all runs right—then we shall glorify, becomingly." [12] A sober pillar of the Church, Mr. Dickinson was capable of scenes like the one Emily described to Austin in June 1853:

> The rest have gone to meeting, to hear Rev Martin Leland. I listened to him this forenoon in a state of mind very near frenzy, and feared the effect too much to go out this afternoon. The morning exercises were perfectly ridiculous, and we spent the intermission in mimicking the Preacher, and reciting extracts from his most memorable sermon. I never heard father so funny. . . . Father said he didn't dare look at Sue – he said he saw her bonnet coming round our way, and he looked "straight ahead" – he said he ran out of meeting for fear somebody would ask him what he tho't of the preaching. He says if anyone asks him, he shall put his hand to his mouth, and his mouth in the dust, and cry, Unclean – Unclean!
>
> [I, 251–52]

The awe which the Dickinsons felt for their father did not prevent them from expressing their disagreement with him at times. In 1853 Emily wrote to Austin, "I do think it's so funny – you and father do nothing but 'fisticuff' all the while you're at home, and the minute you are separated, you become such devoted friends . . ." [I, 231]. Emily usually wrote about family disagreements in satirical or comic terms. As a result her letters conceal her occasional bursts of temper. Vinnie, more outspoken, described an angry morning to Austin in 1852: "Oh! dear! Father is killing the horse. I wish you'd come quick if you want to see him alive. He is whipping him because he did'nt look quite *'umble* enough this morning. Oh! Austin, Emilie is screaming to the top of her voice. She's so vexed about it." [13]

The abyss between generations can be taken for granted. The younger Dickinsons were none too pleased by encroachments on their privacy. "I dont love to read your letters all out loud to father –" Emily wrote to Austin in 1853; "it would be like opening the kitchen door when we get home from meeting Sunday, and are sitting down by the stove saying just what we're a mind to, and having father hear" [I, 243]. Two years before, she had complained that she didn't have enough jokes or poetry, "father having made up his mind that its pretty much all *real life*. Fathers real life and mine sometimes come into collision, but as yet, escape unhurt!" [I, 161.]

Emily and her father never met intellectually. The one surviving letter from Edward Dickinson to his daughter after her childhood (dated July 26, 1854, and found among Austin's papers) is entirely domestic in subject matter. [14] Edward Dickinson was too busy with his briefs, Emily said, to notice what she did. He assumed that his daughters, like his wife, cared more about puddings than poetry. Of course none of the family, not even Austin, ever realized that there was a great poet among them. When Emily and her father talked about books, the conversation was limited to the father's scorn for "modern literati" and the daughter's defense of them. Inevitably, the elder Dickinsons disapproved of the doings of "the present generation." Just as inevitably, Emily fought back, whether the subject was literature or not. When a group of relatives "hoped every young man who smoked would take fire," she "respectfully intimated that [she] thought the result would be a vast conflagration . . ." [I, 250].

For a vivid picture of family life nothing surpasses one

of Emily's 1852 letters to Austin. The time was late winter; Mr. Dickinson was confined to the house with rheumatism, and his wife and daughters were bearing his presence "with a good deal of fortitude."

Soon after tea, last night, a violent ring at the bell – Vinnie obeys the summons – Mr Harrington, Brainerd, would like to see me at the door. I come walking in from the kitchen, frightened almost to death, and receive the command from father, "not to stand at the door" – terrified beyond measure, I advance to the outside door – Mr. H. has an errand – will not consent to come in, on account of my father's sickness – having dismissed him hastily, I retreat again to the kitchen – where I find mother and Vinnie, making most desperate efforts to control themselves, but with little success – once more breathe freely, and conclude that my lungs were given me, for only the best of purposes. Another ring at the door – enter Wm Dickinson – soon followed by Mr Thurston! I again crept into the sitting room, more dead than alive, and endeavored to *make conversation*. Father looked round triumphantly. I remarked that "the weather was rather cold" today, to which they all assented—indeed I *never witnessed* such *wonderful unanimity*. Fled to my mind again, and endeavored to procure something equally agreeable with my *last happy remark*. Bethought me of Sabbath day, and the Rev. Mr Bliss, who preached upon it – remarked with wonderful emphasis, that I thought the Rev. gentleman a very remarkable preacher, and discovered a strong resemblance between himself & Whitfield, in the way of remark – I confess it *was rather* laughable, having never so much as seen the *ashes* of that gentleman – but oh such a look as I got from my rheumatic sire. You should have seen it – I can never find a language vivid enough to portray it to you – well, pretty soon, another pull at the bell – enter *Thankful Smith,* in the furs and robes of her ancestors, while *James* brings up the rear.

Austin, my cup was full – I endeavored to shrink away into primeval nothingness – but sat there large as life, in spite of every effort. Finally Father, accompanied by the cousins, adjourned to the kitchen fire – and Vinnie and I, and our friends enjoyed the rest of the evening.

[1, 185–86]

Letters like this, while they show that Emily was somewhat shy, make it clear that her father did not deprive her of a "normal" social life. The position of the Dickinsons in the community, of course, isolated them somewhat from intimate contact with the town at large. Emily's grandfather, father, and brother were all lawyers, all important figures in town and college affairs. The grandfather, Samuel Fowler Dickinson, had become bankrupt in his efforts to establish Amherst College firmly. Emily's father inherited only pride and a pile of debts. It was his own hard work that rebuilt the family's financial standing and made possible the repurchase of the homestead, though he also devoted much of his time to his duties as college treasurer. Edward Dickinson did not consider everyone good enough for his children's affections. In general, Emily's early friends were the daughters of college faculty members. The young men who visited her or took her out riding were usually students or graduates of the college.

The prominence of the family subjected it to the usual small-town criticism. The Dickinsons, sure of their position and worth, ordinarily overlooked gossip. It was only when their sense of duty was attacked that they became angry. In 1853 the four orphaned daughters of Edward Dickinson's sister, Mrs. Mark Newman, arrived in Amherst. The older two went to another uncle, but the younger girls, Clara and Anna, were under Mr. Dickinson's supervision. At first an aunt, Mrs. Samuel Fay, cared for them; they did not live with the Dickinsons. The neighbors, especially Mrs. Luke Sweetser, disapproved of the arrangement. In March 1854 Vinnie wrote to Austin,

> Sue was here this afternoon & told me a long story that Mrs. Sweetser had told Harriet about us this morning. . . . She says we dont treat the Newmans with any attention & that Mrs. Fay has talked with her about it & all such stuff. I shall first go to Mrs. Luke & give her a piece of my mind, then Mrs. Fay another piece & see what effect will come of it.

Austin replied,

> *Will* those desiring have an opportunity to view the *remains* of the mischievous lady of the woods when you get through with her, what few there may be left!
>
> My own notion would be, Vinnie, not to say a single word to Mrs. Sweetser on the subject. She is not our master, nor are we in any way responsible to her for anything we are, or have.[15]

Austin's attitude was typical of the Dickinsons. Their private affairs were not the business of neighbors to whom they owed nothing.

Emily tended to give character and intellect more weight than social position in her judgments. Thus she wrote to Austin about the orphaned cousins, "The Newmans seem very pleasant, but they are not *like us*. What makes a few of us so different from others? It's a question I often ask myself" [I, 245]. When she thought someone to be "like us," social considerations were set aside. Her friendship with Susan Gilbert—the beginning of a tragedy which outlived all the Dickinsons—is a case in point.

Emily wrote her first surviving letter to Sue Gilbert late in 1850. Sue was an exact contemporary—nine days younger than Emily—and the friend who came closest to

Emily's intelligence level. Like Emily, she wrote poems (some of which are now in the Dickinson collection at Harvard). In 1856 Sue married Austin and became, in name if not in spirit, a Dickinson.

The differences between Sue and Emily far outweigh their similarities. Students of Emily Dickinson's art and life have been presented several contradictory Sues; it is sometimes hard to separate them. Sue's daughter, Martha Dickinson Bianchi, fostered the image of "Sister Sue," Emily's *alter ego* with a "sixth sense for Emily's real meaning." [16] In doing so, she misdated poems and letters until it seemed that Emily had praised Sue in prose and verse from the mid-eighteen forties to the end of her life.[17] Vinnie, on the other hand, claimed that Sue's cruelties had shortened Emily's life by at least ten years.[18] Emily herself, in her early twenties, imagined Sue to be almost a twin, but her letters reveal a gradual disillusionment and eventually a series of breaks and reconciliations.

The actual Sue Gilbert was not a second Emily. She had a grief of origin which Emily, secure in birth and family, overlooked. There were memories of a tavern-keeper father who had died an alcoholic, of life as an orphan shunted for years from one relative to another. Along the way ambition replaced love. Sue must shine; she must be Emerson's or Beecher's hostess when the great men came to Amherst; she must assert herself in brilliant conversation, no matter how much her wit hurt those around her.[19] She must live on a scale of extravagance which kept Austin continually worried about money. Sue could never accept or disdain local eminence with the aplomb of the Dickinsons. The failure of her marriage (in all but outward appearance) had much to do with her incessant glory-getting.

It would be a mistake to consider Susan Gilbert Dickinson's life less than a tragedy, though the tragedy she made for others takes away much of one's pity. Austin's deletion of all references to Sue in the letters Emily wrote him [20] suggests what he must have undergone. The final illness of Vinnie may have been precipitated by, of all things, Sue's theft of her manure pile.[21] Sue had intellect and charm: as late as 1883 Emily could write to her, "To be Susan is Imagination, To have been Susan, a Dream – What depths of Domingo in that torrid Spirit!" [III, 791]. But Sue's ability to love had been stunted early. It was this incapacity which gradually darkened her life and the lives of all the Dickinsons.

The letters Emily wrote to Sue in the early eighteen fifties were sentimental extravagances. Because they had much in common, Emily assumed that she and Sue were alike. The two pleased themselves, Emily wrote, "with the fancy that we are the only poets, and everyone else is *prose* . . ." [I, 144]. Emily almost envied Sue's background, so much more like romantic fiction than her own. In April 1852 she wrote,

> I have parents on earth, dear Susie, but your's are in the skies, and I have an earthly fireside, but you have one above, and you have a "Father in Heaven" where I have *none* – and *sister* in heaven, and I know they love you dearly, and think of you each day.
> Oh I wish I had half so many dear friends as you in heaven – I could'nt spare them now – but to know they had got there safely, and should suffer nevermore – Dear Susie!
>
> [I, 202]

Romanticism also shaped Emily's descriptions of her affection for Sue. Many of the letters make embarrassing reading. Friendship was stated in a way which sounds abnormal to the twentieth-century ear. The 1852 letter just quoted begins, "So sweet and still, and Thee, Oh Susie, what need I more, to make my heaven whole? Sweet Hour, blessed Hour, to carry me to you, and to bring you back to me, long enough to snatch one kiss, and whisper Good bye, again" [I, 201]. In another letter Emily wrote, "Susie, will you indeed come home next Saturday, and be my own again, and kiss me as you used to?" [I, 215]. Resisting the current critical fashion for treating all great writers as sexual misfits, one finds in such letters simply the romantic conventions of an era when women fainted and men wept at the slightest provocation —or liked to think they did. At twenty-one, Emily expected to marry in due time. When she spoke of marriage in her letters to Sue, the conventions of romanticism molded her speech:

> Those unions, my dear Susie, by which two lives are one, this sweet and strange adoption wherein we can but look, and are not yet admitted, how it can fill the heart, and make it gang wildly beating, how it will take *us* one day, and make us all it's own, and we shall not run away from it, but lie still and happy! . . . How dull our lives must seem to the bride, and the plighted maiden, whose days are fed with gold, and who gathers pearls every evening; but to the *wife*, Susie, sometimes the *wife forgotten*, our lives perhaps seem dearer than all others in the world; you have seen flowers at morning, *satisfied* with the dew, and those same sweet flowers at noon with their heads bowed in anguish before the mighty sun; think you these thirsty blossoms will *now* need naught but – dew? No, they will cry for sunlight, and pine for the burning noon, tho' it scorches them, scathes them; they have got through with peace – they know that the man of noon, is *mightier* than the morning and their life is henceforth to him.
>
> [I, 209–10]

Portrait of Emily Dickinson

Here were the themes of future poems like "I'm 'Wife'"
and "The *Sun – just touched* the morning," but Emily
Dickinson had not yet learned to make them her own.

Emily's early letters to Sue are less interesting than the
ones to Austin. Sentimentality was never her forte. When
she was speaking in her own mocking voice, however, the
letters became bright. In January 1854 she satirized her
shyness as she described to Sue a church service:

> I walked – I ran – I turned precarious corners – One mo-
> ment I was not – then soared aloft like Phoenix, soon as
> the foe was by – and then anticipating an enemy again,
> my soiled and drooping plumage might have been seen
> emerging from just behind a fence, vainly endeavoring
> to fly once more from hence. . . . How big and broad
> the aisle seemed, full huge enough, before, as I quaked
> slowly up – and reached my usual seat!
>
> In vain I sought to hide behind your feathers – Susie
> – feathers and *Bird* had flown, and there I sat, and
> sighed, and wondered I was scared so. . . . After the
> opening prayer I ventured to turn round. Mr Carter
> immediately looked at me – Mr Sweetser attempted to do
> so, but I discovered *nothing*, up in the sky somewhere,
> and gazed intently at it, for quite half an hour. During
> the exercises I became more calm, and got out of church
> quite comfortably. Several roared around, and sought
> to devour me, but I fell an easy prey to Miss Lovina
> Dickinson, being much too exhausted to make any far-
> ther resistance. . . . The singing reminded me of the
> Legend of "Jack and Gill," allowing the Bass Viol to
> be typified by *Gill*, who literally tumbled after, while
> Jack – i e the choir, galloped insanely on. . . .

[1, 283–85]

Austin and Sue became engaged—secretly at first—early
in 1853. For some time Austin had been attracted to both
Sue and Martha Gilbert. Drafts of his letters to the shy
"Mat" (who hid when she heard Mr. Dickinson coming)

show that he was especially fond of her in 1851 and 1852.[22] Sue, however, endeared herself to Mr. Dickinson and Emily. No doubt their support helped Austin to decide in favor of Sue. Emily kept reassuring her brother with comments like this:

> Father went home with Sue. I think he and mother both think a great deal of her, and nobody will make me believe that they don't think she is their's, just as much as Vinnie or you or me. Perhaps I am mistaken, but I can most always tell anything that I want to.
>
> [I, 242]

Emily's tone is a hint that doubt existed about Sue's alliance with the Dickinsons. For one thing, Vinnie did not get along well with Sue, nor would she ever. To please Austin, however, she tried to overcome her antagonism and was able to write to him, "I love *Sue* most dearly and will try never to do her injustice again." [23] Outside the household, there was gossip. The town was not pleased to see its prize bachelor go to the daughter of a drunken tavern keeper. On June 9, 1853, Emily wrote to Austin, "I hope you wont trouble yourself about any remarks that are made. . . . Nobody'll dare to harm dear Susie, nobody'll dare to harm you" [I, 252–53].

The family, with Sue's help, managed to convince Austin that his choice was right. On Thanksgiving Day 1853 Austin and Sue announced their engagement, though they did not marry until July 1856. Austin thought Sue "sober, thoughtful, noble, loving—deeper, truer than any 'gay girl' ever dreamed of," [24] an opinion strengthened by the continual propaganda of Emily's letters. Both Austin and Emily were mistaken in their estimate of Sue. The Dickinsons were, as Emily said, "unlike most everyone," and Sue was not really like the Dickinsons. From her viewpoint it was Austin who was getting a bargain and she who must apologize for not making a better match. In January 1854 she wrote to her brother Frank, "I see no reason, viewing the subject as I try to, without prejudice, why you wont like Austin and find in him all you could desire as the companion of your sister—He is poor and young and in the *world's* eyes these are great weaknesses—but he is strong, manly, resolute—understands human nature and will take care of me." [25]

Emily came to realize, even before the marriage which none of the Dickinson family seems to have attended, that Sue was not all she had imagined in the first ardor of friendship. About 1854 a serious disagreement arose. For one thing, Sue was incapable of understanding friendship in Emily's terms. As her letter to her brother shows, she tried to place reason above loyalty. For another thing, Sue was conventionally pious and Emily was not. Emily made her position clear to Sue in the following strong letter:

> Sue – you can go or stay – There is but one alternative – We differ often lately, and this must be the last.
>
> You need not fear to leave me lest I should be alone, for I often part with things I fancy I have loved, – sometimes to the grave, and sometimes to an oblivion rather bitterer than death – thus my heart bleeds so frequently that I shant mind the hemorrhage, and I only add an agony to several previous ones, and at the end of the day remark – a bubble burst!
>
> Such incidents would grieve me when I was but a child, and perhaps I could have wept when little feet hard by mine, stood still in the coffin, but eyes grow dry sometimes, and hearts get crisp and cinder, and had as lief burn.
>
> Sue – I have lived by this. It is the lingering emblem of the Heaven I once dreamed, and though if this be taken, I shall remain alone, and though in that last day, the Jesus Christ you love, remark he does not know

me – there is a darker spirit will not disown it's child.

Few have been given me, and if I love them so, that for *idolatry* they are removed from me – I simply murmur *gone*, and the billow dies away into the boundless blue, and no one knows but me, that one went down today. We have walked very pleasantly – Perhaps this is the point at which our paths diverge – then pass on singing Sue, and up the distant hill I journey on.

[1, 305–06]

The disagreement, however, did not last long. Emily was too loyal to Austin to remain at odds with the girl she had helped convince him to marry. Her many reconciliations with Sue in later years may have been motivated by similar ideas: family loyalty and a sense of guilt for her part in Austin's unhappy marriage.

Until Austin married Sue, the family remained an unbroken unit. Its various members were not always at home, of course. All of Edward Dickinson's children went away to school, and Austin was gone for the better part of two years while he was teaching in Sunderland and Boston. Mrs. Dickinson liked to visit relatives for several weeks at a time. Her husband, whose political activities included two years as a U. S. Representative, was often absent.

When Emily Dickinson left home for Mount Holyoke Female Seminary in 1847, she did not go far; the school was only eight miles from Amherst, just out of sight behind the Holyoke Range. Even so, she found an environment quite different from the one she had known. Mary Lyon, who had founded the seminary ten years before, was a vigorous intellectual woman accustomed to have her own way, which she regarded as God's. To Emily's mother, the will of God was the will of Edward Dickinson. At Mount Holyoke everyone was expected to speak freely and in detail about her deepest beliefs and unbeliefs—subjects the Dickinsons considered private.

At first Emily was well satisfied with the school. On October 27, 1847, she wrote to Austin, "I had a great mind to be homesick after you went home, but I concluded not to, & therefore gave up all homesick feelings" [I, 48]. She was rooming with her cousin Emily Norcross: that helped. Although she missed the news and asked Austin if he knew of any nation about to besiege South Hadley, the family had shown its affection for her, each member perfectly in character. "Tell mother," she wrote, "that she was very thoughtful to inquire in regard to the welfare of my shoes. Emily has a large shoe brush & plenty of blacking, & I brush my shoes to my heart's content. Thank Viny 10,000 times for the beautiful ribbon & tell her to write me soon. Tell father I thank him for his letter & will try to follow its precepts" [I, 49].

After Thanksgiving vacation Emily wrote, "Never did Amherst look more lovely to me & gratitude rose in my heart to God, for granting me such a safe return to my *own DEAR HOME*" [I, 58]. The brief vacation had induced the homesickness which Emily had evaded earlier. By the middle of February she was telling Austin, "Home was always dear to me & dearer still the friends around it, but never did it seem as dear as now. All, all are kind to me but their tones fell strangely on my ear & their countenances meet mine not like home faces, I can assure you, most sincerely" [I, 62]. On March 25 the family learned that Emily was sick, and Austin was sent to bring her home. Several weeks later, back at school, Emily wrote to Abiah Root, "Father is quite a hand to give medicine, especially if it is not desirable to the patient, and I was dosed for about a month after my return home, without any mercy, till at last out of pity my cough went away . . ." [I, 66]. Meanwhile her father had decided that she should stay at home the following winter.

Emily's gradual dissatisfaction with Mount Holyoke

probably came neither from sickness nor homesickness. She had no trouble with her studies, after the first few weeks, even when she neglected her geometry. "Emily was never floored," Vinnie recalled. "When the Euclid examination came and she had never studied, she went to the blackboard and gave such a glib exposition of imaginary figures that the dazed teacher passed her with the highest mark." [26] Part of the trouble with the seminary was that such occasions were the only ones when Emily could freely use her imagination.

The core of the problem, though, was religion. Emily went to Mount Holyoke for education; Mary Lyon had founded the school with a different intention. "It was the end and aim of all her efforts," wrote President Hitchcock of Amherst College, "to make the seminary a nursery to the church. She diligently prayed and sought that all the genius and learning, talent and tact there gathered, might be baptized into the spirit of the gospel." [27] One of Miss Lyon's mottoes (she had hundreds, to suit all occasions) was "Acquire knowledge that you may do good." [28] She and her staff taught their students well, but a poetic imagination seemed to them useless unless it was devoted to promoting the faith.

The influence of Mary Lyon and Mount Holyoke upon Emily Dickinson's writing is not a specific one. Some of the seminary catchwords—"rebellion," "unsubdued will," "female propriety and sedate deportment"—appear as humor in her letters. She reacted to the underlying ideas less lightly. Early in 1848 she wrote to Abiah Root, "I have not yet given up to the claims of Christ, but trust I am not entirely thoughtless on so important & serious a subject" [I, 60]. Wholehearted surrender to Mary Lyon's God was impossible, but it may be that the year at Mount Holyoke, with its daily emphasis on the relationship between man and God, established in Emily her lifelong habit of searching for the Creator who nearly always eluded her.

The God the Dickinsons worshiped seems almost a member of the family in Emily's letters. New England religion in the mid-nineteenth century was neither a matter of church membership nor a "patriotic duty." It was at the core of daily life and thought. Twice-on-Sunday church attendance, and mealtime, morning, and evening prayers were not tokens of unusual devotion; they were as much a part of ordinary existence as business and house-cleaning. Biblical quotations were convenient channels of thought because everyone knew them. Emily's use of scriptural language is striking only because she applied it to daily situations in an unusual manner.

Deeper than any surface appearance of religion lay the New England conscience. By the middle of the nineteenth century the burning urgency of the individual conscience—most clearly seen, perhaps, in Cotton Mather's diary—had subsided to a duller glow. Most New Englanders of Emily's generation felt no need to justify each daily act as proof or disproof of their election by Calvin's God. Occasional "revival" blotted out any number of sins in one grand gesture. Mary Lyon, however, insisted not only on revival but on accountability for each day's life: "Every act that is performed, every word as it is spoken, every thought as it passes through the mind, takes its foreseen place in the infinite series of events out of which God will evolve the glory of his great name. . . ." [29] She impressed the importance of small acts on her students in a daily ritual which Emily described to Abiah Root. "At 3¾ I go to Sections, where we give in all our accounts for the day, including, Absence – Tardiness – Communications – Breaking Silent Study Hours – Receiving Company in our rooms & ten thousand other things . . ." [I, 54–55].

In the Dickinson home, religion was an inward matter. Open confession did not suit so reticent a family. Outward indications of faith seemed showy—"ostensible" was Emily's word for it. Edward Dickinson did not become a church member until he was forty-seven; his decision had nothing to do with daily prayers and weekly church attendance, which he took as a matter of course. Rather, it meant that he had reached a state of belief which his conscience could accept as genuine.

Emily never became a church member. She could not reconcile the God of church and home with the overpowering deity of *Revelation*. Nevertheless, religious thought saturated hundreds of her poems and letters. Readers who enjoy or deplore her iconoclasm may fail to see the strength of her belief. Emily Dickinson played with concepts of God, just as she poked fun at her father in her letters to Austin. Her awe of each was sufficiently deep to allow a little fun at the foot of the august throne. Her family, she told Higginson in 1862, were all religious but her, and addressed "an Eclipse, every morning – they call their 'Father'" [II, 404]. But an eclipse is a darkened reality, not a void. Emily sensed a power in God's apparent darkness:

> Though the Great Waters sleep,
> That they are still the Deep,
> We cannot doubt –
> No Vacillating God
> Ignited this Abode
> To put it out –
>
> [III, 828]

Strong in essential faith—though it was often "that Religion/ That doubts – as fervently as it believes"—Emily joked about details. She told her "Master" that Thomas' faith in anatomy was stronger than his faith in faith. She was capable of describing the doctrine of the Trinity in terms of "The Courtship of Miles Standish": God the Father sends Christ to woo the human soul, but if the soul accepts, God

> Vouches, with hyperbolic archness –
> "Miles" and "John Alden" were Synonyme.[30]

Emily enjoyed her joke, no doubt, but her imagery was no odder than Jesus' parables of the lost coin or the talents.

Like many of her mature friends, Emily was trying to define a God whose orthodox definition no longer satisfied her. Her friend Samuel Bowles once wrote, "I have great faith in man, and faith in God is perfect, only it cannot describe and take hold of the object." [31] When Emily found words that could "take hold of the object," even in the form of humor, she was quick to use them.

The application of religious ideas to daily life—perhaps instilled by Mary Lyon—pervades much of Emily's prose and poetry. Like Thoreau, Emily Dickinson has seemed to many a "nature writer"; it was the nature of religion, not the religion of nature, that interested her. If she sometimes found God in nature, she also discovered Him in other parts of her life. While she was at Mount Holyoke she told Abiah Root that she could not be happy away from home. In October 1851 she wrote to Austin, "Home is a holy thing – nothing of doubt or distrust can enter it's blessed portals. . . . Here seems indeed to be a bit of Eden which not the sin of *any* can destroy . . ." [I, 150–51]. Nineteen years later she wrote, "Home is the definition of God" [II, 483].

Like home, love became holy to Emily. The quatrain, "Love is like life, merely longer," exists (as Millicent Todd Bingham has pointed out) in an alternate form which substitutes "Faith" for "Love." [32] The Biblical "God

is love" meant to Emily that love was God. The human
and divine aspects of love mingled in her mind until both
lover and deity were equally God:

If "God is love" as he admits
We think that he must be
Because he is a "jealous God"
He tells us certainly

If "All is possible with" him
As he besides concedes
He will refund us finally
Our confiscated Gods – [33]

The gradual hallowing of love can be illustrated by two
excerpts from Emily's letters. About 1861 she wrote to
"Master," "I heard of a thing called 'Redemption –' which
rested men and women. You remember I asked you for
it – you gave me something else. I forgot the Redemption . . ." [II, 374]. By 1877, when Colonel Higginson's
first wife died, love was no longer "something else." Emily
wrote to him, "Do not try to be saved – but let Redemption find you – as it certainly will – Love is it's own rescue,
for we – at our supremest, are but it's trembling Em-
blems " [II, 594].

The name Emily chose for the man she loved in 1861,
"Master," suggests a theological relationship. It does not
follow (as I shall try to show in later chapters) that the
man so identified was a minister, or even an orthodox be-
liever. The hallowing occurred in Emily's mind. Her final
love, Judge Lord, was an agnostic; Emily wrote to him,
"While others go to Church, I go to mine, for are you not
my Church, and have we not a Hymn that no one knows
but us?" [III, 753.]

By the end of her life Emily Dickinson had developed
an image of God quite unlike the God of her father or

Mary Lyon. The Calvinist heritage, however, survived in her sense of each moment's importance in eternity. Her poems and the aphoristic scraps of prose from which she constructed letters were her "accounts," her daily attempts to justify her own "election." The goal might be art, or love, or fame, or heaven, but in each she felt that

> Eternity will be
> Velocity or Pause
> Precisely as the Candidate
> Preliminary was — [34]

We play at Paste –
Till qualified, for Pearl –
Then, drop the Paste –
And deem ourself a fool –

The Shapes – though – were similar –
And our new Hands
Learned *Gem*-Tactics –
Practicing *Sands* –

                                    —Emily Dickinson

2
Growth

It would be convenient to take Emily Dickinson's 1845
warning to Abiah Root—"Don't let your free spirit be
chained"—as proof of her childhood revolt against society.
Her growth as an individual did indeed lead her to reject
the artistic standards of her time, but it was a less dramatic evolution. Emily was exposed to a number of conventions, accepted each of them for a time, and gradually
decided that none of them was for her.

The subject matter and style required by Amherst
Academy were standard for their time. Emily was expected to write papers like one which she described to her
friend Jane Humphrey in May 1842, when she was
eleven:

> there was one young man who read a Composition the
> subject was think twice before you speak – he was de-

scribing the reasons why any one should do so – one was – if a young gentleman – offered a young lady his arm and he had a dog who had no tail and he boarded at tavern think twice before you speak. Another is if a young gentleman knows a young lady who he thinks nature has formed to perfection let him remember that roses conceal thorns he is the sillyest creature who ever lived I think. I told him that I thought he had better think twice before he spoke –

[1, 7]

"A young lady . . . nature has formed to perfection": this was the style children were expected to learn and write. Emily remained herself in her letters to Austin, but sometimes a great deal of the conventional diction crept into the letters to conventional Abiah Root. "Your soliloquy on the year that is past and gone," Emily wrote to Abiah in February 1845, "was not unheeded by me. Would that we might spend the year which is now fleeting so swiftly by to better advantage than the one which we have not the power to recall!" [I, 9.]

As other letters of the same year show, Emily already had another use for high-flown phrases: humor. Probably she could not get away with too much lightness in her school compositions—in May 1845 she described one of them as "exceedingly edifying"—but she and her friends were in the habit of writing for their own enjoyment. Emily said that a paper Abiah had written was "so sharp I was afraid of cutting off some of my fingers," and added, "Please send me a copy of that Romance you was writing at Amherst. I am in a fever to read it. I expect it will be against my Whig feelings" [I, 11–12]. In Emily's letters the stock rhetoric of the classroom could become the source of humor if taken literally:

Since I wrote you last, the summer is past and gone, and autumn with the sere and yellow leaf is already upon us. I never knew the time to pass so swiftly, it seems to me, as the past summer. I really think some one must have oiled his chariot wheels, for I don't recollect of hearing him pass, and I am sure I should if something had not prevented his chariot wheels from creaking as usual. But I will not expatiate upon him any longer, for I know it is wicked to trifle with so reverend a personage, and I fear he will make me a call in person to inquire as to the remarks which I have made concerning him.

[I, 20]

Emily's Amherst Academy schoolmates could remember fifty years later how much her compositions had delighted them. Several girls contributed to a handwritten newspaper, *Forest Leaves*. According to Emily Fowler Ford, Emily Dickinson was one of the two wits of the school, and a humorist of the "comic column." She often wrote comic sermons in a standard pattern, "the art of which consisted in bringing most incongruous things together, . . . ending always with the same refrain, 'He played on a harp of a thousand strings, sperrets of just men made perfec'.' Emily's combinations were irresistible . . ."[1]

All of the compositions and *Forest Leaves* have been lost, but Emily's early letters probably resemble them. The mock-sermon, for instance, has parallels in Emily's "vision" of her uncle Joel Norcross in hell, or her valentine letters and verses—at least to the extent of bringing together incongruities. Another type of humor, the tall tale based on a short fact, can be seen in Emily's description of a cold, written to Abiah Root in January 1850. The length of the piece makes it a fair substitute for one of the lost compositions.

I am occupied principally with a cold just now, and the dear creature *will* have so much attention that my time slips away amazingly. It has heard *so* much of New Englanders, of their kind attention to strangers, that it's come all the way from the Alps to determine the truth of the tale – it says the half was'nt told it, and I begin to be afraid it was'nt. . . . Neither husband – protector – nor friend accompanied it, and so utter a state of loneliness gives friends if nothing else. . . . I stayed at home all Saturday afternoon, and treated some disagreeable people who insisted upon calling here as tolerably as I could – when evening shades began to fall, I turned upon my heel, and walked. Attracted by the gaiety in the street I still kept walking till a little creature pounced upon a thin shawl I wore, and commenced riding – I stopped, and begged the creature to alight, as I was fatigued already, and quite unable to assist others. It would'nt get down, and commenced talking to itself – "cant be New England—must have made some mistake, disappointed in my reception, dont agree with accounts, Oh what a world of deception, and fraud – Marm, will you tell me the name of this country—it's Asia Minor, isn't it. I intended to stop in New England." By this time I was so completely exhausted that I made no farther attempt to rid me of my load, and travelled home at a moderate jog, paying no attention to it, got into the house, threw off both bonnet, and shawl, and out flew my tormenter, and putting both arms around my neck began to kiss me immoderately, and express so much love, it completely bewildered me. Since then it has slept in my bed, eaten from my plate, lived with me everywhere, and will tag me through life, for all I know. I think I'll wake first, and get out of bed, and leave it, but early, or late, it is dressed before me, and sits on the side of the bed looking right in my face with such a comical expression it almost makes me laugh in spite of myself. I cant call it interesting, but it certainly is curious – has two peculiarities which would quite win your heart, a huge pocket-handkerchief, and a very red nose. The first seems so *very* abundant, it gives you the idea of independence, and prosperity in business. The last brings up the "jovial bowl, my boys," and such an association's worth the having. If it *ever* gets tired of *me*, I will forward it to *you* – you would love it for *my* sake, if not for it's own, it will tell you some queer stories about me – how I sneezed so loud one night that the family thought the last trump was sounding, and climbed into the currant-bushes to get out of the way – how the rest of the people arrayed in long night-gowns folded their arms, and were waiting – but this is a wicked story, it can tell some *better* ones. Now my dear friend, let me tell you that these last thoughts are fictions – vain imaginations to lead astray foolish young women.

[1, 86–88]

Emily's light approach to her cold belies the seriousness of all sickness to her and her family. The mortality rate among young people was high: every illness, no matter how trivial, held the possibility of death. As Millicent Todd Bingham has shown by listing the deaths of Emily's Amherst contemporaries in the early eighteen fifties, it was fact, not morbid imagination, which led Emily to write so often of "death's tremendous nearness." [2]

Books of the day, especially popular fiction and religious writings, dwelt on death as persistently as books a century later would dwell on sex. It was predictable that death should become a literary convention and that readers should apply the convention to reality. Young people "pined away" like their fictional heroes and heroines, uttering "last words" to those who wept at the melodramatic bedside. One of Emily's Mount Holyoke schoolmates, Emily Washburn, died in May 1848; her final words, a message for her absent parents, were these: "Tell them that Jesus called me, and I could not wait for them; for Christ says, 'He that loveth father or mother more than me is not worthy of me.'" [3]

The conventions of death appear in Emily Dickinson's letters. At the age of fifteen she was familiar enough with the clichés to write an earnest string of them to Abiah Root:

> I cannot realize that the grave will be my last home – that friends will weep over my coffin and that my name will be mentioned, as one who has ceased to be among the haunts of the living, and it will be wondered where my disembodied spirit has flown. I cannot realize that the friends I have seen pass from my sight in the prime of their days like dew before the sun will not again walk the streets and act their parts in the great drama of life. . . .
>
> [I, 28]

In the same year, 1846, Emily spoke to Abiah about the death two years before of fifteen-year-old Sophia Holland. The actual event had so disturbed Emily that her parents had sent her to visit relatives in Boston and Worcester. Memory had clothed the terrible reality in conventional phrasing. Sophia now seemed to have been "too lovely for earth." Emily's genuine distress had become "a fixed melancholy" which "was gnawing at my heart strings." It was not until the death of Ben Newton and the serious illness of Samuel Bowles that Emily found the clichés of death impotent to tell her grief. Sophia Holland had lain on her deathbed "mild & beautiful as in health & her pale features lit up with an unearthly – smile" [I, 32]. By 1862 Emily could approach the same subject—the lifelike appearance of a dead child—and make original poetry of it:

> She lay as if at play
> Her life had leaped away –
> Intending to return –
> But not so soon –

Her merry Arms, half dropt –
As if for lull of sport –
An instant had forgot
The Trick to start –

Her dancing Eyes – ajar –
As if their Owner were
Still sparkling through
For fun – at you –

Her Morning at the door –
Devising, I am sure –
To force her sleep –
So light – so deep – [4]

During Emily's early years religious revivals moved like
thunderstorms across New England. Preachers clouded
the spirits of college students and schoolgirls by describing
the torments of those who died without Christ. In a time
when so many died young, examples of "good" and "bad"
deaths were close at hand to give immediacy to the preaching. The excitement of revival grew until the sudden
lightning of conversion struck. One child, one adult after
another "gave his life to Christ." College towns became
centers of piety: from 1845 to 1866 Amherst College experienced ten revivals.[5] During the 1850 revival in Amherst, "the whole aspect of the College was changed at
once, with almost the suddenness of an electric flash." [6]
To those who remained "without hope," it seemed as if all
but themselves had been transfigured with joy. After a
few weeks the revival subsided as quickly as it had come,
leaving life much as it had been before. A year or two
later, most of the "saved" had to become Christians all
over again.

Luckily for her art, Emily Dickinson saved herself from
salvation. She seems to have succumbed once, in 1846,

but to have recovered her balance almost immediately. In 1848, when she was at Mount Holyoke, she was one of the last even to "indulge a hope" (she did not give in completely) and one of the first to recant.[7] Her quick rebound kept her from being immersed in the stock phrases of revival. The rhetoric of conversion is typified by a letter Vinnie wrote to Austin during the revival of 1850:

> Oh, if you have *not* yet given yourself to Christ wholly and entirely, I entreat you in the name of the blessed Jesus, to delay no longer, to deprive yourself of *that* happiness, the Joy, *no* longer but my Dear Brother, *now*, while pardon is offered you & while the precious Saviour is waiting to receive you, *come*, yes, now. . . . Do not faint by the *way*, & thus fail of entering in to the Kingdom, but oh! strive & struggle against Sin, as your *greatest enemy*! [8]

Such language might be useful to an evangelist or a missionary, but it would be (and often was) fatal to a poet's art. Emily came close to the jargon of salvation when she described her 1846 experience to Abiah Root:

> I think of the perfect happiness I experienced while I felt I was an heir of heaven as of a delightful dream, out of which the Evil one bid me wake & again return to the world & its pleasures. Would that I had not listened to his winning words! . . . I determined to devote my whole life to [God's] service & desired that all might taste of the stream of living water from which I cooled my thirst. But the world allured me & in an unguarded moment I listened to her syren voice.
>
> [1, 30]

Later revivals disturbed Emily, but her prose style was less affected by them. Perhaps she realized at Mount

Holyoke that belief could be intense without demanding stilted words. Mary Lyon depicted hell to her students "in the natural, but low, deep tones with which men talk of their wills, their coffins, and their graves." [9] When Emily wrote to Jane Humphrey about the revival of 1850, she was in command of her own voice. She even employed the strong three-stress metre which was her first individual device of style. As a result her refusal of salvation is a good deal more convincing than Vinnie's acceptance of it. It is also an interesting description of the oppressive thunderstorm aura of revival.

> How lonely this world is growing, something so desolate creeps over the spirit and we dont know it's name, and it wont go away, either Heaven is seeming greater, or Earth a great deal more small, or God is more "Our Father," and we feel our need increased. Christ is calling everyone here, all my companions have answered, even my darling Vinnie believes she loves, and trusts him, and I am standing alone in rebellion, and growing very careless. . . . In the day times it seems like Sundays, and I wait for the bell to ring, and at evening a great deal stranger, the "still small voice" grows earnest and rings, and returns, and lingers, and the faces of good men shine, and bright halos come around them; and the eyes of the disobedient look down, and become ashamed.
>
> [1, 94]

When Emily described her near-conversion of 1848 to Abiah Root, she wrote, "It is hard for me to give up the world." Her friend Abby Wood, she said, was near salvation and only desired to be good. "How I wish I could say that with sincerity, but I fear I never can" [I, 67–68]. It was not "the world" which Emily Dickinson refused to relinquish so much as it was the sanctity of her own mind. Revivalism demanded an instant, visible, total conversion.

Emily would not pretend that such a change had come to her, even in the enthusiasm of revival. Until she felt it sincerely, she preferred to be "one of the lingering *bad* ones."

In rejecting a public declaration of faith, Emily was turning toward an older New England attitude. She was never fond of people who spoke of hallowed things aloud; they embarrassed her dog, she said. Emily Fowler Ford remembered, many years later, that Emily had asked her if it did not make her shiver to hear many people talk: they took "all the clothes off their souls." [10] A faith which was too glib seemed to Emily, as it had to her Puritan forebears, a denial of real faith. Adult repentance, according to Calvin, was "too late to be plausible" [II, 520]. Eventually her attitude toward all things "ostensible" led her to the opposite extreme. As a mature poet she did not publish. She had others address many of her letters for her, as if even the appearance of her handwriting in public took the clothes off her soul. Her distaste for overt emotion, during the years when her own inward "conversion" was at its peak, may be counted as one of the reasons for her gradual seclusion.

Hunting for Emily Dickinson's first poetry by examining her prose is somewhat like detecting an unknown planet by measuring aberrations in a familiar orbit. At a distance of more than a century, the forces which acted upon the letters are often difficult to chart. Books that Emily never mentioned, conversations she failed to record, and the daily fluctuations of her hidden mind all shaped the course of her writing. The following suggestions, therefore, are speculations based on short arcs of a circle which is lost forever.

Emily was writing metrical prose in a three-stress pattern by the beginning of 1850. She employed the rhythm for all kinds of subject matter, but easily slipped back into ordinary prose. In her letter of January 11, 1850, to Joel Norcross, she delivered her mock-apocalypse almost entirely in three-foot units. The rest of the letter was less consistent:

> Would you like to try a duel – or is that too quiet to suit you – at any rate I shall kill you – and you may dispose of your affairs with that end in view. . . . Uncle Loring – and Aunt Lavina *will* miss you some to be sure – but trials *will* come in the best of families – and I think they are usually for the best – they give us new ideas – and *those* are not to be laughed at. . . . How do you sleep *o nights* – and is your appetite waning? These are infallible symptoms, and I only thought I'd inquire – no harm done I hope.
>
> [1, 79]

The appearance of verse measures in the most prosaic of prose can only mean that Emily was thinking about poetry, and presumably trying to write it. Her "tutor" in this adventure was her father's law student, Benjamin Franklin Newton. Ben Newton came to Edward Dickinson's law office in the autumn of 1847, while Emily was at Mount Holyoke. For two years he learned law by apprenticeship. During this time he introduced Emily to the poems of Emerson, whose religious views were still considered heretical by most New Englanders. Newton departed in 1849 for Worcester, marriage, and untimely death by consumption. If Emily was in love with him, as some have suggested, her letters during his lifetime give no hint of it.

On January 23, 1850, Emily wrote to Jane Humphrey that she had received a letter and a copy of Emerson's *Poems* from Newton: "I should love to read you them both – they are very pleasant to me. I can write him in about three weeks – and I *shall*" [I, 84]. There is no doubt that Ben saw Emily's first poetry and criticized it. Not long before his death in 1853 he wrote to her that he would like to live until she became a poet [II, 408]. Ben encouraged Emily, but he refrained from praising her beyond her worth. The letter she was eager to read to Jane Humphrey may have spoken of her poems.

If the winter of 1849–50 marks the beginning of Emily's poetic career, the atmosphere in which she first wrote is far from the Dickinson Myth. As Emily described it to Jane Humphrey, her life was unusually gay in January 1850:

> There is a good deal going on just now – the last two weeks of vacation were full to the brim of fun. Austin was reading Hume's History – and his getting through was the signal for general uproar. Campaign opened by a sleigh ride on a very magnificent plan . . . a party of ten from here met a party of the same number from Greenfield – at South-Deerfield the evening next New Year's – and had a frolic, comprising charades – walking around *indefinitely* – music – conversation – and supper – set in the most modern style; got home at two o'clock – and felt no worse for it the next morning – which we all thought was very remarkable. Tableaux at the President's followed next in the train – a Sliding party close upon it's heels – and several cozy sociables brought up the rear. To say nothing of a party *universale* at the house of Sydney Adams – and one *confidentiale* at Tempe Linnell's.
>
> [1, 83–84]

In February Emily sent to Austin's friend George Gould the valentine letter which he published. The three verses in it, unlike the majority of Emily's early poems that have survived, are in tetrameter. But the unrhymed three-stress lines are present in profusion. Emily demands an interview "In gold, or in purple, or sackcloth – I look not upon the *raiment*. With Sword, or with pen, or with plough –

the weapons are less than the *wielder*. In coach, or in wagon, or walking, the *equipage* far from the *man*. With soul, or spirit, or body, they are all alike to me" [I, 92]. Three months later Emily applied her new style to the subject of religious revival in letters to Jane Humphrey and Abiah Root. To the latter she wrote, "What shall we do my darling, when trial grows more, and more, when the dim, lone light expires, and it's dark, so very dark, and we wander, and know not where, and cannot get out of the forest – whose is the hand to help us, and to lead, and forever guide us, they talk of a 'Jesus of Nazareth,' can you tell me if it be he?" [I, 98.]

The rhythms of 1850 persisted intermittently for several years. Although Emily afterward employed the metres of poetry in her prose, the galloping three-foot line which begins with a dactyl or anapest is almost entirely confined to the prose of the eighteen fifties. It is not surprising that Emily's poems should follow much the same pattern. One poem (perhaps in reality two, separated by two prose lines in the same metre) occurs in a letter of October 1851 to Austin: ". . . there is *another* sky ever serene and fair, and there is *another* sunshine, tho' it be darkness there – never mind faded forests, Austin, never mind silent fields – *here* is a little forest whose leaf is ever green, here is a *brighter* garden, where not a frost has been, in its unfading flowers I hear the bright bee hum, prithee, my Brother, into *my* garden come!" [I, 149.]

The following examples of the three-stress unit in Emily Dickinson's prose are typical of the style. By 1858 four-beat measures were adding variety to the usual device. Thereafter a mixture of rhythms was customary.

To Susan Gilbert (about February 1852)

    But what can I do towards you? – *dearer* you *cannot* be, for I love you so already, that it almost

breaks my heart – perhaps I can love you *anew,*
every day of my life, every morning and evening –
Oh if you will let me, how happy I shall be!

[I, 177]

To Mrs. J. G. Holland (September 15 1854)

Three days and we are there – happy – very happy!
Tomorow I will sew, but I shall think of you, and
Sunday sing and pray – yet I shall not forget you,
and Monday's very near, and here's to me on Tuesday! . . . Once more, if it is fair, we will come on
Tuesday, and you love to have us, but if not convenient, please surely tell us so.

[I, 308]

To "Master" (Samuel Bowles?) (about 1858)

I would that all I love, should be weak no more.
The Violets are by my side, the Robin very near,
and "Spring" – they say, Who is she – going by
the door –

Indeed it is God's house – and these are gates of
Heaven, and to and fro, the angels go, with their
sweet postillions –

[II, 333] [11]

By the time Ben Newton died, in March 1853, Emily
was exchanging poems with Henry Vaughan Emmons, a
close Amherst College friend of her beloved cousin John
Graves. Emmons was two years younger than Emily:
there was no tutor-pupil relationship this time. The two
met socially for some time before Emily admitted she was
writing poetry. Emily wrote to Austin on February 6,
1852, that she had gone for a ride the previous evening
"with *Sophomore Emmons,* alone . . ." [I, 174], and
soon afterward told Sue that she had "found a beautiful,
new, friend . . ." [I, 183]. A year later she began to
write letters to Emmons which make clear the literary
nature of their friendship. She sent him flowers, regretting

that they could not compare with the "immortal blossoms" he had sent her. But she added, "If 'tis ever mine to gather those which fade not, from the garden we have not seen, you shall have a brighter one than I can find today" [I, 246]. Soon afterward, Emily showed Emmons her poems: "Thank you, indeed, Mr. Emmons, for your beautiful acknowledgement, far brighter than my flowers; and while with pleasure I *lend* you the little manuscript, I shall beg leave to claim it, when you again return" [I, 247].

Vaughan Emmons, who later became a minister, had literary ambitions during his college years. Emily did not regard him strictly as a man of letters (in 1854 she seems to have worried about a misunderstanding between him and John Graves),[12] but she wrote him letters of peculiar stiffness. Since she began her correspondence with Higginson later in about the same style, it is safe to conclude that this was her idea of the way to speak as one writer to another. In the letters to Emmons, Emily chose her words with care and aimed at a terse dignity which contrasted acutely with the easy informality she had been cultivating for years. By August 1854, when she thanked Emmons for a book (possibly by Poe, if the list of jewels is acrostic), Emily had advanced far toward her mature prose manner. Formality, strong rhythms which still followed the three-stress metre but were becoming iambic, and economy of words all give the letter a distinct Dickinsonian flavor:

> I find it Friend – I read it – I stop to thank you for it, just as the world is still – I thank you for them all – the pearl, and then the onyx, and then the emerald stone.
>
> My crown indeed! I do not fear the king, attired in this grandeur.
>
> Please send me gems again – I have a flower. It looks like them, and for it's bright resemblances, receive it.

> A pleasant journey to you, both in the pathway home,
> and in the longer way – *Then* "golden morning's open
> flowings, *shall* sway the trees to murmurous bowings,
> in metric chant of blessed poems" –
> Have I convinced you Friend?
>
> [I, 303]

The quotation in the letter, a variation on lines of a poem
which Emmons had recently published in the *Amherst
Collegiate Magazine,* is evidence enough that Emily
Dickinson got no part of her poetic style from Vaughan
Emmons.

Emily's letters to Emmons help to document a transi-
tional period between her youth and maturity. Emily was
now serious about her writing; her view of marriage was
becoming that of a permanent bystander. When Emmons
became engaged to Susan Phelps in the summer of 1854
Emily wrote, "My heart is full of joy, Friend – Were not
my parlor full, I'd bid you come this morning, but the
hour must be *stiller* in which we speak of *her.* Yet must I
see you, and will love most dearly, if quite convenient to
you, to ride a little while this afternoon – " [I, 301].

A ride alone with an engaged man was somewhat im-
proper for a girl of the eighteen fifties. Emily was paying
less attention to conventions as time passed, though her
sense of individuality as "royalty" had not yet asserted itself. In October 1854 her friend Eliza Coleman wrote to
John Graves, "I know you appreciate [Emily] & I think
few of her Amherst friends do. They wholly misinterpret
her, I believe. . . ." [13] Graves, who knew Emily best at
this time, recalled long afterward, "She was different.
Emily Dick had more charm than anyone I ever saw." [14]
His daughter Louise writes, ". . . a sort of *aura* hovered
over him at the mere mention of her name." When asked
for a detailed description of Emily, Graves could only say,

"unlike everyone else—a grace, a charm." [15] To friends like Graves and Emmons, Emily's "difference" was no liability.

In August 1854 Henry Vaughan Emmons left Amherst. Emily may have missed him, but she is not known to have written to him again. She had signed her last letter to him, "Pleasantly, Emily." The relationship had been a pleasant one, and it was over. A few weeks before, Emily had brought another friendship to an end, apparently, when she wrote to her childhood friend Abiah Root, "I don't go from home, unless emergency leads me by the hand, and then I do it obstinately, and draw back if I can. Should I ever leave home, which is improbable, I will with much delight, accept your invitation; till then, my dear Abiah, my warmest thanks are your's, but dont expect me. I'm so old fashioned, Darling, that all your friends would stare" [I, 298-99].

Former ties were breaking, but new ones began to replace them. On July 10, 1853, Emily wrote to Austin that Dr. and Mrs. J. G. Holland had spent a day with the Dickinsons, and that she and Vinnie had promised to visit them in Springfield [I, 262]. The arrival of the Hollands, appropriately celebrated with champagne, was the beginning of Emily's lifelong friendship with Elizabeth Holland, though she had met Dr. Holland before. Soon Emily was writing regularly to the Hollands.

Josiah G. Holland, physician-turned-writer, had been associate editor of the *Springfield Republican* since 1850. From the first, he and Samuel Bowles, the editor, complemented one another. Bowles was a "born journalist," but had begun his newspaper career at seventeen and lacked for some time the literary taste of Holland. On the other hand, Holland's piety sometimes got the better of him and he needed Bowles's news sense near at hand to keep him from turning an excellent paper into a religious journal.

> The two men [writes Bowles's biographer, George S. Merriam] worked together harmoniously, but never came into personal intimacy. Dr. Holland had not a little of the clerical attributes. While in his social tastes he was democratic, he avoided the companionship of men whose moral standards were different from his own. . . . Mr. Bowles, on the other hand, was always ready to hob-nob with any man, saint or sinner, in whom he found any likable quality. His highest aspirations, his finest feelings, were not carried in sight of the world, —they were seldom openly expressed in his writings or in his ordinary conversations. . . . No doubt Holland often thought Bowles irreverent, not to say heathenish, and Bowles thought Holland something of a prig.[16]

This comparison of Holland and Bowles is interesting because both were close friends of Emily Dickinson. It is easy to see why she found Bowles the more stimulating of the two. Even so, she always honored Holland. After his death in 1881 she wrote to Mrs. Holland, "I have rarely seen so sincere a modesty on a mature Cheek as on Dr Holland's – and one almost feels an intrusiveness in proclaiming him, lest it profane his simplicity" [III, 718].

When Emily and Vinnie visited the Hollands in 1853 they were impressed by the cheer of the Springfield home. The Dickinson household was bound together by a love which was seldom spoken aloud; the Hollands did not conceal their affection for one another, nor for the God who seemed to Emily quite unlike the austere deity her father prayed to. Twenty-eight years later she wrote to Mrs. Holland, "I shall never forget the Doctor's prayer, my first morning with you – so simple, so believing. *That* God must be a friend – *that* was a different God – and I almost felt warmer myself, in the midst of a tie so sunshiny" [III, 713].

Emily's letters to Mrs. Holland—after the eighteen fifties she seldom wrote to the doctor—contain much of her finest prose. The friendship took a median course. Little Mrs. Holland (smaller even than Emily, who described herself as "small, like the Wren") was intelligent and vivacious, and Emily could express herself in subtleties or witticisms which would have been over the heads of her faithful but dull Norcross cousins. Yet Mrs. Holland did not evoke the self-consciousness of Emily's correspondence with T. W. Higginson, or the frightened ardor of her letters to Samuel Bowles. In later years, when Mrs. Holland was nearly blind, Emily took special care to write bright letters to her "little Sister." Theodora Ward, the Hollands' granddaughter, writes, "The arrival of each letter from Emily was an occasion of excitement for the whole family. Because of their mother's impaired sight, one of the girls usually read the letters aloud, and my mother became expert in deciphering the strongly individual handwriting, even though some of Emily's expressions were beyond her understanding." [17] Emily's late letters show an unusual amount of interest in the Hollands' children, perhaps because of their part in the correspondence with their mother.

The first letters to the Hollands set the tone of Emily's long friendship with them. Domestic affairs, humor, and spiritual problems appear in quick succession. Dr. and Mrs. Holland—respectively eleven and seven years older than Emily—were in a middle ground between contemporaries and elders. Emily felt she could speak freely to them, especially since they were neither relatives nor neighbors. Already she had begun to need an outlet for emotions she could not discuss at home. In November 1854 she wrote to the Hollands,

> The minister today, not our own minister, preached about death and judgment, and what would become of those, meaning Austin and me, who behaved improp-

erly – and somehow the sermon scared me, and father
and Vinnie looked very solemn as if the whole was
true, and I would not for worlds have them know that
it troubled me, but I longed to come to you, and tell
you all about it, and learn how to be better. He preached
such an awful sermon, though, that I didn't much think
I should ever see you again until the Judgment Day,
and then you would not speak to me, according to his
story. The subject of perdition seemed to please him,
somehow. It seems very solemn to me.

[I, 309]

Dr. Holland was the first professional writer Emily
knew. The letters to him and his wife were not overtly
literary, nor were they stiff like the letters to Emmons.
But Emily was aware enough of her audience to make
sure that she wrote carefully. In the earliest known letter
to the Hollands, late in 1853, Emily said, "I wrote to you
last week, but thought you would laugh at me, and call me
sentimental, so I kept my lofty letter for 'Adolphus
Hawkins, Esq.'" [I, 264] (Hawkins was a sentimental
poet in Longfellow's novel *Kavanagh*.) A year later Emily
worked into a letter part of her poem "I have a bird in
spring," disguising it as prose, and used two sentences
which a day or two later appeared in a letter to Sue: "Today has been a fair day, very still and blue. Tonight the
crimson children are playing in the west, and tomorrow
will be colder" [I, 310].

By 1856 a subtle change in style had appeared. Letters
essentially like those of 1853 and 1854 contain phrases
which have the ring of Emily's mature prose. Two passages from a letter of January 1856 illustrate the mingled
tone:

Your voice is sweet, dear Mrs. Holland – I wish I
heard it oftener.

One of the mortal musics Jupiter denies, and when indeed its gentle measures fall upon my ear, I stop the birds to listen.

. . . still we keep our father's house, and mother lies upon the lounge, or sits in her easy chair. I don't know what her sickness is, for I am but a simple child, and frightened at myself. I often wish I was a grass, or a toddling daisy, whom all these problems of the dust might not terrify — and should my own machinery get slightly out of gear, *please,* kind ladies and gentlemen, some one stop the wheel, — for I know that with belts and bands of gold, I shall whizz triumphant on the new stream!

[II, 322–24]

The effects of Emily's reading on her changing prose style were probably slight. Her lifelong mainstays, the Bible and Shakespeare, may account for the simplicity and majesty of her best writing, but she had come to them early. Likewise the foundations of her prosody, Watts's hymns, had been part of her consciousness since childhood. Bible and hymns can be taken for granted; as proof of Emily's acquaintance with undiluted Shakespeare there are the recollections of Emily Fowler Ford.

We had a Shakespeare Club—a rare thing in those days, and one of the tutors proposed to take all the copies of all the members and mark out the questionable passages. . . . We told the men to do as they liked— "we shall read everything." I remember the lofty air with which Emily took her departure, saying, "There's nothing wicked in Shakespeare, and if there is I don't want to know it." The men read for some three meetings from their expurgated editions, and then gave up their plan, and the whole text was read out boldy.[18]

Though her insistence on the complete Shakespeare does her credit, Emily Dickinson was primarily a poet, not a critic. She read what her teachers and friends read. After 1853 the Hollands had some influence on her reading; later she also relied on the judgments of Samuel Bowles and T. W. Higginson. Thomas H. Johnson points out that all her literary opinions strikingly parallel those of Dr. Holland.[19] Generally this is true, unfortunately, though Emily certainly got her taste for Emerson from Ben Newton and her liking for Theodore Parker from Samuel Bowles. Neither writer would have been recommended by Holland in the eighteen fifties. A pious author himself, Holland was inclined to judge other writers by their orthodoxy. Once, in a single sentence of uncanny inaccuracy, he predicted oblivion for the writings of Poe, Whitman, and Thoreau.[20] He may have been the author of a long editorial in the *Republican* on June 16, 1860, entitled " 'Leaves of Grass'—Smut in Them,"—an editorial which probably accounts for Emily's statement to T. W. Higginson that she had been told Whitman was disgraceful.[21] Holland's statement that Emily's own poems were "too ethereal" to publish [22] probably means that he thought Emily did not moralize enough. Like Higginson, Dr. Holland was a man of his time: within the limits the age imposed, his taste was excellent.

The books which most appealed to Emily in her youth were sentimental. In an April 1852 letter to Sue Gilbert she commented on the faults of the books she was reading, and thereby made clear what she admired:

> I have just read three little books, not great, not thrilling – but sweet and true. "The Light in the Valley," "Only," and "A House upon a Rock" – I know you would love them all – yet they dont *bewitch* me any. There are no walks in the wood – no low and earnest voices, no moonlight, no stolen love, but pure little lives, loving God, and their parents, and obeying the

laws of the land; yet read, if you meet them, Susie, for they will do one good.

[1, 195]

One book that did bewitch Emily was *The Reveries of a Bachelor* by Ik Marvel (Donald G. Mitchell). The *Reveries* were published in 1849–50 and became popular at once. Emily seems to have named her dog Carlo after the hero's dog, and by 1851 she was looking forward to *Dream Life*, the second Ik Marvel book:

> It is such an evening, Susie, as you and I would walk and have such pleasant musings, if you were only here – perhaps we would have a "Reverie" after the form of "Ik Marvel?" indeed I do not know why it would'nt be just as charming as of that lonely Bachelor, smoking his cigar – and it would be far more profitable as "Marvel" *only* marvelled, and you and I would *try* to make a little destiny to have for our own. Do you know that charming man is dreaming *again*, and will wake pretty soon – so the papers say, with *another* Reverie – more beautiful than the first?
>
> Dont you hope he will live so long as you and I do – and keep on having dreams and writing them to us; what a charming old man he'll be, and how I envy his grand-children, little "Bella" and "Paul"! We will be willing to die Susie – when such as *he* have gone, for there will be none to interpret these lives of our's.
>
> [1, 144]

The last sentence is a clue to the hold the book had on Emily. The sentimental fantasies of the *Reveries* seemed to be her own. As Whicher says, the reticent young people of 1850 were starved for open expression of their loves and fears; "this bible of a sentimental age," subtitled "A Book of the Heart," allowed them to release their emotions vicariously.[23]

Much of Emily's prose in the early eighteen fifties—especially the letters to Sue—has a general flavor of the *Reveries*. Emily was too original to imitate "Ik Marvel" outright, but in method and tone she often approximated his style. The Bachelor continually imagines vignettes involving his friends and himself; a good example of Emily's "reveries," using the same technique, is found in an 1852 letter to Sue. "Oh Susie, my child," Emily writes, "I sit here by my window, and look each little while down toward that golden gateway between the western trees, and I fancy I see you coming, you trip upon the green grass, and I hear the crackling leaf under your little shoe; I hide behind the chair, I think I will surprise you, I grow eager to see you, I hasten to the door, and start to find me that you are not there" [I, 215].

Occasionally there seem to be echoes of Mitchell in Emily's later letters. The Bachelor says, for instance, "Blessed be letters!— . . . they are the only true heart-talkers! . . . Your truest thought is modified half through its utterance by a look, a sign, a smile, or a sneer. . . . But it is not so of Letters: there you are, with only the soulless pen, and the snow-white, virgin paper. Your soul is measuring itself by itself and saying its own sayings: . . . nothing is present, but you, and your thought." [24] In 1869 Emily wrote to Colonel Higginson in the same vein: "A letter always feels to me like immortality because it is the mind alone without corporeal friend. Indebted in our talk to attitude and accent, there seems a spectral presence in thought that walks alone . . ." [II, 460].

The best American writing which came to Emily's attention was much like her own in spirit. The closest approximations of her prose style are the journals (which she cannot have read) of Emerson. In his poems (which she did read, under Ben Newton's direction) are many of the elements of her own poetic style, and his lectures, like her letters, are often series of aphorisms loosely connected. "The Humble-Bee," which Emily quoted in an 1885 letter to Mabel Loomis Todd [III, 882], sounds like many of her lighter nature poems. If there is any specific Emersonian influence in Emily's poetry, it may be that of the poem "Beauty," which described the ideal poet, and ends,

> He thought it happier to be dead,
> To die for Beauty, than live for bread.[25]

From this to Emily's "I died for Beauty" is only a step.

Emily Dickinson enjoyed Hawthorne's works, though she seems not to have read *The Scarlet Letter*. One of her most surprising literary references is her comparison of the Dickinson homestead and the House of the Seven Gables. In 1851, of course, the Dickinsons had been away from the homestead for more than ten years and had no prospect of returning to it. Recalling the scene in which Judge Pyncheon sits dead in the parlor of the Salem house, Emily wrote to Austin, "I am glad we dont come home as we used, to this old castle. I could fancy that skeleton cats ever caught spectre rats in dim old nooks and corners, and when I hear the query concerning the pilgrim fathers – and imperturbable Echo merely answers *where*, it becomes a satisfaction to know that they are there, sitting stark and stiff in Deacon Mack's mouldering arm chairs" [I, 134–35].

Emily's acquaintance with the writings of Thoreau may have been slight: she mentioned him only twice in her letters. But his biographer Franklin B. Sanborn was one of her correspondents, and she must have read Sanborn's excellent article on Thoreau which the *Springfield Weekly Republican* reprinted from the *Concord Monitor* on June 7, 1862. That Emily Dickinson understood Thoreau is evident in a letter of 1881 to the Norcrosses. "The fire-bells are oftener now, almost, than the church-bells," she wrote. "Thoreau would wonder which did the most harm" [III, 692]. If Emily read *Walden*, it is possible that her locomotive poem, "I like to see it lap the miles," had its source in Thoreau's description of the "fire-steed" which "will reach his stall only with the morning star. . . ." [26]

It is more likely, though, that Emily achieved her image of the Iron Horse by herself. The longer one reads in the books she read, the more one is aware that Emily would "never consciously touch a paint mixed by another person" [II, 415]. Certain mannerisms, like the romantic spelling of her name as "Emilie" from about 1848–60 or her archaic use of capital letters after the mid-eighteen fifties, hint at the influence of books but have no direct bearing on her art. The literary conventions she learned at school she soon abandoned. Most of her reading was sentimental: she became one of the least sentimental poets America has produced. She safely passed the pitfalls of revivalism and its rhetoric. When her "second baptism" finally came, in her late twenties, she had already learned to clothe her thoughts in patterns of words which were unique and her own.

Did Our Best Moment last —
'Twould supersede the Heaven —
A few — and they by Risk — procure —
So this Sort — are not given —

Except as stimulants — in
Cases of Despair —
Or Stupor — The Reserve —
These Heavenly Moments are —

A Grant of the Divine —
That Certain as it Comes —
Withdraws — and leaves the dazzled Soul
In her unfurnished Rooms —
                    —Emily Dickinson

3

Preceptors and Poetry

All her life Emily Dickinson spoke of herself as a student. Long after her schooling ended she relied on "masters" and "preceptors" to guide one phase or another of her spiritual growth. Toward all of them she felt reverence and awe. With some of them she was in love.

The first of Emily's schoolmasters was the only one who actually taught her in school. He was Leonard Humphrey, principal of Amherst Academy in 1846 and 1847. Humphrey was six years older than Emily, and he died in November 1850 at the age of twenty-six. His former pupil mourned him in the rhythmic prose of a letter to Abiah Root: ". . . some of my friends are gone, and some of my friends are sleeping — sleeping the churchyard sleep — the hour of evening is sad — it was once my study hour — my master has gone to rest, and the open leaf of the book, and the scholar at school *alone,* make the tears come, and I cannot brush them away; I would not if I could, for they are the only tribute I can pay the departed Humphrey" [I, 102].

Emily's grief at Humphrey's death was genuine, but it was the grief the young feel for all who die young, and her phrasing was conventionally romantic. Her first soul-shaking bereavement came after the death in March 1853 of Ben Newton. Ben's death surprised Emily. He had written to her, only a week before, "If I live, I will go to Amherst—if I die, I certainly will" [II, 551]. Emily had not understood his hint. The distraction she experienced when friends were ill and distant in later years may have grown out of this early shock. She explained to Colonel Higginson in 1863, "Perhaps Death – gave me awe for friends – striking sharp and early, for I held them since – in a brittle love – of more alarm, than peace" [II, 423].

Nine months after Ben Newton died, Emily wrote to his pastor, Edward Everett Hale. In rather formal language she asked for Hale's assurance that Ben had been willing to die. "The Dead was dear to me," she said, "and I would love to know that he sleeps peacefully." She went on to say that she had been a child (childhood for Emily always had indefinite boundaries) when Ben had been in Amherst, but that she had been old enough to learn from him.

> Mr Newton became to me a gentle, yet grave Preceptor, teaching me what to read, what authors to admire, what was most grand and beautiful in nature, and that sublimer lesson, a faith in things unseen, and in a life again, nobler, and much more blessed –
>
> Of all these things he spoke – he taught me of them all, earnestly, tenderly, and when he went from us, it was as an older brother, loved indeed very much, and mourned, and remembered.
>
> [I, 282]

As years passed, Emily continued to mourn and remember Ben. Her 1859 poem, "Sexton, my master's sleeping here," is almost certainly in memory of Newton, and "Your Riches – taught me – Poverty," written in 1862, may be as well. In the latter year Emily described to another preceptor, Higginson, the role of Ben Newton in her life.

> When a little Girl, I had a friend, who taught me Immortality – but venturing too near, himself – he never returned – Soon after, my Tutor, died – and for several years, my Lexicon – was my only companion –
>
> [II, 404]

> My dying Tutor told me that he would like to live till I had been a poet, but Death was much of Mob as I could master – then –
>
> [II, 408]

Ben's death may, in Emily's opinion, have slowed her poetic growth, but she went on writing poetry. Most of the poems written before 1858 appear to have been destroyed in that year, when Emily began to assemble her packets—the threaded booklets with fair copies of her poems.[1] Only one poem known to be earlier than 1858 appears in packet form: "On this wondrous sea," sent to Sue in 1852. Packet 82, which contains the poem in 1858 handwriting, is predominantly poetry about flowers. There are fourteen flower poems in a group of twenty-two poems. Apparently Emily was selecting verse from a larger collection and arranging it by subject. It is likely that she copied into the earliest packets her favorite poems, new and old, then destroyed the rest.

Only a handful of Emily's 1855 and 1856 letters survive. Therefore both her poetry of the time and the beginning of her long friendship with another preceptor, the Reverend Charles Wadsworth, are hidden. For many years it was supposed that Emily had met Wadsworth on a trip to Washington and Philadelphia in 1854, until Thomas H. Johnson and Theodora Ward published part of an 1854 letter in which Sue Gilbert described staying with Emily while the family was in Washington [II, 289]. The newly established date for Emily's trip, February-March 1855, has the backing of the guest-arrivals lists for Willard's Hotel, published in *The Washington Evening Star;* all the people Emily is known to have met at Willard's are listed as arrivals during February, and on February 10 the following arrival is listed: "E. Dickinson and daughters"—though the place of origin is given as New Hampshire rather than Massachusetts.

The change in date makes Emily's letters euphemistic, to say the least. It is difficult to reconcile Emily's "Sweet and soft as summer, . . . maple trees in bloom and grass green in the sunny places . . ." in a letter now dated February 28, 1855, with *The Washington Evening Star's* report for that day: "Another fine bracing day greets us this morning, and the long cold spell has almost blocked up the Potomac." The highest temperature of the month, on the afternoon of February 14, was only 53° F.[2] This is hardly consistent with Emily's claim that "one soft spring day we glided down the Potomac in a painted boat," though the boats to Mount Vernon were indeed running every Wednesday and Friday when the weather permitted.

After they left Washington, Emily and Vinnie spent more than two weeks in Philadelphia. They stayed at the home of their friend Eliza Coleman, and undoubtedly went to the Arch Street Presbyterian Church with the Colemans. Though Emily may not have spoken with the minister, Dr. Charles Wadsworth, she must have been impressed by his preaching. At some time in the next three or four years she needed spiritual help, remembered Wadsworth, and wrote to him for advice.

So much has been said about Emily Dickinson's dependence on Dr. Wadsworth that his real relationship with her has become obscure. He is supposed to have been the "lover" who "inspired" Emily's poems. He is brought forward as the reason for her later seclusion. Evidence to the contrary—and there is a great deal of it—has been overlooked or twisted to fit a single romantic theory. Quite aside from the reasons for Emily Dickinson's poetic stature, a number of dates and statements make it impossible for Wadsworth to have been "the man," at least during the crucial years 1858–65.

Each point of doubt must be settled in its appropriate place. But there are several facts to consider. Emily was in Philadelphia in 1855. Dating of the poems by handwriting has demolished Martha Dickinson Bianchi's claims that Emily wrote her finest love poems immediately after her return to Amherst.[3] The first powerful poetry of love did not come until about 1860. The point at which Emily discovered, as she thought, that her "Master" returned her love was "a day at summer's full" in 1860. Wadsworth did not have a summer meeting with Emily until 1880.

When Mabel Loomis Todd was editing Emily's poems and letters she asked Austin and Vinnie point-blank if Emily had been in love with Wadsworth. They both thought not.[4] Drafts of letters to Judge Otis P. Lord tell how much Emily loved *him* during years when she was still writing to Wadsworth. After the minister died, Emily eulogized him in letters to Mrs. Holland and the Clark brothers, but she continued to write love letters to Judge Lord; indeed, her first comment on the death of Wadsworth appears in one of them.

What, then, was Emily's relationship with her "dearest earthly friend," Dr. Wadsworth, "whom to know was life?" Emily answered the question herself. Late in 1883, eighteen months after Wadsworth died, she sent his friend Charles Clark the poem, "The Spirit lasts – but in what mode –": a statement of her doubts about immortality. She prefaced this poem with a note: "These thoughts disquiet me, and the great friend is gone, who could solace them" [III, 801]. Other letters of 1882 and 1883 describe the Reverend Charles Wadsworth as "my shepherd from 'Little Girl' hood," "my Clergyman," and "my 'Heavenly Father.'"

Dr. Wadsworth was orthodox in belief, strong in conviction. Except for Dr. Holland, who preached in his books and articles a good-natured orthodoxy, Emily's closest friends shared her doubts about traditional Christianity. Speculation was essential to Emily, but when her doubts overwhelmed her, she needed a guide whose faith was firm to rescue her. Though she could not wholly accept Wadsworth's theology (just as she could not follow Higginson's literary advice), it comforted her. His sermons attracted her: sometimes his language, drawn from the Apocalypse, was much like her own. Some of her favorite metaphors appear, for instance, in a published 1877 sermon, "The Bright Side."

> And how near, then, heaven is to us! Who talks of a "land afar off in its beauty?"
>
> Far away! Why, where is eternity? Transcendental —transsepulchral, in the remote distances and silences of the Infinite? O no, no. All around you. Just behind this cloud-veil of things seen and temporal. And see! See how this curtain seems to stir—to tremble, as if the risen and beloved Dead were breathing behind it; as if invisible hands were even now lifting it—parting it. And there! There! is your prepared place—your white robe, and sceptre, and diadem! [5]

The effect of Wadsworth's sermons on Emily may have
been the emotion she described in "He fumbles at your
soul": stunning by degrees, and, just as the brain begins
to cool, dealing "one imperial thunderbolt / That scalps
your naked soul." [6] The kind of advice he gave her survives in a single undated letter, perhaps written in December 1877 during the final illness of Samuel Bowles: [7]

> My Dear Miss Dickenson [sic]
>   I am distresssed beyond measure at your note, received
> this moment,—I can only imagine the affliction which
> has befallen, or is now befalling you.
>   Believe me, be what it may, you have all my sym-
> pathy, and my constant, earnest prayers.
>   I am very, very anxious to learn more definitely of
> your trial—and though I have no right to intrude upon
> your sorrow yet I beg you to write me, though it be
> but a word.
>
> > In great haste
> > Sincerely and most
> > Affectionately Yours—
> >
> > [II, 392]

Wadsworth did not sign the letter. He and Emily must
have been corresponding for some time, though not frequently, to judge by his misspelling of her name. Had she
been writing love letters to him it is not likely that he
would have spoken in terms of "sympathy," "your sorrow," or "the affliction . . . be what it may."

The Reverend Charles Wadsworth was Emily Dickinson's spiritual preceptor. She loved him as such. She knew
almost nothing about his personal life because her correspondence with him was that of parishioner and minister.
"To turn a relationship such as that of Dr. Wadsworth
and Emily Dickinson into a love affair," Millicent Todd
Bingham wrote when she published Wadsworth's letter,
"is not only misleading; it is false." [8]

Emily's friendship with "Master," almost certainly Samuel Bowles, began in the late eighteen fifties and subsided somewhat by about 1865. In this case (discussed at length below) the student-tutor relationship was secondary to the mingling of love and fear, but Emily still asked for advice. In June 1862 she transferred part of her allegiance to T. W. Higginson when she asked him, "Will you be my Preceptor, Mr. Higginson?" [II, 409].

Higginson, as preceptor, was the friend to whom Emily turned for literary advice. Loyalty to her previous masters—Wadsworth and Bowles and perhaps others, still unrecognized—persisted. It was not until 1872, ten years after he became "Preceptor," that Higginson became "Master" as well.

There is some evidence that Emily had other schoolmasters during her middle years. The poem, "Because that you are going," written in the winter of 1873–74, seems an autobiographical farewell to a man Emily loved. None of her known "tutors" or other friends died or took significant journeys at this time. In the summer of 1877 Emily wrote to Higginson, "I have a friend in Dresden, who thinks the love of the Field a misplaced affection – and says he will send me a Meadow that is better than Summer's" [II, 588]. The identity of this man remains a mystery.

By late 1878 Emily was in love with Judge Otis Lord, and continued to be until his death in 1884. After Lord died, she wrote to his friend Benjamin Kimball, "you are a Psychologist, I, only a Scholar who has lost her Preceptor" [III, 861]. Not long before, she had spoken of her dead nephew Gilbert as "prattling Preceptor." Her letters to others, the correspondents she considered "sacred," make plain her continuing devotion to the memory of earlier masters.

The number of Emily Dickinson's master-preceptors

seems confusing at first. When the myth of "one great love" is laid aside, however, the pattern of her life is clearer. Emily Dickinson, quite simply, chose to describe many kinds of friendship, dependence, and love as scholar-schoolmaster relationships. In an 1860 poem, "I shall know why – when Time is over," she wrote,

> Christ will explain each separate anguish
> In the fair schoolroom of the sky – [9]

The bond between student and teacher lay somewhere between a daughter-father kinship and the friendship of equals, between the filial loyalties of childhood and the marital tie. Whether an individual preceptor seemed to Emily the teacher of her literary, religious, or erotic "scholarship," all were important to her. Speculation about which master fulfilled which need must be based on evidence in Emily's letters and poems, not on sentimental theory. Above all, the idea that any friendship or love can account for the quality of Emily Dickinson's art demands rational examination.

Not a single letter or poem by Emily Dickinson can safely be dated 1857. The gap in biography is unfortunate because it may obscure the event or events which turned a bright young woman into a major poet. To add to the problem, there are no poems and few letters of 1855 and 1856, and no datable letters of 1858 before June. On one side of the darkness is the familiar Emily of the earlier letters, gay and sentimental by turns, accurate in phrase but not profound in thought. On the other side is a young woman perfecting her skill in poetry which is coming to her more and more often until she begins to fear for her sanity. The meanings she discovers in her everyday life cannot be satisfied in terms of that life. She is also beginning to write letters to a man she calls "Master."

Undoubtedly the growth of Emily Dickinson's talent was gradual; 1858, the year she began to assemble her packets of poems, was the year when a long-simmering intellect came to a boil. Everything in Emily's character—even the evidence of her slowly changing handwriting—suggests the natural evolution of a mind. The biographical gap of 1857 is neither mysterious nor meaningful: it only dramatizes the changes.

Several biographers have drawn upon sentimental fictions to explain Emily's inward growth. She was, they maintain, in love. Great poetry followed. Unfortunately the argument is circular, deriving biography from poetry, then using this biography to explain the poetry. "Emily wrote poetry about a hopeless love," the argument runs; "therefore she was unrequitedly in love. Because of her hopeless love she wrote poetry."

The love existed, of course, though it was at least as religious and symbolic as it was erotic. Emily's inability to fulfill herself in marriage may account for the subject matter and the number of poems she wrote during the critical years 1858–65. But the quality of the poetry depends on her genius and on her years of practice in expressing her thoughts on paper. Unrequited love often results in verse, but never in genius.

A more likely source of Emily Dickinson's poetry is the repeated experience which she described in poems like the one which heads this chapter, and the following:

> The Soul's Superior instants
> Occur to Her – alone –
> When friend – and Earth's occasion
> Have infinite withdrawn –
>
> Or She – Herself – ascended
> To Too remote a Hight
> For lower Recognition
> Than Her Omnipotent –

This Mortal Abolition
Is seldom – but as fair
As Apparition – subject
To Autocratic Air –

Eternity's disclosure
To favorites – a few –
Of the Colossal substance
Of Immortality [10]

Such overwhelming moments help to account for much that seems strange in Emily's manner of life. Why, for instance, was she sometimes unable to receive visitors whom at other times she welcomed? Mere caprice cannot be the answer: Emily Dickinson lived too deliberately for that. Nor was the reason always her fear of losing self-control in the presence of a friend who "needed light and air," as Samuel Bowles did when Emily first refused to see him, in 1861. Her own answer after one attempted interview helps to explain her feelings. The year was 1883; the friend was Professor Joseph K. Chickering, who had shown special kindness to Emily and Vinnie after their mother's death a few months before. Emily wrote to Chickering, "I had hoped to see you, but have no grace to talk, and my own Words so chill and burn me, that the temperature of other Minds is too new an Awe –" [III, 758]. To this letter may be added part of Emily's August 1870 conversation with Colonel Higginson. "If I read a book and it makes my whole body so cold no fire can ever warm me I know *that* is poetry. If I feel physically as if the top of my head were taken off, I know *that* is poetry. These are the only way I know it. Is there any other way?" [II, 473–74.]

These are the words of a poet. Emily Dickinson appraised all poetry by its ability to produce in her the same effect as her own moments of creation. Her experience of "the soul's superior instants" is not unique, of course. It is recorded again and again throughout the history of all the arts. Calling it mysticism, William James devoted a chapter to it in *The Varieties of Religious Experience*. Malcolm Cowley has detected it as a factor in the poetry of Whitman. In Cowley's words, "Such ecstasies consist in a rapt feeling of union or identity with God (or the Soul, or Mankind, or the Cosmos), a sense of ineffable joy leading to the conviction that the seer has been released from the limitations of space and time and has been granted a direct vision of truths beyond argument." [11] Emily Dickinson brought to such ecstatic moments her years of practice in verse, and thereby caught "Eternity's disclosure" in words. Perhaps she had enough experience with them to gauge their frequency and regulate her life, including visitors, accordingly.

The question of love in "superior instants" remains. Again, Emily supplies an answer:

> To pile like Thunder to it's close
> Then crumble grand away
> While Everything created hid
> This – would be Poetry –
>
> Or Love – the two coeval come –
> We both and neither prove –
> Experience either and consume –
> For None see God and live – [12]

"The two coeval come": love and poetry. Neither was cause, neither result of the other. Rather, both seemed to Emily the results of a single consuming inward experience, a "signal esoteric sip / Of sacramental wine." Repeated many times, such experiences made Emily Dickinson the poet whose life and words are worth our notice. When the shattering moment coincided with a thought about nature, Emily wrote poetry of nature. When it came while love was in her mind, love poems were the result. The finest passages in her letters may show that poetry was not the only art such glimpses of great light could produce in her. But whatever the result in art, the source was Emily's own amazing mind.

The crucial years of Emily Dickinson's life were 1858–65—approximately the period between her twenty-seventh and thirty-fifth birthdays. In 1858 she copied into booklets about fifty poems, new and old. During the next seven years she wrote at least a thousand. The letters of these years and the poems enclosed in them (or sent as messages) reflect the growing tensions in Emily's mind and the heightening quality of her thought. Her growth as a prose artist lagged behind her poetic maturing; the letters retained some of their earlier characteristics for several years.

Former correspondences were all but ended now. Even in that era of long engagements and late marriages Emily was passing the usual age for marriage. Girlhood friends and the young men of Amherst College like Emmons and John Graves had moved away or settled into domestic life. Austin and Sue were living next door in the house Edward Dickinson had built for them before their marriage, and Emily saw them too often to send more than occasional notes. Only the letters to the Hollands continued past the 1857 chasm. Even these are missing—with one possible exception—through all of the Civil War.

Emily began several new correspondences during the years when she became a poet. The first important group of letters, beginning in 1858, were written to Samuel Bowles and his wife. In 1859 Emily first wrote to her cousins Louisa and Frances Norcross, who at the time were respectively seventeen and twelve. Gradually Loo and Fanny Norcross became Emily's most intimate correspondents. The letters to Thomas Wentworth Higginson began in 1862. Minor correspondences—some of them essentially minor, others so because few of the letters survive—are those with the Reverend Edward Dwight (pastor from 1853–60 at Amherst), Sue's friend Kate Scott, Mrs. Joseph Haven, and Vinnie (during Emily's 1864 and 1865 eye treatments in Boston). It would not be amiss to recall that other letters have been lost. During the eight years of her greatest poetic growth Emily was certainly writing to her cousin William H. Dickinson and the Reverend Charles Wadsworth, and probably to her father's closest friend, Judge Lord.

Emily became friendly with Samuel Bowles and his wife about 1858. Bowles was not much older than Emily (he was born in 1826, the same year as her girlhood friend Emily Fowler) but already he had turned his family's newspaper, the *Springfield Republican*, into a journal of national reputation. Brilliant, high-spirited, and devoted to his family and friends (if sometimes irascible at work), Samuel Bowles sought out men and women of similar qualities—the more so because his wife Mary did not share his intellectual interests. His "vital, fructifying personality," as described by others, is at once apparent in his letters to Austin Dickinson and Maria Whitney. His biographer wrote, "All analysis will seem cold and all praise meager to those who knew and loved him best. Their common sentiment toward him was expressed by one who wrote, 'Not to see you sometimes, not to hear from you, is a kind of eclipse.'" [13] In spirit, even in phrasing, this was the attitude of Emily Dickinson toward Bowles.

Bowles and Austin had first met in 1850 at Monson; they became friends several years later. In her reminiscences, "Annals of the Evergreens," Susan Dickinson said that Bowles was the first guest in her "newly married home"—presumably in the summer of 1856.[14] Emily's acquaintance with the Bowleses may have begun then, or perhaps not until a visit early in the summer of 1858, when Mrs. Bowles had given birth to a stillborn child and her husband was trying to divert her grief by trips to friends' homes. It was in 1858, at any rate, that Emily began to write to the Bowleses. Her first surviving letter was addressed to both, though she was speaking only to Samuel Bowles. Afterwards she always wrote to wife and husband separately, in tones appropriate for each. Emily's delight in Bowles is apparent from the first:

> Dear Friends.
> . . . Tonight looks like "Jerusalem." I think Jerusalem must be like Sue's Drawing Room, when we are talking and laughing there, and you and Mrs. Bowles are by. I hope we may all behave so as to reach Jerusalem.
> . . . I hope your tour was bright and gladdened Mrs Bowles. Perhaps the Retrospect will call you back some morning.
>
> [II, 334]

The cheerful tone of this letter does not betray Emily's growing inward storm. At about the same time, however, her narrowing life was confining her more to the homestead. She explained to Mrs. Joseph Haven, using her parents' needs as her excuse, "I should love to pass an hour with you, and the little girls, could I leave home, or mother. I do not go out at all, lest father miss me, or miss some little act, which I might forget, should I run away –" [II, 337]. To her uncle Joseph Sweetser she revealed more:

> Much has occurred, dear Uncle, since my writing you – so much – that I stagger as I write, in sharp remembrance. Summers of bloom – and months of frost, and days of jingling bells, yet all this while this hand

upon our fireside. Today has been so glad without, and yet so grieved within – so jolly, shone the sun – and now the moon comes stealing, and yet it makes none glad. I cannot always see the light – please tell me if it shines.

[II, 335]

In prose like this, Emily was tightening her words toward the compact intensity of her poems, though traces of the old three-stress rhythm remain. Emily was aware that she sounded strange: at the end of the same letter she wrote, "I hardly know what I have said – my words put all their feathers on – and flutter here and there" [II, 336].

As the summer of 1858 ended, Emily wrote to thank Samuel Bowles for a pamphlet he had sent her. Her tone was poetic. One paragraph of apparent prose was actually the poem, "I would distill a cup." She was intimate and epigrammatic; this letter belongs with her mature prose. Here too is the first of Emily's many descriptions to Bowles of the meaning of friendship.

> My friends are my "estate." Forgive me then the avarice to hoard them! . . . God is not so wary as we, else he would give us no friends, lest we forget him! The Charms of the Heaven in the bush are superceded I fear, by the Heaven in the Hand, occasionally. Summer stopped since you were here. . . . Doubtless, the fields are rent by petite anguish. . . . But this is not for us. Business enough indeed, our stately Resurrection! . . . Good night, Mr. Bowles! this is what they say who come back in the morning, also the closing paragraph on repealed lips. Confidence in Daybreak modifies Dusk.
>
> [II, 339]

Only one 1859 letter from Emily Dickinson to Samuel Bowles is known to exist, though Emily said, "I write you frequently, and am much ashamed" [II, 352]. She wrote several times to Mrs. Bowles; only occasionally do the letters reveal the poet, for Mary Bowles was an unexciting correspondent. The sole remaining letter to Samuel Bowles tells Emily's sorrow at missing him on his visit to Amherst and promises to send him a bottle of wine. Then Emily continues, "Will you not come again? Friends are gems – infrequent. Potosi is a care, Sir. I guard it reverently, for I could not afford to be poor now, after affluence" [II, 352]. One of the four poems sent to Bowles about 1859 also begs him to return:

Heart, not so heavy as mine
Wending late home –
As it passed my window
Whistled itself a tune –
A careless snatch – a ballad –
A ditty of the street –
Yet to my irritated Ear
An Anodyne so sweet –
It was as if a Bobolink
Sauntering this way
Carolled, and paused, and carolled –
Then bubbled slow away!
It was as if a chirping brook
Upon a dusty way –
Set bleeding feet to minuets
Without the knowing why!
Tomorrow, night will come again –
Perhaps, weary and sore –
Ah Bugle! By my window
I pray you pass once more. *Emily*.[15]

Several of Emily's 1859 letters to her friends dwell on personal relationships. As Emily became a poet she valued all friendships more than before, though she discussed friendship most often with Bowles. In February, when Vinnie was in Boston caring for her sick aunt Lavinia Norcross, Emily wrote to Mrs. Haven, "I would like more sisters, that the taking out of one, might not leave such stillness. Vinnie has been all, so long, I feel the oddest fright at parting with her for an hour, lest a storm arise, and I go unsheltered" [II, 346]. The same month Emily asked Mrs. Holland to read and approve a note of apology to Judge Reuben Chapman of Springfield, a mutual friend. With Vinnie away, Emily was uncertain whether she had offended Chapman by hiding when he rang the homestead bell. She had not been alone; Sue's friend Kate Scott was her "confederate" in the escape. But Austin had been angry, and Emily did not want to displease Chapman, who discussed books with her.

Flights from doorbells did not mean that Emily was already a recluse. "I ran, as is my custom," she told Mrs. Holland, but she thoroughly enjoyed evenings of company at Austin's house. She fled from Chapman only because she thought a stranger was at the door.

In March 1859 Emily wrote to Kate Scott, who had left Amherst. The tone of the letters to Kate is extravagant, witty, and sentimental, apparently to match the impression Kate made on Emily. The March letter is a little more extravagant than the others:

> Sweet at my door this March night another candidate – Go Home! We don't like Katies here! Stay! My heart votes for you, and what am I indeed to dispute her ballot? – What are your qualifications? Dare you dwell in the *East* where we dwell? Are you afraid of the Sun? – When you hear the new violet sucking her way among the sods, shall you be *resolute*? All *we* are *strangers* – dear – The world is not acquainted with us, because we are not acquainted with her. And Pilgrims! Do you hesitate? And *Soldiers* oft – some of us victors, but those I do not *see* tonight owing to the smoke. – We are hungry and thirsty, sometimes – We are barefoot – and cold –

[II, 349]

Although there are elements of poetry in the letter, it seems more a regression in style than an advance. The rhetoric and rhythms recall the valentine letters of the early eighteen fifties. Kate was not the only friend to receive such a message in March 1859. Emily wrote to Mrs. Holland,

> People with *Wings* at option, look loftily at hands and feet, which induces watchfulness! How gay to love one's friends! How *passing* gay to fancy that they reciprocate the whim, tho' by the Seas divided, tho' by a single Daisy hidden from our eyes! . . . Vinnie is yet in Boston. . . . I am somewhat afraid at night, but the Ghosts have been very attentive, and I have no cause to complain. Of course one cant expect one's furniture to sit still all night, and if the Chairs do prance – and the Lounge polka a little, and the shovel give it's arm to the tongs, one dont mind such things! From fearing them at first, I've grown quite to admire them, and now we understand each other, it is most enlivening! How near, and yet how far we are! The new March winds could bring me, and yet "whole legions of Angels" may lie between our lips!
>
> [II, 351]

Both letters bring up death, fear, whimsy, and joy in quick succession. The reason for the sudden play of words is not clear. Perhaps they have something to do with one of Emily's "ecstatic moments" and the anguish which followed "in keen and quivering ratio / To the ecstasy." One thing is certain: Emily's poetry was growing in both quantity and quality at the time.

Later—probably in the fall of 1859—Emily wrote again to Kate Scott. "I remember you," she said, "as fires begin, and evenings open at Austin's, without the Maid in black, Katie, without the Maid in black. Those were unnatural evenings. – *Bliss* is unnatural. How many years, I wonder, will sow the moss upon them, before we bind again, a little altered it may be, older a little it *will* be, and yet the same as suns, which shine, between our lives and loss" [II, 355]. The sense of bliss was one which Kate Scott shared. Emily probably chose the word because it was one of Kate's favorites. She had written to Sue in 1855, "I take the words of that Sweet Kate Scott, I have never seen – and say 'It is too blissful'" [II, 315]. In 1917, when she alone lived to remember them, Kate recalled "the old blissful evenings at Austin's! Rare hours, full of merriment, brilliant wit, and inexhaustible laughter, Emily with her dog, & Lantern, often at the piano playing weird & beautiful melodies, all from her own inspiration, oh! she was a choice spirit . . . Those heavenly nights are gone forever! One can only live on the memory of them!" [16]

According to Martha Dickinson Bianchi, these were the times when Samuel Bowles and Kate Scott "played battle-dore and shuttlecock to the *crescendo* of Emily's counting. . . ." [17] Bowles was certainly a part of the blissful memory; his presence may account for Emily's fervent recollection of the "unnatural evenings." In the letters Bowles wrote to Austin he spoke fondly of Kate. She, in return, was "flirtatious"—or so Bowles described her.

While Emily recalled delightful evenings at Austin's, she was also aware of her growth as an individual. The poetry which was now a part of her daily life made her continually aware of her separation from those around her. The wonder of each separate life is the theme of a letter to the Hollands in September 1859. In prose as in poetry, Emily could now find words to convey delicate distinctions.

> Vinnie is sick tonight, which gives the world a russet tinge, usually so red. It is only a head-ache, but when

the head aches next to you, it becomes important. When she is well, time leaps. When she is ill, he lags, or stops entirely.

Sisters are brittle things. God was penurious with me, which makes me shrewd with him.

One is a dainty sum! One bird, one cage, one flight; one song in those far woods, as yet suspected by faith only! . . . Indeed, this world is short, and I wish, until I tremble, to touch the ones I love before the hills are red – are gray – are white – are "born again"! If we knew how deep the crocus lay, we should never let her go. Still, crocuses stud many mounds whose gardeners till in anguish some tiny, vanished bulb. . . .

We talk of you together, then diverge on life, then hide in you again, as a safe fold. Don't leave us long, dear friends! You know we're children still, and children fear the dark.

Are you well at home? Do you work now? Has it altered much since I was there? Are the children women, and the women thinking it will soon be afternoon? We will help each other bear our unique burdens.

[II, 354]

No one could share Emily's unique burden with her, the burden of genius. But the love and trust of friends helped her find strength to bear the weight herself.

The word "genius," as it was used in the nineteenth century, had not yet become simply the upper end of a numerical scale of intelligence. Rather, it was the name for individual creative power raised to the level of the universal. As such, it belongs to Emily Dickinson. Emerson considered genius the universal soul (or Over-Soul, or God) breathing through the individual intellect, the same power which was virtue if it came through the will, or love if it came by way of the affections. Emily Dickinson tended to treat all heightened experience—intellectual, religious, and emotional—as forms of genius. Love and poetry "coeval come," she wrote; each was "a grant of the divine." Late in her life she placed love above intellect. In the spring of 1881 she quoted to the Norcross cousins the words of a correspondent already dead (Samuel Bowles?) on the subject. "The beautiful words for which Loo asked were that genius is the ignition of affection – not intellect, as is supposed, – the exaltation of devotion, and in proportion to our capacity for that, is our experience of genius" [III, 692].

As she matured Emily continued to search for the God she had been unable to accept in orthodox interpretations. Among the poems sent to Samuel Bowles in 1859 is one which expresses her doubts about immortality. She and Bowles, who shared her skepticism of the answers given in church, were discussing religion at the time: that Christmas Bowles introduced her to the writings of Theodore Parker by giving her one of Parker's books. Here are Emily's doubts, phrased in the language of a schoolgirl:

> Good night, because we must,
> How intricate the dust!
> I would go, to know!
> Oh incognito!
> Saucy, Saucy Seraph
> To elude me so!
> Father! They wont tell me,
> Wont you tell them to? [18]

A religious subject, used in quite another way, became Emily's metaphor for her friendship with the Bowleses. The poem was actually sent to Mrs. Bowles, though not at all like Emily's letters to her. Assuming that the poem was intended for Mrs. Bowles alone, there may have been a strain in her friendship with Emily which is not recorded elsewhere. The word "Daisy," a pseudonym Emily used in her love poems and her letters to "Master," appears here for the first time in a message to the Bowleses.

> "They have not chosen me," he said,
> "But I have chosen them!"
> Brave — Broken hearted statement —
> Uttered in Bethleem!
>
> I could not have told it,
> But since *Jesus dared* —
> Sovreign! Know a Daisy
> Thy dishonor shared! [19]

By early 1860 Emily Dickinson's friendship with Samuel Bowles was so close that she could write to him without explaining herself. Her cryptic messages would have meaning for Bowles alone. Necessity is a possible reason for such obscurity. Bowles was often absent from Springfield; his mail was opened by others. When Emily sent him "A feather from the Whippowil," for instance, an unidentified assistant or servant, "F. H. C.," put aside the sprig of white pine enclosed and forwarded the poem to Bowles [II, 364].

Whatever Emily had to say to Bowles, it was not for the eyes of others. One letter of 1860 illustrates the oblique method of writing she adopted:

> Dear Mr. Bowles.
> Thank you.
>
> > "Faith" is a fine invention
> > When Gentlemen can *see* —
> > But Microscopes are prudent
> > In an Emergency.
>
> You spoke of the "East." I have thought about it this winter.

> Dont you think you and I should be shrewder, to take the *Mountain Road?*
>
> That *Bareheaded Life* – under the grass – worries one like a Wasp.
>
> The Rose is for Mary.
>
> > Emily.
>
> > > [II, 364]

Such a letter, with its vague references to religion and death, leaves the modern reader as mystified as any 1860 intruder on Emily's privacy might have been.

In March 1860 Vinnie went to Boston to attend her dying aunt Lavinia Norcross. No more than a few days after Vinnie left, Emily received a visit from Dr. Wadsworth.[20] Because of Vinnie's absence, the only account of the visit is one which Emily wrote twenty-five years later, and it tells very little. "When he first came to see me," she wrote to his friend James Clark, "there was Black with his Hat. 'Some one has died,' I said. 'Yes' – he said, 'his Mother.' 'Did you love her,' I asked. He replied with his deep 'Yes'" [III, 742]. Probably these were the opening words of the interview. During the talk Wadsworth mentioned his friend James Clark of Northampton: it was Clark, therefore, who became Emily's "sacred" correspondent many years later, when the minister was dead.

The one surviving letter which Emily wrote during the spring of 1860—to Vinnie, after Aunt Lavinia died—is a rather conventional reaction to the aunt's death. It does not mention the interview with Dr. Wadsworth. That the minister's visit meant a great deal to Emily is evident in her exact recollection of it so long afterward. Her need for spiritual guidance at the time is attested by her poems and her letters to Samuel Bowles. But the great event of 1860, for Emily, did not come until midsummer, when Dr. Wadsworth was again distant.

If I amazed your kindness – My Love is my
only apology. To the people of "Chillon" –
this – is enough. I have met no others.
Would you – ask less for your *Queen* –
Mr Bowles?

　　　　　　　—Emily Dickinson

4
Crisis

Amherst College Commencement in 1860 came the week
of August 5. Loo and Fanny Norcross were staying at
Austin's house. Samuel Bowles arrived to report the
week's events for the *Republican.* Before the final flurry
of preparation for Edward Dickinson's guests, Governor
and Mrs. Banks, Emily had time for conversation with
Bowles, made fun of the feminist movement and, as she
thought, offended him:

　　　　　　　　　　　　　　　　Sunday night
Dear Mr Bowles.
　　I am much ashamed. I misbehaved tonight. I would
like to sit in the dust. I fear I am your little friend no
more, but Mrs Jim Crow.
　　I am sorry I smiled at women.
　　Indeed I revere holy ones, like Mrs. Fry and Miss

Nightingale. I will never be giddy again! Pray forgive me now: Respect little Bob o' Lincoln again!

My friends are very few. I can count them on my fingers – and besides, have fingers to spare.

I am gay to see you – because you come so scarcely, else had I been graver.

Good night, God will forgive me – Will you please to *try*?

Emily.

[II, 366]

It is unlikely that Bowles was deeply offended. As his letters to his closest woman friend, Maria Whitney, show, he enjoyed discussion with women—even arguments—on topics of social, religious, or philosophical interest. If Emily "smiled" at the subject of women's rights, she probably did so with her customary wit, the very quality that attracted Bowles to her.

A few days later, when the Governor arrived, Emily sent a hasty note to Sue. It is a unique glimpse into Emily's life at a moment when she had no time to choose words with her usual care:

God bless you for the Bread! Now – can you spare it? Shall I send it back? Will you have a Loaf of mine – which is spread? Was silly eno' to cut six, and have three left. Tell me just as it is, and I'll send home your's, or a loaf of mine, *spread*, you understand –

Great times –

Love for Fanny.

Wish Pope to Rome – that's all –

Emily.

Esqr in parlor –

[II, 366–67]

Emily was immersed in the week's events. Besides the preparation for the Bankses, there was Edward Dickinson's annual Commencement reception—presumably the reason for the six cut loaves of bread. As usual, Emily was expected to make conversation with the guests. One of the Commencement speakers, Dr. Joseph P. Thompson, made a mistake which Emily recalled a month later to Fanny and Loo: "In the event of my decease, I will still exclaim 'Dr. Thompson,' and he will reply, 'Miss Montague'" [II, 367]. Sometime in the week of festivity, Emily was introduced to John Dudley, the fiancé of her friend Eliza Coleman.

These were the outward events. They did not leave much time for a poet's inner life. Nevertheless, this Commencement Week of 1860 may have brought to a crisis the situation Emily described in several of her poems. The crucial event came on "a day at summer's full" in 1860; many years later Emily wrote, "It sometimes seems as if special Months gave and took away – August has brought the most to me . . . in incessant instances –" [III, 744].

By 1860 Emily Dickinson was overwhelmingly drawn to a man she was calling "Master" in poems and drafts of letters. The first of three surviving "Master" letters had been written in 1858 or 1859. It begins, "Dear Master I am ill, but grieving more that you are ill, I make my stronger hand work long eno' to tell you. I thought perhaps you were in Heaven, and when you spoke again, it seemed quite sweet, and wonderful, and surprised me so – I wish that you were well." In style this letter is quite unlike the two later "Master" letters with their terrible tensions and distorted rhetoric, although the master was sick. He had written to Emily to ask what the flowers she had sent him said: "then they were disobedient – I gave them messages. They said what the lips in the West, say, when the sun goes down, and so says the Dawn" [II, 333].

Only one of Emily's regular correspondents is known to have been ill at this time: Samuel Bowles. From 1857 to the end of his life Bowles suffered from chronic illness, the result of overwork and nervous strain. At first his ailments were intermittent (Emily refers in one letter to "the strong man we first knew"). The health of "Master" gradually became a theme in Emily's love poems, though not as early as 1858.

Among the 1860 poems of Emily Dickinson are several almost delirious with joy: "At last, to be identified!"; "Come slowly, Eden!"; "For this – accepted Breath –"; and " 'Tis so much joy! 'Tis so much joy!" are some of them. Images of wealth and royalty became frequent. Scattered among these poems in Emily's booklets are others opposite in tone, including "To learn the Transport by the Pain –"; "A *Wounded* Deer – leaps highest –"; "I shall know why – when Time is over –"; and "Just lost, when I was saved!" Between extremes of joy and grief is the first of many poems in which Emily considers herself married, in spirit at least:

> I'm "wife" – I've finished that –
> That other state –
> I'm Czar – I'm "Woman" now –
> It's safer so –
>
> How odd the Girl's life looks
> Behind this soft Eclipse –
> I think that Earth feels so
> To folks in Heaven – now –
>
> This being comfort – then –
> That other kind – was pain –
> But why compare?
> I'm "Wife"! Stop there! [1]

Ever since Emily Dickinson's poetry came to public attention there has been speculation about the events that led to poems like "I'm 'wife.'" Did Emily or did she not have sexual relations with her master? Almost certainly she did not. One 1860 poem, "Did the Harebell loose her girdle," shows that she debated the possibility of such intimacies in future terms. But her accounts of the crucial event indicate that "Master" only held her on his knee: intimacy enough for Emily. In later years she chose to wear at all times the symbolic white of the virgin bride.

Whatever it was that happened to Emily in the summer of 1860, it brought her a moment of joy and almost at once a new sadness. A year later, in the poem, "One year ago – jots what?" she described the event:

> I tasted – careless – then –
> I did not know the Wine
> Came once a World – Did you?
> Oh, had you told me so –
> This thirst would blister – easier – now –
> You said it hurt you – most –
> Mine – was an Acorn's Breast –
> And could not know how fondness grew
> In shaggier Vest –
> Perhaps – I couldn't –
> But had you looked in –
> A giant – eye to eye with you, had been –
> No Acorn – then – [2]

Although it is dangerous to take Emily's poems too literally as autobiography, she seems to be describing a conversation with a man who has declared deep friendship and suddenly discovers his words have been misinterpreted by a woman in love. "You said it hurt you – most –": a protest appropriate for a man caught in a situation he would like to escape. The ardor was Emily's, not her master's. By 1861 Emily realized this, at least in part:

> The *Sun – just touched* the Morning –
> The *Morning* – happy thing –
> Supposed that he had come to *dwell* –
> And Life would all be *Spring*!
>
> She felt herself *supremer* –
> A *Raised – Etherial Thing*!
> Henceforth – for Her – *What Holiday*!
> Meanwhile – Her wheeling King –
> Trailed – slow – along the Orchards –
> His *haughty – spangled* Hems –
> Leaving a *new nescessity*!
> The *want* of *Diadems*!
>
> The Morning – *fluttered – staggered* –
> Felt *feebly* – for her *Crown* –
> Her *unanointed forehead* –
> Henceforth – her *only* One! [3]

Like "I'm 'wife'" and many other love poems, this poem treats individual fulfillment as royalty. "Master" is king; Emily is his queen, crowned or uncrowned as he responds to her or rejects her.

Sometime in 1860 Emily wrote a cryptic message to Samuel Bowles:

> I cant explain it, Mr Bowles.
>
> > Two swimmers wrestled on the spar
> > Until the morning sun,
> > When one turned, smiling, to the land –
> > Oh God! The other One!
> > The stray ships – passing, spied a face
> > Upon the waters borne,

> With eyes, in death, still begging, raised,
> And hands – beseeching – thrown!
>
> [II, 363]

This poem can be read as a statement, in sea imagery rather than light and royalty, of the theme of "The *Sun – just touched* the Morning." The aftermath of the situation is plain enough (and now in terms of royalty) in an 1861 poem:

> Mr Bowles –
>
> > I'll send the feather from my Hat!
> > Who knows – but at the sight of *that*
> > My Sovreign will relent?
> > As trinket – worn by faded Child –
> > Confronting eyes long – comforted –
> > Blisters the Adamant! [4]

The pleading in the two poems just quoted is carried to an extreme in another poem of about 1860 which Emily sent to Samuel Bowles. In this case Emily's art was insufficient to rescue her private emotion.

> What shall I do – it whimpers so –
> This little Hound within the Heart
> All day and night with bark and start –
> And yet, it will not go –
> Would you *untie* it, were you me –
> Would it stop whining – if to Thee –
> I sent it – even now?
>
> It should not tease you –
> By your chair – or, on the mat –
> Or if it dare – to climb your dizzy knee –
> Or – sometimes at your side to run –

When you were willing –
Shall it come?
Tell Carlo –
He'll tell *me!* [5]

The biographer of Samuel Bowles, G. S. Merriam, described the kind of women Bowles chose as friends. Though his generic description certainly was modeled on Maria Whitney, it is an accurate portrait of Emily Dickinson also.

> His closest intimacies were with women of a characteristic New England type. There is in that section a class of such who inherit a fine intellect, an unsparing conscience, and a sensitive nervous organization; whose minds have a natural bent toward the problem of the soul and the universe; whose energies, lacking the outlet which business and public affairs give to their brothers, are constantly turned back upon the interior life, and who are at once stimulated and limited by a social environment which is serious, virtuous, and deficient in gayety and amusement. . . . In the many cases where they remain unmarried, the fervor and charm of womanhood are refined and sublimated from personal objects and devoted to abstractions and ideals. They are platonic in their attachments, and speculative in their religion; intense rather than tender, and not so much soothing as stimulating.[6]

To these women—to all his intimate friends, men or women—Bowles gave freely of his vivacity and sensibility. Reticent to the point of harshness at the *Republican* office, he unburdened himself to friends. His letters to Austin and Sue repeatedly tell his dependence on them. "The gift of friendship," he wrote to Austin about 1862, "is a holy one, & its proofs stimulate and sadden, as the most delicate of responsibilities." [7] If Emily Dickinson was in love with Bowles she could easily mistake his characteristic words on friendship for evidence of another kind of love.

Emily's first surviving letter to Bowles after their meeting during the 1860 Commencement Week was written months later: perhaps in February, or early in the spring.[8] Bowles was in poor health again. Emily disguised her personal feelings by using "we" instead of "I," but some of her sentences make it clear that the "we" was herself.

> We voted to remember you – so long as both should live – including Immortality. To count you as ourselves – except sometimes more tenderly – as now – when you are ill – and we – the haler of the two – and so I bring the Bond – we sign so many times – for you to read, when Chaos comes – or Treason – or decay – still witnessing for Morning. . . . We hope our joy to see you – gave of it's own degree to you – We pray for your new health – the prayer that goes not down – when they shut the church. . . .
>
> [II, 371]

The appearance of Emily's handwriting becomes more chaotic during 1861. In prose as in poetry, dashes between phrases are now profuse. Sometimes they are substitutes for punctuation, sometimes rhythmic devices which make the sentences seem breathless. More and more words are capitalized or underlined: the letters to Bowles and poems like "The *Sun – just touched* the Morning" convey Emily's fear and excitement by their appearance as well as their words.

The great national event of 1861, the Civil War, scarcely touched Emily Dickinson as an artist. Her deepening perceptions moved continually inward. While other poets mobilized their talents against slavery and secession, Emily was true to a poem she had written about 1859:

> To fight aloud, is very brave –
> But *gallanter*, I know
> Who charge within the bosom
> The Cavalry of Wo – [9]

Victory or defeat, as she understood them, lay only within. Her attitude toward most public events she summed up in an 1870 letter to Mrs. Holland: "What Miracles the News is! Not Bismark but ourselves" [II, 483].

Emily's letters, like her poems, avoid the war almost completely. Only two events, the death of a soldier she knew and Colonel Higginson's part in the war, evoked more than casual comment. These were mortality and friendship: problems her mind could weigh in its accustomed scales. But the atmosphere of war, no matter how distant, may be counted as an essential tension during the years when Emily Dickinson came to maturity as a poet.

During 1861 Emily and Sue were drawing apart. The birth on June 19 of Edward Dickinson (nicknamed Jacky—for Union Jack—at first, but afterward called Ned) inspired a gay, dreadfully inartistic poem by Emily, but increased the distance between the new mother and the new aunt. Busy with an infant, Sue had little time to discuss poetry with her sister-in-law. The child had suffered prenatal or birth injuries; from infancy his health was precarious.

In 1860 Emily had written two poems addressed to Sue by her pet name, "Dollie." One of them, "You love me – you are sure –" bluntly tells of disagreement, and ends,

> Be sure you're sure – you know –
> I'll bear it better now –
> If you'll just tell me so –
> Than when – a little dull Balm grown –
> Over this pain of mine –
> You sting – again! [10]

The real source of tension between the two was Austin's disappointment in his marriage. Apparently Sue did not want children: the orphaned Newman girls, Anna and Clara, now living with Austin and Sue, were bother enough. Austin and his father, of course, hoped that the family name would continue. With Emily and Vinnie both past the usual age for marriage, Edward Dickinson could count on no grandchildren but those born to Austin and Sue. Sue's social climbing was another source of distress. She was a delightful but rather imperious hostess who took advantage of her position as the wife of "young Squire" Dickinson; she was also extravagant. Emily's first delight in the marriage of Austin and Sue had been tempered by Austin's unhappiness.

Nevertheless, Emily continued to send poems to Sue. In the summer of 1861, not long after Ned was born, Sue was discussing "Safe in their Alabaster Chambers" with Emily. The second stanza of the 1859 poem, beginning "Light laughs the breeze in her castle above them," was not to Sue's liking. Emily wrote an entirely new stanza, "Grand go the Years – in the Crescent – about them –" and added a note: "Perhaps this verse would please you better – Sue –"

Sue's objections to the new stanza show that Emily had reason to call on her for literary advice. Susan Dickinson was ambitious and sometimes ruthless, but her mind was acute. She wrote,

> I am not suited Dear Emily with the second verse – It is remarkable as the chain lightening that blinds us hot nights in the Southern sky but it does not go with the ghostly shimmer of the first verse as well as the other one – It just occurs to me that the first verse is complete in itself it needs no other, and can't be coupled – Strange things always go alone – as there is only one Gabriel and one Sun – You never made a peer

for that verse, and I *guess* your kingdom doesn't hold
one – I always go to the fire and get warm after thinking of it. . . .

[II, 379–80]

Emily replied with another second stanza, one beginning
"Springs – shake the Sills – / But – the Echoes – stiffen – "
and asked, "Is *this frostier?*" adding, "Your praise is good –
to me – because I *know* it *knows* – and *suppose* it *means* –
Could I make you and Austin – proud – sometime – a
great way off – 'twould give me taller feet – " [II, 380].

"I *know* it *knows* – and *suppose* it *means*": this was
one reason for Emily's need of preceptors. She trusted
Sue's judgment but not her candor. For the rest of her
life Emily would send poems to Sue, but for criticism she
would turn to others.

In the spring or summer of 1861 Emily wrote to Loo
and Fanny Norcross, "The seeing pain one can't relieve
makes a demon of one." One of her 1861 poems begins,

A single Screw of Flesh
Is all that pins the Soul
That stands for Deity, to Mine,
Upon my side the Vail – [11]

Another, in which terror is disciplined to verse, but apparent in punctuation and underlining, opens with an appall-
ing fear:

If *He dissolve* – then – there is *nothing – more*
Eclipse – at *Midnight* –
It was *dark – before* – [12]

Apparently Emily confided some of her fears to Sue, who
replied, "If you have suffered this past Summer I am
sorry. . . . If a nightingale sings with her breast against
a thorn, why not *we?*" [13]

In July 1861 Samuel Bowles, exhausted by overwork and recurring sciatica, drove to the White Mountains with his friend Charles Allen for several weeks of rest. He returned to Springfield in August, but after a short time another rest was necessary. On October 17 he went to Dr. E. E. Denniston's "Water Cure" in Northampton, and soon wrote to Austin Dickinson that Dr. Denniston took "new views of my case—which have been on my mind before, but which no other physician encouraged. There is a serious doubt in it—involving the heart—" [14]

Emily was afraid Bowles would die. Fear pervades most of her letters to him. Austin visited Bowles at the "water cure," and when he felt well enough, Bowles came to Amherst. Emily refused to see him. Though she had often fled from strangers, she had never before purposely avoided a close friend. Her own account of this strange action suggests that she was afraid she would lose control of her emotions at a time when Bowles needed "light and air." The next day she wrote to him,

> Perhaps you thought I didn't care – because I stayed out, yesterday, I *did* care, Mr Bowles. I pray for your sweet health to "Alla" – every morning – but something troubled me – and I knew you needed light – and air – so I didn't come.
>
> . . . It's little, at the most – we can do for our's, and we must do that – flying – or our things are *flown!* Dear friend, I wish you were well –
>
> It grieves me till I cannot speak, that you are suffering. Could I bring you something? My little Balm might be *o'erlooked* by wiser eyes – you know – . . .
>
> [II, 382]

Emily signed the letter, " 'Swiveller' may be sure of the 'Marchioness.' " She was referring to the little servant girl in Dickens' *The Old Curiosity Shop* who nurses Dick

Swiveller (whom she loves) back to health after an almost fatal illness. In gratitude for her love and care, Swiveller marries the small "Marchioness."

In November Samuel Bowles went home from Northampton, though by no means well. Mrs. Bowles was about to give birth, and her husband had decided to take her to New York for special care during her confinement —three children had been stillborn in the previous five years. Early in December Emily wrote to Samuel Bowles, speaking of herself as "we" and so wording parts of her message that only Bowles would understand them:

> It grieves us – that in near Northampton – we have now – no friend – and the old-foreigner – look blurs the Hills – *that* side – It will be bravest news – when our friend is well – . . .
>
> The hallowing – of pain – makes one afraid to convalesce – because they differ – wide – as *Engines* – and *Madonnas*. . . .
>
> I think the Father's Birds do not all carol at a time – to prove the *cost* of *Music* – not doubting at the last each Wren shall bear it's "Palm" –
>
> To take the pearl – costs Breath – but then a pearl is not impeached – let it strike the East!
>
> Dear Mr Bowles – We told you we did not learn to pray – but then our freckled bosom bears it's friends – in it's own way – to a simpler sky – and many's the time we leave their pain with the "Virgin Mary."

> Jesus! Thy Crucifix
> Enable thee to guess
> The smaller size –
>
> Jesus! Thy *second* face
> Mind thee – in paradise –
> Of Our's.

[II, 382–83]

The final paragraph and poem are not as enigmatic as they seem. "Virgin Mary," like "Alla" in the previous letter, is God. Emily's message—minus its unique phrasing—is this: "Though my beliefs are unorthodox, I pray in my own way for friends in pain. Jesus understands human pain because he suffered it, and perhaps his immortal body will remind him of our mortal ones." But Emily's "pearl" (perhaps immortality, or the gates of heaven, or "that perfect pearl / The man upon the woman binds") is still obscure. So is the "east," a private symbol Emily had used before.

A son was born to the Bowleses on December 19, and named for his father's friend Charles Allen. Emily thought he should be called Robert after Robert Browning, and for some time pretended he had been so named. The little joke was one of her few reliefs from the almost unbearable tensions of the winter.

Emily Dickinson wrote the second of her three letter-drafts to "Master" about 1861. The following sentences, which offer the only clue to the time of year, raise the single serious doubt about identifying Samuel Bowles as "Master." "Could you come to New England – this summer – " Emily wrote (then she crossed out "this summer") "would you come to Amherst – Would you like to come – Master?" [II, 375.] Dr. Wadsworth, who had never been in Amherst on "a day at summer's full," was indeed outside New England. Much of the year Bowles was not. Due to his illness, however, his plans were vague enough to make Emily's question appropriate to him. In January 1861 he was in New York and wrote to Charles Allen,

> . . . I mean to spend the winter as easily as possible, spending another week in New York with Mary, and perhaps several in Washington. . . . Then if, when spring opens, there comes no substantial relief, I shall break away more thoroughly—go abroad, if circumstances

invite—make a trip to the Plains—spend some weeks or
months in the country or at a water-cure—or make a
long trip on horseback, with Mrs. Bowles in the carriage,
through New England.[15]

The outbreak of war plus the pregnancy of Mrs. Bowles
brought changes in these far-ranging plans. By December,
in far worse health, Bowles was again in New York and
again talking of spending several months abroad. At
either end of the year Emily would have had reason to
beg him to come to New England.

There are other slight hints of the master's identity in
Emily's second letter-draft. Ones which suggest Dr. Wadsworth are the statement that Emily had asked "Master"
for redemption, and the following words: "To come
nearer than presbyteries – and nearer than the new Coat –
that the Tailor made – . . . is forbidden me" [II, 374].
That Emily was also talking about redemption with
Bowles is evident in her letters and love poems to him.
"The new Coat" is not the sort of thing Wadsworth is
known to have mentioned to Emily: he did not talk about
himself, according to Emily, and after his death she had
to ask the Clark brothers for the most overt facts of his
life. As to "presbyteries," Millicent Todd Bingham commented when she published the "Master" letters, "the
word 'presbytery' cannot be taken literally any more than
words like 'Himmaleh' or 'Calvary,' which were often
used in a metaphorical sense." [16]

A slight clue in Bowles's favor is the master's beard:
Bowles was handsomely bearded while Wadsworth was
clean-shaven. Here, of course, Emily may simply have
been distinguishing man from woman by a figure of
speech. More convincing is the childlike pleading tone, so
similar to that in "What shall I do – it whimpers so," one
of the poems to Bowles: "if I had the Beard on my cheek –

like you – and you – had Daisy's petals – and you cared
so for me – what would become of you? Could you forget
me in fight, or flight, or the foreign land? Couldn't Carlo,
and you and I walk in the meadows an hour – and nobody
care but the Bobolink – and *his* – a *silver* scruple?" [II,
374.]

Most convincing of all is a paraphrase of part of this
"Master" letter in a letter to Bowles, written in 1861 or
early 1862. Since Emily saved the draft of her message to
"Master," contrary to her custom at the time, she may
never have mailed a fair copy of the entire letter. The
edges of the letter to Bowles have been torn away, but
only one word remains in doubt. Emily wrote to "Master," "if I wish with a might I cannot repress that mine
were the Queen's place – the love of the Plantagenet is
my only apology – . . . 'Chillon' is not funny" [II, 374].
To Bowles she wrote,

> If I amazed your kindness – My Love is my only apol-
> ogy. To the people of "Chillon" – this – is enough. I
> have met no others. Would you – ask less for your *Queen*
> – Mr Bowles?
>
> Then – I mistake – my scale – To Da (?) 'tis *daily* to
> be granted and not a "Sunday Sum" Enclosed is my
> defence –
>
> Forgive the Gills that ask for Air – if it is harm – to
> breathe!
>
> To *"Thank" you* – shames my thought!

> Should you but fail at – Sea –
> In sight of me –
> Or doomed lie –
> Next Sun – to die –
> Or rap – at Paradise – unheard
> I'd *harass God*
> Until he let you in!

> [II, 393] [17]

Emily Dickinson considered herself Samuel Bowles's *"Queen,"* throneless and accustomed to "Chillon," like Byron's prisoner, but still hoping to be recognized as royalty. The one word which cannot be reconstructed may be "Daisy": "To Daisy 'tis *daily* to be granted and not a 'Sunday Sum.'" No other word seems nearly as appropriate in context. Emily was telling Samuel Bowles that he should expect no smaller apology than love from his "Queen," no matter how she amazed his kindness. As long as she was Daisy (her name in love poems and the "Master" letters) she claimed the apology of love as a daily right.

The edges of this letter are gone, but there is direct proof elsewhere that Emily Dickinson wrote as "Daisy" to Samuel Bowles. In 1863 or 1864 she sent him a letter-poem pinned around a stub of pencil; in spite of her impersonal pronouns there can be no doubt this plea for a letter was a message to her Master.

> If it had no pencil
> Would it try mine –
> Worn – now – and *dull* – sweet,
> Writing much to thee.
> If it had no word,
> Would it make the Daisy,
> Most as big as I was
> When it plucked me? [18]

Unless Emily was "Daisy" to more than one man, and called more than one man "sweet," Samuel Bowles was "Master," the man she loved when she became a poet. The fact that she called herself his queen is itself almost enough proof of her love. Dozens of her love poems (some of them sent to Bowles) play on the theme of royalty. Many years later, Austin, who did not believe Emily had fallen in love with Dr. Wadsworth, said that she had loved Samuel Bowles "beyond sentimentality." [19]

The year 1862, as a graph of Emily Dickinson's poetic output will show, was the continental divide of her life. She wrote an average of a poem a day. Never before or after did she concentrate so much of her energy in poetry. Since the dating of the poems is only approximate, Emily's letters are the surest clues to the reasons for the number and subject matter of her poems during this momentous year.

On January 2, 1862, Emily wrote to her former pastor, the Reverend Edward Dwight, to apologize for a mistake. She had "mis-enveloped" two letters—one to him and one to an unidentified man. She would not have mentioned the error to him, she told Dwight, "except the familiar address – must have surprised your taste – I have the friend who loves me – and thinks me larger than I am – and to reduce a Glamour, innocently caused – I sent the little Verse to *Him*. Your gentle answer – undeserved, I more thank you for" [II, 389]. The friend who "thinks me larger than I am" may well have been "Master." An 1862 poem begins, "That first Day, when you praised Me, Sweet," and there is an 1863 love poem, "You said that I 'was Great' – one Day – " There are two reasons, neither of them far-fetched, to connect Samuel Bowles with the "mis-enveloped" letter. In April Emily wrote to T. W. Higginson, "Two Editors of Journals came to my Father's House, this winter – and asked me for my Mind – and when I asked them 'Why,' they said I was penurious – and they, would use it for the World – " [II, 404–05]. Bowles and Holland are the two editors Emily is most likely to have seen. Apparently they wanted to publish some of her poetry. The "little Verse" intended to "reduce a Glamour, innocently caused" may be the following love poem which Emily sent to Bowles at about this time:

> The Drop, that wrestles in the Sea –
> Forgets her own locality –
> As I – toward Thee –
>
> She knows herself an incense small –
> Yet *small* – she sighs – if *All* – is *All* –
> How *larger* be?
>
> The Ocean – smiles – at her Conceit –
> But *she*, forgetting Amphitrite –
> Pleads – "Me?" [20]

Emily Dickinson felt herself "an incense small" at one moment, royal the next. Her love poems waver between the picture of "the daisy low" to whom "The Himmaleh was known to stoop" and the sort of grandeur typified by a poem which she sent to Samuel Bowles early in 1862 as a letter of explanation:

> Title divine – is mine!
> The wife – without the Sign!
> Acute Degree – conferred on me –
> Empress of Calvary!
> Royal – all but the Crown!
> Betrothed – without the swoon
> God sends us Women –
> When you – hold – Garnet to Garnet –
> Gold – to Gold –
> Born – Bridalled – Shrouded
> In a Day –
> "My Husband" – women say –
> Stroking the Melody –
> Is this – the way?

Heres – what I had to "tell you" – you will tell no other?
Honor – is it's own pawn –

[II, 394]

Empress of Calvary: was it the pain or the redemption of
the cross to which Emily Dickinson, Samuel Bowles's
"Queen," imagined herself married, or both? A year before, she had linked the pain of the crucified Jesus to her
concern for Bowles's health. But the image of divinity,
the distant stately lover God, the heavenly Master, is
always a part of Emily's love poetry. Emily had asked her
master for redemption; he had given her something else,
but still she looked for the face of deity in mortal form.
One of her marriage poems, "A Wife – at Daybreak – I
shall be – " ends, in the packet copy,

> Eternity – I'm coming – Sir –
> Master – I've seen the Face – before – [21]

In the first weeks of 1862 two of Emily's friends were
thinking of traveling far from home. On January 11,
Philadelphia newspapers reported that the Reverend
Charles Wadsworth had received a call from Calvary
Church in San Francisco. Six days later Samuel Bowles,
still in New York, wrote to a *Republican* associate that he
had been thinking of "going abroad early, say in March,
to come back in early Fall. I believe I have made up my
mind to do it, if my fears and not my hopes are realized. . . ." [22]

Emily's reaction to Wadsworth's call (which he did
not accept until March) cannot be known. Some of her
letters and letter-poems to Bowles can be dated only by
handwriting, so their exact order is in doubt. Emily was
more and more afraid for Bowles: this much is clear in
the datable letters. Since June he had put aside his work
twice on account of his health, and perhaps he had also

had some rest during the weeks in New York. With each unsuccessful rest cure Emily's anxiety had heightened. When Bowles decided on his long visit to Europe, Emily must have been terrified.

Her first 1862 letter to Bowles, in the middle of January, combines fear for Bowles with her own poetic tension. Probably she enclosed a poem and was referring to it in her opening line.[23]

> Dear friend.
>
> Are you willing? I am so far from Land – to offer *you* the cup – it might some Sabbath come *my* turn – Of wine how solemn – full!
>
> . . . While you are sick – we – are homesick – Do you look out tonight? The Moon rides like a Girl – through a Topaz Town – I dont think we shall ever be merry again – you are ill so long –
>
> When did the Dark happen?
>
> I skipped a page – tonight – because I come so often – now – I might have tired you.
>
> That page is fullest – tho'. . . .
>
> [II, 390]

The expression "I am so far from Land" is Emily's figurative description of her troubled state of mind. She dwelt on sea imagery many times during her years of crisis. About 1859 she told Kate Scott, "I am pleasantly located in the deep sea . . ." [II, 356]. When the long engagement of Susan Phelps and Henry Vaughan Emmons was broken in May 1860, Emily comfortingly paraphrased Isaiah 43:2 to Susan: "When thou goest through the Waters, I will go with thee" [II, 364]. She employed the theme in various poems to Bowles: "Two swimmers wrestled on the spar," "Should you but fail at sea," and "The Drop, that wrestles in the Sea."

Another frequent image of this period is Calvary. George F. Whicher theorized that the word, which appears in seven poems of 1861–63, referred to Dr. Wadsworth's Calvary Church in San Francisco. When Whicher wrote *This Was a Poet* in 1938, the evidence at hand pointed to Wadsworth as the man Emily had loved in the eighteen sixties. The Bowles copy of "Title divine – is mine!" had not yet been published, nor had the "Master" letters, Wadsworth's letter to Emily, "If it had no pencil," and the mutilated letter to Bowles beginning "If I amazed your kindness . . ." Whicher did not know that on January 2, 1862, Emily had sent the "Calvary" stanza of "There came a day at summer's full" to the Reverend Edward Dwight, adapting it to the memory of Mrs. Dwight: proof that the poem was completed before Wadsworth received his call from Calvary Church.

The Calvary identification becomes more tenuous still with the discovery that Emily also used it in speaking of Judge Lord more than twenty years later [III, 761].[24] Aside from "Daisy" and "Master," Emily Dickinson was not in the habit of playing on words which identified specific persons. If she had been, a number of poems with the word "lord" might be expected during the years when she loved the judge; actually she employed "lord" most often in 1862.

The Bowleses returned from New York with their baby at the end of January. Sometime during the next month Samuel Bowles visited Amherst. It may have been just before this visit that Emily wrote him another letter of gratitude and fear:

> I cant thank you any more – You are thoughtful so many times, you grieve me *always* – *now*. The old words are *numb* – and there a'nt any *new* ones – Brooks – are useless – in *Freshet* – *time* –
>
> "*Speech*" is a prank of *Parliament* –
> "*Tears*" – a trick of the *nerve* –

> But the Heart with the heaviest freight on –
> Doesn't – always – move –

[II, 395]

Emily's continual thanks in her letters to Bowles may mean that he was offering some kind of literary advice. Emily still had hopes of publication, and "two Editors of Journals" had spoken of giving her "mind" to the world. On March 1, Bowles printed "Safe in their Alabaster Chambers" in the *Republican,* with the second stanza of 1859, which had not been frosty enough for Sue. He did not name the poet, but printed instead, "Pelham Hill, June, 1861." The place must have had some private meaning to poet and editor; the date may have been the month when Emily gave Bowles the poem. It was the only poem by Emily Dickinson published during her most productive year.

The day the poem appeared, Bowles made a trip to Washington. Emily had just written to ask that he do some errand for her, and now wrote Mary Bowles to apologize in case *she* had tried to fulfill the errand. The letter is informal but not intimate. Emily and Mrs. Bowles were not close friends. Indeed, Mrs. Bowles does not seem to have got along well with any of the Dickinsons. After one disastrous visit to Amherst, Bowles wrote to Austin, "I want you to understand & appreciate & love Mary—to do this, you must make more allowances for her peculiarities,— & judge her by what she means, rather always than by what she says." [25] Another letter mentions a specific problem. "Mary will not come, of course. It could hardly be expected, since Sue has not been to see her, even though she has been in Springfield two or three times." [26] Emily often mentioned Mary Bowles at the end of letters to her husband, but usually only as a dutiful afterthought. Now she tried to be more friendly with the

woman who shared her fears for the life of Samuel
Bowles. Still, she was quite willing to believe that Mrs.
Bowles had opened a letter addressed to Mr. Bowles.

On March 14 young Frazar Stearns, son of the president of Amherst College, was killed in action. In December Emily had written to the Norcross cousins, "Frazer
[sic] Stearns is just leaving Annapolis. His father has
gone to see him today. I hope that ruddy face won't be
brought home frozen" [II, 386]. Now Frazar was dead,
and the distant war was suddenly very near. A week later
his body was brought home. Emily wrote to Loo and
Fanny, "Just as he fell, in his soldier's cap, with his sword
at his side, Frazer rode through Amherst. Classmates to
the right of him, classmates to the left of him, to guard
his narrow face!" She added, "Austin is stunned completely. Let us love better, children, it's most that's left to
do" [II, 397–98].

Austin's shock carried over into a letter to Bowles in
which Emily pretended in turn that she was her brother
and that she was writing at his request. The opening sentences ask Bowles to address and mail an enclosed letter—
perhaps to Wadsworth, whose acceptance of the San Francisco pulpit was announced March 15.

> Will you be kind to *Austin* – again? And would you
> be kinder than sometimes – and put the name – on – too
> – He tells me to tell you – He could not thank you –
> Austin is disappointed – He expected to see you –
> today –
> He is sure you wont go to Sea – without first speak-
> ing to Him. I presume if Emily and Vinnie knew of his
> writing – they would entreat Him to ask you – not –
> Austin is chilled – by Frazer's murder – He says –
> his brain keeps saying over "Frazer is killed," just as
> Father told it – to Him. Two or three words of lead –
> that dropped so deep, they keep weighing –

Tell Austin – how to get over them!
He is very sorry you are not better – He cares for you
– when at the Office – and afterwards – too – at Home –
and sometimes – wakes at night, with a worry for you
– he didn't finish quite – by Day –

[II, 398–99]

Then Emily turned to the practical problem of a drinking
flask Sue wanted to give Bowles for his journey, and asked
him to be sure not to buy one. The poet was all but absent from this letter. The situation was too frightening for
poetic prose. Only in poetry could Emily master fear. The
"two or three words of lead," within the discipline of
verse, could be repeated until shock stilled into art:

It dont sound so terrible – quite – as it did –
I run it over – "Dead," Brain, "Dead."
Put it in Latin – left of my school –
Seems it dont shriek so – under rule.[27]

The editors of *Letters* suggest that the death of Frazar
Stearns may have occasioned Emily's one attempt at free
verse, "Victory comes late." The handwriting is of 1861
or 1862, and the poem was sent to Samuel Bowles. In view
of Emily's other letter-poems to Bowles, it seems more
likely that that "victory" was inward, and had more to
do with love for "Master" than with the Civil War.

Dear Mr Bowles.

Victory comes late,
And is held low to freezing lips
Too rapt with frost
To mind it!
How sweet it would have tasted!
Just a drop!
Was God so economical?

His table's spread too high
Except we dine on tiptoe!
Crumbs fit such little mouths –
Cherries – suit *Robins* –
The Eagle's golden breakfast – *dazzles them*!
God keep his vow to *"Sparrows,"*
Who of little love – know how to starve!

Emily.

[II, 399–400]

The date of Bowles's departure for Europe was set for April 9. He was too ill to make a final trip to Amherst on the day he planned, and Emily did not hide her anxiety:

The Hearts in Amherst – ache – tonight – You could not know how hard – They thought they could not wait – last night – until the Engine – sang – a pleasant tune – that time – because that you were coming the flowers waited – in the vase – and love got peevish, watching – A Rail Road person, rang, to bring an evening paper – Vinnie tipped Pussy – over – in haste to let you in – and I, for joy – and Dignity – held tight in my chair – My Hope put out a petal –

. . . *Please* do not take our *spring* – away – since you blot Summer – out! . . .

Dear friend – we meant to make *you* – brave – but moaned – before we thought. If we should play 'twas *Austin* – perhaps we couldn't let *him* go – to do Good night – to you – If you'll be sure and get well – we'll try to bear it – If we could only care – the less – it would be so much easier – Your letter, troubled my throat. It gave that little scalding, we could not know the reason for, till we grow far up.

I must do my Good night, in *crayon* – I *meant* to – in Red. Love for Mary.

[II, 402]

The love and anguish in this letter, hidden only a little by Emily's "we," make it easier to understand why there were times when Emily could not meet Bowles face to face. Her fear that Bowles would leave without a final visit turned out to be needless: On April 5 he was well enough to visit Amherst. Three days later, in New York, he wrote to Mrs. Bowles his own mixed hopes and fears about his health: "I have faith that it will all work out rightly and happily for my happiness and health. At any rate, we must both act and live as though we expected and believed that." [28]

Next morning Samuel Bowles sailed on the *China*. A few moments before departure he wrote to Austin his "last & hurried goodbye." He spoke of his trip to Amherst and his appreciation of "Emily's considerate attentions & full words." [29] No matter how full Emily's words had been then, no matter how well she had controlled her emotions, she was almost speechless, almost hysterical as she wrote to Mary Bowles,

> When the Best – is gone – I know that other things are not of consequence – The Heart wants what it wants – or else it does not care –
> You wonder why I write – so – Because I cannot help – I like to have you know some care – so when your life gets faint for it's other life – you can lean on us – We wont break, Mary. We look small, but the Reed can carry weight.
> Not to see what we love, is very terrible – and talking does'nt ease it – and nothing does – but just itself.
> The Eyes and Hair, we chose – are all there are – to us – Is'nt it so – Mary?
> I often wonder how the love of Christ, is done – when that – below – holds – so –

[II, 405–06]

I rose – because He sank –
I thought it would be opposite –
But when his power dropped –
My Soul grew straight.
                    —*Emily Dickinson*

5
Royalty

On April 15, 1862, six days after Samuel Bowles sailed on the *China,* Emily Dickinson wrote her first letter to Thomas Wentworth Higginson. Tormented as she was by events impending or just past, she chose her words with special care:

> Mr. Higginson,
>   Are you too deeply occupied to say if my Verse is alive?
>   The Mind is so near itself – it cannot see, distinctly – and I have none to ask –
>   Should you think it breathed – and had you the leisure to tell me, I should feel quick gratitude –
>   If I make the mistake – that you dared to tell me – would give me sincerer honor – toward you –
>   I enclose my name – asking you, if you please – Sir – to tell me what is true?

That you will not betray me – it is needless to ask – since Honor is it's own pawn –

[II, 403]

The final words enjoining secrecy are the ones Emily had written to Bowles when she sent him "Title divine – is mine!"

Above the salutation Emily pasted return postage: two red three-cent stamps. She wrote her name on a card and enclosed it within its own small envelope. She also sent four poems: "I'll tell you how the Sun rose," "Safe in their Alabaster Chambers," "The nearest Dream recedes unrealized," and "We play at Paste."

The immediate reason for Emily's letter was Higginson's article, "Letter to a Young Contributor," in the April *Atlantic Monthly*. The article was unsigned, but the *Springfield Daily Republican* had identified its author in a March 29 review:

> The Atlantic Monthly for April is one of the best numbers ever issued; not of that popular periodical merely, but of magazine literature since its first inception. . . . Its leading article, T. W. Higginson's Letter to a Young Contributor, ought to be read by all the would-be authors of the land. . . . It is a test of latent power. Whoever rises from its thorough perusal strengthened and encouraged, may be reasonably certain of ultimate success.[1]

The *Weekly Republican* reprinted the review on April 5, the day Bowles made his farewell visit to Amherst.

"I read your Chapters in the Atlantic –" Emily told Higginson in her second letter to him, "and experienced honor for you – I was sure you would not reject a confiding question –" [II, 405]. The article so impressed her that she could quote part of it from memory long afterward. Early in 1877 she wrote to Higginson, "Often, when troubled by entreaty, that paragraph of your's has saved me – 'Such being the Majesty of the Art you presume to practice, you can at least take time before dishonoring it' . . ." [II, 573].[2] In 1862 "majesty" was a word certain to catch Emily Dickinson's attention.

Writing to a total stranger was not easy for Emily. The strain is evident in her taut prose. Perhaps she strengthened herself to the task by recalling that Charlotte Brontë, like herself an unknown poet unsure if her verses breathed, had asked the same kind of advice from Southey. But like the "Yorkshire Girl," Emily Dickinson was too thoroughly individual to be guided much by anyone. Higginson had laid stress, for instance, on the appearance of the Young Contributor's manuscript: ". . . send your composition in such a shape that it shall not need the slightest literary revision before printing." "Reduce yourself to short allowance of parentheses and dashes. . . ."[3] Emily paid no attention to his warnings. Higginson's reaction, as he remembered it in 1891, was predictable. The letter "was in a handwriting so peculiar that it seemed as if the writer might have taken her first lessons by studying the famous fossil bird-tracks in the museum of [Amherst College]. Of punctuation there was little; she used chiefly dashes. . . ."[4] He also noticed the odd archaic use of capitals. As to the enclosed poetry, he commented on April 17 to James T. Fields, editor of the *Atlantic*, "I foresee that 'Young Contributors' will send me worse things than ever now. Two such specimens of verse as came yesterday & day before fortunately *not* to be forwarded for publication!"[5] Nevertheless, Higginson was sufficiently interested by Emily's poems and letters to reply immediately.

Emily Dickinson's second letter to Higginson, ten days after the first, was carefully written but fairly expansive.

She thanked him for his criticism of her poems—"surgery,"
she called it—and told him a good deal about her family
and her reading. Yet she intended him to imagine her as
the Young Contributor of his *Atlantic* article, not as a
woman of 31. "You asked how old I was?" she wrote. "I
made no verse – but one or two – until this winter – Sir – "
[II, 404]. Thus Emily eluded the question and belied the
three hundred or more poems already in her hand-sewn
booklets. She admitted that several years had passed since
her "Tutor" (Ben Newton) had died, but said he had
taught her immortality when she was a little girl.[6]

If there is much pose in this letter, there is also much
truth. The great flow of poetry was shaking Emily daily.
Two mainstays, Sue and Samuel Bowles, had withdrawn
their support by respective indifference and distance. Passages from this and the next three letters to Higginson
express the loneliness and doubts which Emily felt.

> I had a terror – since September – I could tell to none
> – and so I sing, as the Boy does by the burying Ground
> – because I am afraid –
>
> [II, 404]

> My dying Tutor told me that he would like to live
> till I had been a poet, but Death was much of Mob as I
> could master – then – and when far afterward – a sud-
> den light on Orchards, or a new fashion in the wind
> troubled my attention – I felt a palsy, here – the Verses
> just relieve –
>
> [II, 408]

> Will you tell me my fault, frankly as to yourself, for
> I had rather wince, then die. Men do not call the sur-
> geon, to commend – the Bone, but to set it, Sir, and
> fracture within, is more critical.
>
> [II, 412]

Royalty

I had no Monarch in my life, and cannot rule myself,
and when I try to organize – my little Force explodes –
and leaves me bare and charred –

[II, 414]

The "terror since September" may have begun when
Samuel Bowles found that his health was no better after
a long summer rest, and decided to try Dr. Denniston's
water cure. Or perhaps the death of Mrs. Edward Dwight
in Maine was more of a shock to Emily than extant letters
indicate. The series of Confederate victories which had
begun in July at Bull Run may have frightened Emily, or
the danger to the Amherst townsmen and students who
had enlisted. Whatever the source of the winter's terror,
Emily Dickinson felt that she "had no Monarch" now.
She had lost the preceptor who had replaced Ben Newton.
"I found one more," she wrote to Higginson on April 25,
"but he was not contented I be his scholar – so he left the
Land" [II, 404]. As she wrote, Emily knew how soon yet
another guide would be leaving the land. Dr. Wadsworth,
who had been released from his Philadelphia church on
April 3, was preparing to sail for California, via Panama,
on May 1.

What Emily needed now was not the spiritual guidance
of Wadsworth nor the friendship of Bowles, important as
both were to her. The poems were coming faster—sometimes several in one day, as Emily told Sue in verse.

I send Two Sunsets –
Day and I – in competition – ran –
I finished Two, and several Stars
While He – was making One – [7]

From Higginson Emily expected the objectivity of a critic
who would not praise her—as Bowles and Dr. Holland
might—unless her poems deserved praise. One of the

poems enclosed in her first letter to him, "Safe in their Alabaster Chambers," was a sort of yardstick. The previous summer she had been grateful for Sue's comments on the poem, but had wondered how sincere they were. This same poem had found favor enough with Samuel Bowles to appear in the *Republican*. Obviously Emily was fond of it herself. Now, in the hands of a stranger whose judgment Emily trusted, the poem would serve as the measure of her friends' opinions and her own.

For many years critics armed with hindsight have attacked Higginson for being less acute than Emily thought him. A wiser man, they argue, would have been aware that he had found a poet infinitely superior to the literary idols of the day. He would have brought the Amherst spinster's art to public attention, and perhaps have pried Emily out of her gradual seclusion.

It is fair to ask (using the same hindsight) whether Emily Dickinson could have found a better preceptor. At the moment when she most needed help, his *Atlantic* article appeared and she "experienced honor" for him. Though Higginson was, as usual, preoccupied with any number of causes—chief of them the recruiting of a Negro regiment—he took time to reply to the unsolicited letter and poetry from Amherst. As a minor Transcendentalist and champion of women's rights, he was more likely than most critics to respond to her pleading. If his praise of Emily Dickinson was heavily qualified, it was still praise. The "surgery," she said, "was not so painful as I supposed."

There can be no doubt that Higginson performed a great service for Emily in the spring of 1862. He restored the sense of balance she had all but lost. For several years Emily had stabilized her griefs and terrors in poetry: they seemed not to "shriek so, under rule." When her feelings of royalty were strong, she knew that the poems she was creating made up for whatever she was denied or had forsworn. But when she doubted the worth of her art, the other problems were too much for her. Such was the case when the April *Atlantic* arrived; at the time, Emily wrote, "I could not weigh myself – Myself – My size felt small – to me –" Higginson assured Emily that her poetry *was* art, and thereby helped to save both the poet and her poems from disaster. Seven years later Emily wrote to Higginson, "Of our greatest acts we are ignorant – You were not aware that you saved my Life" [II, 460].

Even so, Higginson's censures led Emily Dickinson to decide against publication. In 1861 she had written "I'm nobody – who are you?" to disclaim any desire to croak her name, froglike, to an admiring bog. If she were to be published, she must come before the public anonymously. The separate enclosure of her name with an unsigned letter hinted as much to Higginson. But as late as March 1862 she and Sue spoke of the poems as a fleet waiting to be launched.[8] Publication of some sort was still in Emily's thoughts.

By June 7 she made up her mind. Higginson's second letter had praised her poems more than the first, so much that she told him, "I have had few pleasures so deep as your opinion, and if I tried to thank you, my tears would block my tongue" [II, 408]. Grateful as she was, Emily saw that Higginson wanted her to obey conventional rules of prosody. In her letter of April 25 she enclosed two poems with a warning: "I bring you others – as you ask – though they might not differ –" [II, 404]. As weeks passed, the reservation grew. Emily wrote on June 7,

> Your second letter surprised me, and for a moment, swung – I had not supposed it. Your first – gave no dishonor, because the True – are not ashamed – I thanked you for your justice – but could not drop the Bells

whose jingling cooled my Tramp – Perhaps the Balm,
seemed better, because you bled me, first. . . .
   You think my gait "spasmodic" – I am in danger –
Sir –
   You think me "uncontrolled" – I have no Tribunal.

                                               [II, 408–09]

Emily Dickinson knew now that she could write by no
rules but her own. Her sense of royalty was returning. If
publication could come only at the cost of her poetic in-
tegrity she thought the price too high. Still, she could not
offend the kindly Higginson. She worded her decision so
that he would not know his part in it. "I smile when you
suggest that I delay 'to publish' – "she wrote, "that being
foreign to my thought, as Firmament to Fin – If fame belonged to me, I could not escape her – if she did not, the
longest day would pass me on the chase – and the approbation of my Dog, would forsake me – then – My Barefoot
Rank is better – " [II, 408]. Then Emily outlined her
terms for her future relationship to Higginson. "If I might
bring you what I do – not so frequent to trouble you – and
ask you if I told it clear – 'twould be control, to me" [II,
409]. She did not say she would follow his advice. At the
end of the letter Emily asked for Higginson's consent to
such an arrangement: "But, will you be my Preceptor,
Mr. Higginson?" He replied that he would, and the
friendship, on Emily's terms, continued.

As Higginson and Emily became closer friends the preceptor tried again and again to be tutor to the woman as
well as the poet. Emily evaded him. His first letter had
elicited as much as Emily cared to tell about herself:

   You inquire my Books – For Poets – I have Keats – and
   Mr and Mrs Browning. For Pross – Mr Ruskin – Sir
   Thomas Browne – and the Revelations. I went to school
   – but in your manner of the phrase – had no education. . . .

You ask of my Companions Hills – Sir – and the Sundown – and a Dog – large as myself, that my Father
bought me – They are better than Beings – because they
know – but do not tell – and the noise in the Pool, at
Noon – excels my Piano. I have a Brother and Sister
– My Mother does not care for thought – and Father,
too busy with his Briefs – to notice what we do – He
buys me many Books – but begs me not to read them –
because he fears they joggle the Mind. They are religious – except me – and address an Eclipse, every morning – whom they call their "Father."

[II, 404]

The truth is this unique autobiographical sketch is wildly
distorted at times. Emily, of course, was trying to be Mr.
Higginson's Young Contributor. She described a child's
household, in which brother, sister, piano, and dog were
important and the father controlled the reading of the
young. It is all too clear that Edward Dickinson would not
buy his daughter books, then beg her not to read them.
But his fears that books would "joggle the mind" probably
was real: he had attributed Emily's new exultation and
sadness and solitude to an overdose of reading. Neither he
nor any of the family understood that it was writing, not
reading, which kept Emily so often in her room. Quite
possibly she gave reading as an excuse. Even Vinnie was
to be amazed at the number of the poems when she discovered them after Emily's death.

Finding that Emily's description of herself avoided
direct answers to his questions, Higginson tried a new
tack. He asked for a picture of Emily. She replied, "Could
you believe me – without? I had no portrait, now, but am
small, like the Wren, and my Hair is bold, like the Chest-
nut Bur – and my eyes, like the Sherry in the Glass, that
the Guest leaves – Would this do just as well?" [II, 411.] [9]

Little as Emily told Higginson about herself, she revealed enough to give him topics for advice. He thought hills, sundown, and Carlo too scant companionship. Emily had warned, speaking of her poems, "When I state myself, as the Representative of the Verse – it does not mean – me – but a supposed person" [II, 412]. Her preceptor could not know that the statement described, at times, her prose art as well. Emily thought of herself as wholly secluded, just as in her poems she imagined herself dressed in the white robes of the Judgment Day. Later she conformed bodily to her artistic image, but not in 1862. Therefore Higginson urged her to spend more time with others. In August Emily explained, "Of 'shunning Men and Women' – they talk of Hallowed things, aloud – and embarrass my Dog – He and I dont object to them, if they'll exist their side. . . . You say 'Beyond your knowledge.' You would not jest with me, because I believe you – but Preceptor – you cannot mean it? All men say 'What' to me, but I thought it a fashion –" [II, 415].

One of the men who said "What?" to Emily must have been "Master." Diplomacy in the presence of a woman in love is difficult enough without that woman's framing her speech in epigram and paradox. About 1862 [10] Emily wrote the last of her three surviving "Master" letters. Like the others it is a draft with deletions and corrections. It remained among Emily's papers. The master is still in shadow, though there are hints of intimacy: "Low at the knee that bore her once to (royal) wordless rest (now) Daisy (stoops) kneels a culprit –" Emily confesses "A love so big it scares her, rushing among her small heart – pushing aside the blood and leaving her faint and white in the gust's arm –" [II, 391].

The letter describes a single biographical event: "Daisy – who never flinched thro' that awful parting, but held her life so tight he should not see the wound – who would have sheltered him in her childish bosom – only it was'nt big eno' for a Guest so large – " By stretch of credulity this parting could be taken as the end of Emily's single interview with Dr. Wadsworth two years before. More likely it was the final visit of Samuel Bowles before his trip to Europe.

There is evidence enough in letters and love poems actually mailed to Bowles to name him as "Master," but this letter-draft offers further confirmation of the identification. First, there is the theme of royalty. Emily asked "Master" to "teach her . . . grace – teach her majesty – " She said her master's knee had once borne her to royal rest. Second, there is the improbability that Dr. Wadsworth would have taken Emily on his knee during his visit to Amherst, when he was in mourning for his mother. Bowles might well have done so, in fun. Such was his charm that his dignified women friends were not offended by words and behavior they would not have tolerated in others. From Europe, in 1862, Bowles wrote to Maria Whitney, "We would 'welcome you with open arms,' and take care not to shock you by closing them—if we could help it!" [11] In 1877 he called Emily a "damned rascal" and she was delighted. For her part, Emily had already suggested to Bowles that she would like to have the "little Hound within the Heart" "climb your dizzy knee."

The letters Emily wrote to Bowles while he was in Europe are far more controlled than those which preceded his departure. For one thing, Samuel Bowles seemed less likely to die. His cheerful letters to the *Republican* and to Austin helped allay Emily's fears—enough, at least, so that she could maintain discipline in prose. Still, she was impatient for his return:

> You go away – and where you go, we cannot come –
> but then the Months have names – and each one comes

but once a year – and though it never seems they could, they sometimes do – go by.

We hope you are more well than when you lived in America – . . . We hope you recollect each life you left behind, even our's, the least –

We wish we knew how Amherst looked, in your memory. Smaller than it did, maybe – and yet things swell, by leaving – if big in themselves – We hope you will not alter, but be the same we grieved for, when the "China" sailed. If you should like to hear the news, we did not die – here – we did not change. We have the same Guests we did, except yourself – and the Roses hang on the same stems – as before you want. Vinnie trains the honeysuckle – and the Robins steal the string for Nests – quite, quite as they used to –

In tone and subject, the letter resembles 1862 poems like "I dreaded that first Robin, so" and "I tie my Hat – I crease my Shawl," in which time passes slowly through the cycle of seasons and routines of daily life for the impatient "Queen of Calvary." The letter to Bowles continues,

I have the errand from my heart – I might forget to tell it. Would you please to come home? The long life's years are scant, and fly away, the Bible says, like a told story – and sparing is a solemn thing, somehow, it seems to me – and I grope fast, with my fingers, for all out of sight I own   to get it nearer

[II, 409–10]

The last sentence may be understood as a reference to the poems Emily was writing. "All out of sight I own" included Samuel Bowles, Dr. Wadsworth, and the dead. Although she could only speculate about death, Emily Dickinson wrote poems in 1862 which brought her living "Master" nearer to her:

I envy Seas, whereon He rides –
I envy Spokes of Wheels
Of Chariots, that Him convey –
I envy Crooked Hills

That gaze upon His journey –
How easy all can see
What is forbidden utterly
As Heaven – unto me!

. . . .

I envy Light – that wakes Him –
And Bells – that boldly ring
To tell Him it is Noon, abroad –
Myself – be Noon to Him –

Yet interdict – my Blossom –
And abrogate – my Bee –
Lest Noon in Everlasting Night –
Drop Gabriel – and Me – [12]

The trouble with Emily's attempts to recall her master in poetry is apparent in the final stanza. There was still the possibility of "Everlasting Night." Her "fainting Prince" (as she described "Master" in "I rose because He sank—") might not live to return to his queen. Darkness as a synonym for absence or death was one of Emily's favorite symbols in her 1862 poems, and she repeated it many times in letters to and about Samuel Bowles. "I dont think we shall ever be merry again – you are ill so long – When did the dark happen?" she wrote to Bowles in January 1862 [II, 390]. Two years later she wrote, "Austin told – Saturday morning – that you were not so well. 'Twas Sundown – all day – . . ." [II, 437]. When Bowles was on his deathbed, Emily told Mrs. Holland, "Dear Mr Bowles is hesitating – God help him decide on the mortal Side! This is Night – now – but we are not dreaming" [II, 596]. A few months later she wrote to Maria Whitney, who had loved Bowles, "I have thought of you often since the darkness, though we cannot assist another's night" [II, 602]. The theme of darkness or midnight occasionally is linked to other friends and events in Emily's letters, but it appears regularly only when Bowles is mentioned.

Emily Dickinson's three correspondences during the summer of 1862 follow three distinct patterns. Emily had always adapted her style to the recipient, but never before had there been such a gulf between art and information. The letters to the Norcross cousins are much like Emily's girlhood letters; those to Higginson are stilted and literary. Between extremes are the letters to Bowles. Each correspondence has its own idiom, its own rhythm. Letters of July and August contain the following contrasts:

To the Norcrosses:

> Loo left a tumbler of sweet-peas on the green room bureau. I am going to leave them there till they make pods and sow themselves in the upper drawer, and then I guess they'll bloom about Thanksgiving time.
>
> [II, 411]

To Samuel Bowles:

> We reckon – your coming by the Fruit. When the Grape gets by – and the Pippin, and the Chestnut – When the Days are a little short by the clock – and a little long by the want – when the Sky has new Red Gowns – and a purple Bonnet – then we say, you will come – I am glad that kind of time, goes by.
>
> [II, 416]

To T. W. Higginson:

> Perhaps you smile at me. I could not stop for that – My
> Business is Circumference – An Ignorance, not of Cus-
> toms, but if caught with the Dawn – or the Sunset see
> me – Myself the only Kangaroo among the Beauty, Sir,
> if you please, it afflicts me, and I thought that instruc-
> tion would take it away.
>
> [II, 412]

In her August letter to Bowles, Emily continued to
speak of herself as "we." There was a faint recurrence of
the winter's disguises as she wrote, "Sue gave me the
paper, to write on – so when the writing tires you – play
it is Her, and 'Jackey' – and that will rest your eyes – for
have not the Clovers, *names*, to the Bees?" [II, 416.]

By late summer Bowles was eager to return, and Emily
kept urging him to do so. Repeatedly she had detailed the
length of her waiting: the number of months which must
pass, the number of crops which must ripen before Bowles
came back. Now the return seemed nearer:

> Summer a'nt so long as it was, when we stood looking
> at it, before you went away, and when I finish August,
> we'll hop the Autumn, very soon – and then 'twill be
> Yourself. . . .
> I tell you, Mr Bowles, it is a Suffering to have a sea –
> no care how Blue – between your Soul, and you. The
> Hills you used to love when you were in Northampton,
> miss their old lover, could they speak – . . .
>
> [II, 416]

Only one letter of Emily Dickinson can be dated between August and November 1862. On October 6 Emily
sent a brief note to T. W. Higginson. "Did I displease
you, Mr. Higginson? But wont you tell me how?" [II,

417.] Emily was soon aware that duty, not displeasure, accounted for Higginson's lapse in correspondence. He had been busy with his troops; in November he led his Negro regiment to South Carolina. For the third time in a year distance and danger were taking one of Emily's preceptors. But as Higginson—Colonel Higginson now—departed, Samuel Bowles returned. Emily wrote to him at once. Perhaps she already knew that he was still unwell —she begged him not to resume work. Once again she felt she must define friendship, this time in terms of life and death. "So few that live – have life – " she wrote, "it seems of quick importance – not one of those escape by Death. And since you gave us Fear – Congratulate us – for Ourselves – you give us safer – Peace. How extraordinary that Life's large Population contain so few of power to us – and those – a vivid species – who leave no mode – like Tyrian Dye."

A few days later Bowles came to Amherst. Emily sent down a note from her bedroom.

> Dear friend
> I cannot see you. You will not less believe me. That you return to us alive, is better than a Summer. And more to hear your voice below, than News of any Bird.
> Emily.
>
> [II, 419]

The message was as tense and formal as some of Emily's letters to Higginson. Bowles did not understand. Emily had been telling him all summer how much she wanted to see him. But he took her refusal lightly, and when he got back to Springfield he sent her "a little bat"—either a dried one or a picture—as an appropriate companion for a woman who hid from him.

Emily tried to explain. She wrote, "Because I did not see you, Vinnie and Austin, upbraided me – They did not

know I gave my part that they might have the more. . . ."
To this false excuse she added the true: "Forgive me if I
prize the Grace – superior to the Sign. . . . My Heart
led all the rest – I think that what we *know* – we can endure that others doubt, until their faith be riper. And so,
dear friend, who knew me, I make no argument – to
you – " Nevertheless, Emily continued the explanation for
her strange behavior, enlarging on it sentence by sentence
until by the end of the letter she had pledged Bowles her
total devotion:

> Did I not want to see you? Do not the Phebes want to
> come? Oh they of little faith. I said I was glad you were
> alive – Might it bear repeating? Some phrases are too
> fine to fade – and Light but just confirms them – Few
> absences could seem so wide as your's has done, to us –
> If 'twas a larger face – or we a smaller Canvas – we need
> not know – now you have come –
>
> We hope often to see you – Our poverty – entitle us –
> and friends are nations in themselves – to supersede the
> Earth –
>
> 'Twould please us, were you well – and could your
> health be had by sacrifice of ours – 'twould be conten-
> tion for the place – We used to tell each other, when
> you were from America – how failure in a Battle – were
> easier – and you here – I will not tell you further –
>
> Perhaps you tire – now – A small weight – is obnox-
> ious—upon a weary Rope – but had you Exile – or
> Eclipse – or so huge a Danger, as would dissolve all
> other friends – 'twould please me to remain –
>
> Let others – show this Surry's Grace –
> Myself – assist his Cross.

[II, 419–20] [13]

The return of Samuel Bowles and Emily's refusal to
see him were the beginning of a new phase of their friendship. During the months when Bowles had seemed near

death, Emily had been writing out her love and fear in hundreds of poems. She had strengthened herself to the point where she could face a life without her "Master." Whether the man she loved should live or die, she could not expect fulfillment of her love. She was convinced that this did not matter as long as she could "sing to use the waiting." As Mabel Loomis Todd said, "Emily was more interested in her poems than in any man." [14]

Emily had come to realize that the joy she had felt when she thought her master returned her love was more important to her than the event which brought the joy. In "The Day that I was crowned" she explained her new position in terms of royalty:

> The Grace that I – was chose –
> To me surpassed the Crown
> That was the Witness for the Grace – [15]

When Bowles returned from Europe, Emily used exactly the same reasoning to explain why she had refused to see him: "Forgive me if I prize the Grace – superior to the Sign." The refusal was not easy. Soon afterward Emily began another poem,

> Renunciation – is a piercing Virtue –
> The letting go
> A Presence – for an Expectation – [16]

Expectation versus present fulfillment appears again in a letter which Emily wrote to Samuel Bowles in 1862 or 1863:

> Dear friend
>   If you doubted my Snow – for a moment – you never
> will – again – I know –

Because I could not say it – I fixed it in the Verse –
for you to read – when your thought wavers, for such a
foot as mine –

> Through the strait pass of suffering –
> The Martyrs – even – trod.
> Their feet – upon Temptation –
> Their faces – upon God –
>
> A stately – shriven Company –
> Convulsion – playing round –
> Harmless – as streaks of Meteor –
> Upon a Planet's Bond –
>
> Their faith – the everlasting troth –
> Their Expectation – fair –
> The Needle – to the North Degree –
> Wades – so – thro' polar Air!

[II, 394–95] [17]

Samuel Bowles could not share Emily's views of "mar-
tyrdom." In January 1862 he had written to Maria Whitney, the woman he loved, "We cannot crucify our earthly
desires,—that has been tried, and it was semi-barbarism.
. . . There are some people—are you not one?—charitable
and loving and generous to everybody else, but hard and
severe to themselves. This is cruel, wicked." [18]

The letters Bowles wrote to Austin Dickinson in the
months after his return from Europe show a progressive
dissatisfaction with Emily's new attitude toward him.
Early in 1863—perhaps late in January—he sent his re-
gards to the family, "and to the Queen Recluse my espe-
cial sympathy—that she has 'overcome the world.' Is it
really true that they sing 'old hundred' & 'alleluia' per-
petually, in heaven—ask her; and are dandelions, aspho-
dels, & Maiden's [joy?] the standard flowers of the
ethereal?" [19]

If Emily saw this letter, it must have hurt her. Bowles

was half joking, half in earnest. He hoped Emily's wit and charm—the qualities he admired in her—would overcome her strange, regal refusal to meet him. Emily had revealed herself to Bowles; she had sent him "Title Divine – is Mine!" in which she was "Empress of Calvary" and had begged him to "tell no other"; she had also called herself his queen. Now Bowles was joking with Austin about her sense of royalty.

Soon Bowles found the situation less funny. His description of Emily in one April letter is not a compliment to her: "I have been in a savage, turbulent state for some time—indulging in a sort of chronic disgust at everything and everybody—I guess a good deal as Emily feels. . . ."[20] At the end of the letter he wrote, "Tell Emily I am here, in the old place. 'Can you not watch one hour?' " The use of Christ's words in Gethsemane was a double barb, for Emily had written in December that she would remain when all other friends "dissolved," to "assist his cross."

It is plain that some situation was deterring Bowles from visiting Amherst in the spring of 1863. In another letter to Austin, probably written a week after the one just quoted, he discussed the reasons. One of them was his health, still poor in spite of his many months of travel and rest. But that was not all:

> Other causes for my reticence—of which you seem sometimes oppressed—you ought to know without my explaining.—I thought to write you of them fully, but I cannot. You certainly are not ignorant of them; I must respect them; so must you. They are not unconquerable —it has seemed to me the wisest thing to put them aside. But that belongs not to me, nor to you. So long as they exist, however, I beg you to be indulgent to my shortcomings in the duties and delights of friendship.[21]

There are two plausible explanations of this "reticence": Emily Dickinson was in love with Bowles, or Sue Dick-

inson and Mary Bowles were at odds. The latter possibility is strengthened by some of the letters from Bowles to
Austin. On the other hand, the fact that Bowles more
than once wrote about the disagreement between his wife
and Sue seems to rule it out as a subject he was unwilling
to discuss. Besides, he had often visited Amherst before
without his wife, and simply had to go there alone, if the
problem involved Mrs. Bowles. There may, of course, be
a third, unknown explanation of Bowles's words.

Only a handful of Emily Dickinson's 1863 letters remain. There are two notes to Bowles: a two-sentence message which accompanied a gift of apples in the fall, and a
single sentence—"I could'nt let Austin's note go – without
a word"—added at the bottom of the poem, "The Zeroes –
taught us – Phosphorus – " [II, 426]. Bowles's April post-
script to Austin, "Tell Emily I am here, in the old place,"
obviously means that Emily had stopped writing to him
for a time.

Correspondence with Colonel Higginson was likewise
confined to two letters, neither of them long. Though her
preceptor was commanding troops in South Carolina,
Emily asked him to come to Amherst in some future summer. "I should have liked to see you, before you became
improbable," she told him. "War feels to me an oblique
place" [II, 423]. It may be that something in this letter
offended Higginson. When Emily next wrote him she
was apologetic and regretted that her friend doubted her
"High Behavior." She had spoken of her fears for the
lives of absent friends; the poem she sent him now, "The
possibility to pass," dealt with the continual imminence
of death. Possibly Higginson, in the midst of war, resented
hearing about death from maiden ladies safe at home. At
any rate, the correspondence stopped until Higginson
returned to New England.

The majority of Emily's 1863 letters were written to

Loo and Fanny Norcross, who were orphaned by the death of their father in January. Emily continued to speak to her cousins as if they were small children, though Louisa was now twenty-one, Fanny sixteen. "Wasn't dear papa so tired always after mamma went, and wasn't it almost sweet to think of the two together these new winter nights? The grief is our side, darlings, and the glad is theirs. Vinnie and I sit down tonight, while mother tells what makes us cry, though we know it is well and easy with uncle and papa, and only our part hurts" [II, 420–21].

The chief value of Emily's letters to the Norcrosses is autobiographical. Emily made the cousins her confidantes, and also told more about her daily life than she considered vital in her intellectual correspondences. According to Mabel Loomis Todd, the Norcross cousins "had the most intimate letters from Emily . . . Louisa pretended to be a reticent person, out of the world like Emily. They adored her like a god. Vinnie wasn't devoted to the Norcrosses. They were such geese." [22] Though the Norcrosses did not allow Mrs. Todd, who was editing Emily's letters in the eighteen nineties, to see anything "too personal" from Emily (they copied out passages for publication, and eventually destroyed the autograph letters), enough remains to show that Emily was still undergoing mental turmoil in 1863. In May she wrote,

> The nights turned hot, when Vinnie had gone, and I must keep no window raised for fear of prowling "booger," and I must shut my door for fear front door slide open on me at the "dead of night," and I must keep "gas" burning to light the danger up, so I could distinguish it – these gave me a snarl which don't unravel yet, and that old nail in my breast pricked me. . . .
>
> [II, 424]

Emily was still writing poems frequently—about 140 of them in 1863—and it may be that poetry accounts for the nervous strain she described to Fanny and Loo. Her reaction to possible dangers, though, seems to be a humorous hint to her cousins that it was her mother's timidity, not her own, which made the nightly precautions necessary. "That old nail in my breast" probably was her love for "Master."

Emily's autumn letters were high-spirited. Though she wrote to the Norcrosses, "Nothing has happened but loneliness, perhaps too daily to relate," she poked fun at her martial Aunt Elisabeth, to whom she must "bid the stiff 'good-night' and the square 'good-morning.'" "The trees stand right up straight when they hear her boots," Emily wrote, "and will bear crockery wares instead of fruit, I fear. She hasn't starched the geraniums yet, but will have ample time, unless she leaves before April" [II, 428]. Daily life, for all its loneliness, had its light moments:

> No one has called so far, but one old lady to look at a house. I directed her to the cemetery to spare expense of moving.
>
> I got down before father this morning, and spent a few moments profitably with the South Sea rose [perhaps Melville's *Typee*]. Father detecting me, advised wiser employment, and read at devotions the chapter of the gentleman with one talent. I think he thought my conscience would adjust the gender.
>
> [II, 427]

These autumn letters do not betray the fact that Emily was ill. Her new discomfort was an unspecified eye ailment. After 1865 Emily ceased to have trouble with her eyes, and she never wore glasses: probably her sickness was an outward symptom of her inward affliction. Twenty years later her reaction to the deaths of Judge Lord and her nephew Gilbert took the form of a physical collapse. At the time of her second letter to Higginson (April 25, 1862), two weeks after Bowles had sailed for Europe and a week before Dr. Wadsworth would leave for California, Emily had been ill for several days. It is impossible to be sure which sicknesses were organic, and the amount of writing Emily must have done in bad light cannot have been good for her eyes. Housework occupied much of the day; Emily read and wrote at night or at daybreak. Whatever the cause of her eye trouble, she was ill by September 1863. The next February she went to Boston to see a specialist, and from April to November 1864 she lived in Cambridge with the Norcross cousins while undergoing a series of treatments.

Life in a Cambridge boardinghouse did not speed Emily's recovery. Poetry was possible, though the doctor had ordered her not to read or write. She wrote in June to Colonel Higginson, who had been wounded and was convalescing in Newport, "I work in my prison, and make guests for myself" [II, 431]. There were nearly two hundred "guests" in 1864: more than in any other year of her life except 1862. But living away from home was not to Emily's taste. There were other boarders and there were trips to the doctor's office in Boston. In May, Emily confessed to Vinnie, "Loo and Fanny take sweet care of me, and let me want for nothing, but I am not at Home, and the calls at the Doctor's are painful, and dear Vinnie, I have not looked at the Spring" [II, 430]. In July she wrote, "I feel no gayness yet. I suppose I had been discouraged so long. You remember, the Prisoner of Chillon did not know Liberty when it came, and asked to go back to Jail" [II, 433].

In time Emily became accustomed to the landlady, Mrs. Bangs, but the arrival of strangers was as disturbing as it had been in Amherst, especially because she could not do much about it. Not long before she returned home in November, Emily wrote, "Anna Norcross lives here, since Saturday, and two new people more, a person and his wife, so I do little but fly . . ." [II, 435]. She took no part in the cultural or social life of the city: her only reference to a local event was an oblique half-sentence about a Cambridge torchlight parade to celebrate Lincoln's re-election —"The Drums keep on for the still Man. . . ." Homesickness troubled her continually. She told Vinnie she would be willing to walk all the way to Amherst and sleep in the bushes. But when it was time to go home, her royalty returned. "I shall go Home in two weeks. You will get me at Palmer, yourself. Let no one beside come" [II, 435]. Cold words to write to her beloved sister, but Emily knew what her state of mind would be if she rode all the way to Amherst and met her whole family at once, after the "publicity" of a railroad coach. Her regal tone was armor against assaults on her timidity.

An 1864 poem sent to Samuel Bowles turns a royal theme to a new use. Bowles probably had chided his "Queen Recluse" for inconsistency when she said she was willing to see him. Emily wrote to him,

> Perhaps you think me *stooping*!
> I'm not ashamed – of *that*!
> *Christ* – stooped – until he *touched the Grave*!
> Do those at *Sacrament* –
> Commemorate *dishonor* –
> Or love – annealed of love –
> Until it bend – as low as *Death*
> *Re-royalized* – above? [23]

It is difficult to trace Emily's friendship with Bowles after early 1863. At that time he seems to have been asking her to write. But by late 1863 or early 1864 the situation was reversed, and Emily wrote her most revealing letter-poem to Bowles, "If it had no pencil," in which she addressed him as "sweet" and asked him, even if he had no message, to draw a daisy, "Most as big as I was, / When it"—Bowles—"plucked me."

Communications between the two seem to have ceased almost entirely. There is no firm evidence that Emily had met Samuel Bowles since April 1862. The one hint that she had is an 1864 poem to him:

> Before He comes, We weigh the Time,
> 'Tis Heavy, and 'tis Light –
> When He departs, an Emptiness
> Is the superior Freight.[24]

Emily's willingness to see Bowles did not mean that she could bring herself to do so when he came to Amherst. When she had apologized for refusing to meet him after his return from Europe, she had written, "We hope often to see you – Our poverty – entitle us – ": another statement of the "Chillon" aspect of her royalty, and a contradiction to her actual behavior during his visit.

In 1864 Bowles again became ill enough to alarm Emily. Without mentioning her own ailment, she wrote to him,

> Austin told – Saturday morning – that you were not so well, 'Twas Sundown – all day – Saturday – and Sunday – such a long Bridge – no news of you – could cross! Teach us to miss you *less* – because the fear to miss you *more* – haunts us – all the time. We did'nt *care* so much – once – I wish it was *then – now –* but you kept tightening – so – it cant be *stirred – today –* You did'nt *mean* to be worse – did you? Was'nt it a *mistake?* Wont you decide soon – to be the strong man we first knew? 'Twould lighten things – so much – and yet *that* man – was not so dear – I guess you'd better *not.*[25]

Whether she would allow herself to see him or not, Emily had not changed in her devotion to Samuel Bowles.

Emily spent the winter of 1864–65 at home, but her eyes continued to give her trouble. She was able to perform only a few household chores, and reported to the Norcrosses that the family considered her "a help": the sort of praise she would not have received if her help had been taken for granted. In April 1865 Emily returned to the city for further treatment. The great tide of poetry in her was ebbing. Personal tensions were no longer dominant in her poems and letters; no doubt she also shared in the general relief which came with the end of the Civil War. Only the quantity of her poetry diminished—her mastery in words never left her. Her finest prose was still to come.

The letters of 1865 (only thirteen of them have been found) are domestic messages to the Norcrosses, Vinnie, Sue, and Mrs. Holland. There are no letters to Bowles, but one poem to him, a variant stanza of "Sweet – You forgot – but I remembered," may have been sent in 1865. Whether it refers to a lapse in correspondence or to Bowles's visits is uncertain.

> Just to be Rich –
> To waste my Guinea
> On so broad a Heart –
> Just to be Poor –
> For Barefoot Pleasure
> You – Sir – Shut me out – [26]

While Emily was in Cambridge, Samuel Bowles was traveling to the far west. Health was not the object of this trip; letters to Austin mention weariness at times, but no alarming sickness. Bowles's travel letters to the *Republican*, published late in the year as *Across the Continent*, described to New Englanders the various aspects of west-

Portrait of Emily Dickinson

ern life, from the Mormon theocracy of Utah to the beauties of Yosemite. One passage on San Francisco must have interested Emily Dickinson; perhaps it was written to please her. "Among the 'orthodox' preachers," Bowles wrote, "Dr. Wadsworth, from Philadelphia, perhaps ranks first; and his society, a Presbyterian one, is probably the largest and richest of that order. He is more of a scholar than an orator, however; but is greatly respected and beloved." [27]

Emily made only one indirect reference to Bowles's journey. In November, when the *Republican* announced that the editor was returning from the west but neglected to name his port of arrival, Emily wrote to Mrs. Holland, "It is hard to be told by the papers that a friend is sailing, not even know where the water lies. Incidentally, only, that he comes to land. Is there no voice for these? Where is Love today?" [II, 444.] [28]

For the time being, Emily let her correspondence with Higginson lapse. His convalescence from war wounds and her own illness precluded a meeting. Emily did not especially need the kind of advice she had sought from Higginson in 1862; she had not yet come to regard him as her "safest friend." The emotional storm involving "Master" was subsiding, if the number and type of love poems are reliable evidence. Emily could not feel herself "crowned" as she had once wished to be, but she had three preceptors, Higginson, Bowles, and Wadsworth, to whom she could turn when she needed help. Without the overwhelming fears of the past several years, she was able at last to rule herself. About 1863 she had written,

Who Court obtain within Himself
Sees every Man a King –
And Poverty of Monarchy
Is an interior thing – [29]

As a poet she had made up for what she was denied as a woman. When the final symptom of the long struggle, her eye condition, abated, the central crisis of her life and art came to an end.

As for Emily, she was not withdrawn or
exclusive really. She was always watching
for the rewarding person to come, but she
was a very busy person herself. She had to
think—she was the only one of us who had
that to do. Father believed; and mother
loved; and Austin had Amherst; and I had
the family to keep track of.
                        —*Lavinia Dickinson* [1]

6

The Queen Recluse

Emily Dickinson returned from Cambridge in October
1865. Her father died in June 1874. Between the two
dates lies a biographical desert. One day in the summer of
1870 is the scholar's oasis: Colonel Higginson came to
visit and recorded Emily's appearance, manners, and conversation. Otherwise nearly ten years of her external life
exist for us as an occasional notation in dressmakers'
ledgers, a few words in letters written by family or friends,
a single published poem.

Emily's mind is less accessible during these years than
before or after. The enormous poetic output of 1861–65
(about 850 poems) was followed by near-silence: in the
next nine years Emily wrote about two hundred poems.
Thoughts and themes of earlier verse were examined and
refined, but never with the urgency of the war years.

Routines of household existence did not change. Emily

and Vinnie became middle-aged spinsters and their parents grew old amid a pattern of cooking and sewing and gardening. The high points of each year were still Thanksgiving and Commencement. The members of the homestead shared vicariously the vigorous life next door at Austin's house, but it was not their own.

Emily's hundred-odd letters of her middle years take on the double role of biography and art. Only in them, for instance, does the pattern of gradually deepening seclusion appear. When she returned form Cambridge Emily Dickinson was leaving the world outside Amherst for the last time. She considered a trip to Boston in 1866, but did not go. In 1869 she wrote to Higginson, "I do not cross my Father's ground to any House or town." Even Austin's house, "a hedge away," eventually seemed too distant to visit. But as Emily told Higginson, "To an Emigrant, Country is idle except it be his own" [II, 460]. When he asked her in 1870 if she never "felt want of employment in seclusion," she replied, "I never thought of conceiving that I could ever have the slightest approach to such a want in all future time," adding, "I feel that I have not expressed myself strongly enough" [II, 474].

Emily might well feel that a stronger expression was necessary. Her posthumous audience has always been limited by the insistence of many readers that such a life could not be sane. Even Higginson, with the advantage of twenty-four years' correspondence and two interviews with Emily, called her "partially cracked."

In an 1891 review of Emily Dickinson's poems, William Dean Howells wrote, "There is no hint of what turned her life in upon itself, and probably this was its natural evolution or involution, from tendencies inherent in the New England, or the Puritan, spirit." [2] Mabel Loomis Todd wrote in 1896 of her friend, "She had tried society and the world, and found them lacking. . . . Her life was the normal blossoming of a nature introspective to a high degree, whose best thought could not exist in pretence." [3] Everything known about Emily's life confirms the opinions of Howells and Mrs. Todd. From early shyness and genius the rest followed. By the time Emily was writing love poems to her "Master," she was already secluding herself from strangers. In her later, shared love affair with Judge Lord, she had every excuse to leave the life she had chosen but declined to do so. Except for her genius, Emily was enough like other intellectual women of New England to fit all the specifications of the "characteristic New England type" which Merriam described in his biography of Samuel Bowles. Emily Dickinson sought the universal within herself: the poems were art by about 1858, the letters reached the level of art soon afterward, and by the late eighteen sixties Emily was consciously turning her daily life toward art.

Emily Dickinson, like Thoreau, wished to live deliberately, to front only the essential facts of life. Thoreau went to Walden Pond; Emily stayed at home. In her opinion the simplest life she could devise was infinitely complex, and any wider existence an unnecessary distraction. She wrote to Mrs. Holland in 1877, "There is not so much Life as *talk* of Life, as a general thing. Had we the first intimation of the Definition of Life, the calmest of us would be Lunatics!" [II, 576.] Sometimes even the talk of life was more than enough. In the same year she sent Samuel Bowles this poem:

> Could mortal lip divine
> The undeveloped Freight
> Of a delivered syllable
> 'Twould crumble with the weight.[4]

Seclusion, then, was true economy to Emily Dickinson. What began as a convenience for the shy girl became a necessity for the mature woman. The fact that the neighbors thought it strange made little difference: the soul selected its own society, then shut the door. In her triumphant individuality Emily sensed, as Thoreau did, the "quiet desperation" of ordinary lives. Emily could find ecstasy in living, she told Higginson; the mere sense of living was joy enough. But she asked her preceptor, "How do most people live without any thoughts? . . . How do they get strength to put on their clothes in the morning?" [II, 474.]

Individuality is the royalty Emily was writing about during her crucial years, though it seemed "uncrowned" without the response of love. Samuel Bowles was joking when he called Emily "the Queen Recluse" in 1863: Emily refused to see him, but had only begun to withdraw from usual company. Still, Bowles was quite right to link Emily's sense of royalty with seclusion. Sovereigns *receive* visitors; they have no obligation to see everyone who knocks at the palace door. Emily Dickinson gradually applied her sovereignty of mind to her daily existence.

The process was slow, and royalty was difficult. Emily did not become a recluse without apology. To the end of her life she kept explaining in letters and poems why she must refuse to see her friends. In 1864 (when she spent more than six months in a Cambridge boardinghouse) Emily was already defending herself in verse:

> My best Acquaintances are those
> With whom I spoke no Word —
> The Stars that stated come to Town
> Esteemed me never rude
> Although to their Celestial Call
> I failed to make reply —
> My constant — reverential Face
> Sufficient Courtesy.[5]

Those around Emily were tolerant of her seclusion, even when they did not understand it. When a friend asked Vinnie if she could not get Emily to go out occasionally, Vinnie replied, "But why should I? She is quite happy and contented as she is. I would only disturb her." [6] Two cousins who entered the Dickinson property by the garden gate caught sight of Emily in the garden. One of them whispered, "Oh, there's Emily; now we can get a good look at her." But both cousins at once sensed that they were being unfair to Emily, so they retreated and banged the gate loudly to give fair warning of their presence.[7]

Only two dozen letters written in 1866–69 survive. Eleven of these are merely sentences or short paragraphs. Outward events worth recording almost ceased. On January 27, 1866, Emily wrote to Colonel Higginson, "Carlo died – E. Dickinson Would you instruct me now?" [II, 449.] Three weeks later, on February 17, the *Springfield Weekly Republican* printed "A narrow fellow in the grass," with a mistake in punctuation. Emily clipped out the poem, which Sue had given to Bowles without her permission, and sent it to Higginson with her opinion of its publication. "Lest you meet my Snake and suppose I deceive," she wrote, "it was robbed of me – defeated too of the third line by the punctuation. The third and fourth were one – I had told you I did not print – I feared you might think me ostensible. If I still entreat you to teach me, are you much displeased?" [II, 450.]

The offending lines, in the clipping, read

> You may have met him – did you not?
> His notice instant is,

although the *Daily Republican* of February 14 had correctly given them as

You may have met him – did you not,
His notice instant is.[8]

Emily thought her anonymity violated by the publication of the poem; Sue and Bowles no doubt thought otherwise. The speaker of the poem is a man who recalls his barefoot boyhood: no reader would have any reason to suspect that a woman wrote the poem.

Aside from the death of Carlo—her "shaggy ally" for so many years—and the publication of "The Snake," nothing but an occasional short illness seems to have disturbed the domestic life of Emily Dickinson for several years. No close friends died. If Samuel Bowles's intermittent sickness alarmed Emily, she said nothing about it in surviving letters. Yet her interest in life and her ability to capture it in words did not diminish. The skills she applied less often to poetry gained strength in her prose. Her letters to Mrs. Holland, for instance, became as firm as those to Higginson, though more domestic. The minute events of the homestead became terse phrases of high quality, as in the following 1866 letter to Mrs. Holland:

Dear Sister,
    After you went, a low wind warbled through the house like a spacious bird, making it high but lonely. When you had gone the love came. I supposed it would. The supper of the heart is when the guest has gone.
    Shame is so intrinsic in a strong affection we must all experience Adam's reticence. I suppose the street that the lover travels is thenceforth divine, incapable of turnpike aims.
    That you be with me annuls fear and I await Commencement with merry resignation. Smaller than David you clothe me with extreme Goliath.
    Friday I tasted life. It was a vast morsel. A circus passed the house – still I feel the red in my mind though the drums are out.

The book you mention, I have not met. Thank **you** for tenderness.

The lawn is full of south and the odors tangle, and I hear today for the first the river in the tree.

You mentioned spring's delaying – I blamed her for the opposite. I would eat evanescence slowly.

Vinnie is deeply afflicted in the death of her dappled cat, though I convince her it is immortal which assists her some. Mother resumes lettuce, involving my transgression – suggestive of yourself, however, which endears disgrace.

"House" is being "cleaned." I prefer pestilence. That is more classic and less fell.

Yours was my first arbutus. It was a rosy boast.

I will send you the first witch hazel.

A woman died last week, young and in hope but a little while – at the end of our garden. I thought since of the power of death, not upon affection, but its mortal signal. It is to us the Nile.

You refer to the unpermitted delight to be with those we love. I suppose that to be the license not granted of God.

> Count not that far that can be had,
> Though sunset lie between –
> Nor that adjacent, that beside,
> Is further than the sun.

Love for your embodiment of it.

Emily.

[ii, 452–53]

Such a letter, with its broad spectrum of interests, allays any suspicion that Emily was bored with the life she chose. No doubt her sense of humor brightened much that was routine. The Commencement which she regarded with humorous terror, however, was becoming a real annual trial for her. Until her father died she had to greet his guests at the reception he customarily gave on Wednesday of Commencement Week. With Mrs. Holland or the Norcrosses at her side she not only managed to do so, but to give the impression that such social events were part of her daily life.[9] The Hollands' daughter Annie recalled to Emily's niece in 1931, "When I was a young girl visiting in Amherst, I went to a reception in your grandparents' house, and met your Aunt Emily. She was so surrounded by people that I had no chance to talk with her. . . ."[10] Apart from such ordeals, Emily's withdrawal from society was slow and steady. After Carlo died, she "explored" little. She tended her garden in summer and her conservatory in winter, sending flowers to friends rather than visiting them. An 1864 poem explains,

> Between My Country – and the Others –
> There is a Sea –
> But Flowers – negotiate between us –
> As Ministry.[11]

In her letters Emily tried to justify her withdrawal, to make it seem to others, as it seemed to her, advance rather than retreat. Late in 1866 she wrote to Mrs. Holland, "I saw the sunrise on the Alps since I saw you. Travel why to Nature, when she dwells with us? Those who lift their hats shall see her, as devout as God" [II, 455.]

Emily's declaration to Higginson in 1869 that she did not leave her father's grounds may have been overstatement. Later in the same year she wrote to Sue, who was out of town, "I humbly try to fill your place at the Minister's, so faint a competition, it only makes them smile" [II, 464]. Even if Emily was actually visiting the minister rather than sending over notes and flowers, the new parsonage was only across the street, opposite Austin's house: Emily had no intention of going to Boston, as Higginson wished. Even as he invited her, Higginson admitted, "It isolates one anywhere to think beyond a certain point or to have such luminous flashes as come to you—so perhaps the place does not make much difference" [II, 461].

Colonel Higginson met Emily for the first time on August 16, 1870. His account of the event, written the same evening to his wife, brings Emily into sharp focus for an hour or two. If the Colonel valued the meeting, his "singular poetic correspondent" did all she could to aid the impression. It may be unfair to call her reception of Higginson a dramatic performance, but the effect was the same. A servant, Maggie Maher, led Higginson into the "dark & cool & stiffish" parlor, and he had time to examine the bookshelves and find two of his own works. Then he heard "a step like a pattering child's in entry & in glided a little plain woman with two smooth bands of reddish hair & a face . . . with no good feature—in a very plain & exquisitely clean white piqué & a blue net worsted shawl. She came to me with two day lilies which she put in a sort of childlike way into my hand & said 'These are my introduction' in a soft frightened breathless childlike voice—" [II, 473].

Emily Dickinson had made an art of her life. In 1861 she had written about becoming "A Woman – white –"; now she dressed in white. An 1862 poem imagining a meeting with "Master" had said,

> I take a Flower as I go,
> My Face to justify – [12]

In manner Emily was still the Young Contributor, though she was nearly forty. Her conversation was like one of her letters come to life. "Is it oblivion or absorption when things pass from the mind?" she asked Higginson. When he was leaving she said, "Gratitude is the only secret that cannot reveal itself" [II, 474].[13]

The effect of such an interview was disagreeable to Higginson, though he had been much impressed. "I was never with any one who drained my nerve power so much," he wrote. "Without touching her, she drew from me. I am glad not to live near her" [II, 476]. A few weeks later Emily told Higginson her own reaction to the visit. "Enough is so vast a sweetness I suppose it never occurs – only pathetic counterfeits," she wrote. "You ask great questions accidentally. To answer them would be events." The words which had drained the Colonel's nerve power had seemed inadequate: "I ask you to forgive me for all the ignorance I had." She asked about books he had mentioned, and added, "If I ask too much, you could please refuse – Shortness to live has made me bold" [II, 480].

It might be asked whether boldness would run upstairs at the sound of a doorbell. Emily's bravery lay in her ability to live as she knew she must. Others had no trouble meeting strangers, but they avoided the stranger within themselves. It cannot have been easy for Emily, as an artist, to see mawkish evasions of essential questions pass for poetry and receive critical acclaim. Since she did not deceive herself, she must have known that Amherst found only eccentricity in the art and life she had achieved.

Eventually Emily had one "disciple": her cousin Louisa Norcross. Without the power of art Louisa suffered a disappointment in love, and in time became a recluse who dressed in white. Loo, indeed, came closer than Emily to the mythical figure Emily is sometimes imagined to have been. But Louisa Norcross had a mediocre mind; she became merely a New England eccentric. As Mabel Loomis

Portrait of Emily Dickinson

Todd put it in 1893, Louisa had "become a recluse after the manner of Emily, but she hasn't any ability as Emily had." [14]

On the basis of Emily's letters to her and a note in *Letters* [II, 500], it appears that Louisa was in love with John Dudley, husband of Emily's friend Eliza Coleman. Fanny and Loo did not allow direct references to this love to be published, but it is not difficult to trace the course of Loo's disappointments in the general advice Emily gave her: advice which tells a good deal more about Emily's attitude toward love than about the problems of the "little cousin."

Emily recognized Louisa's limitations. The style of her letters to the Norcrosses is evidence enough of that. Within the terms of the style, however, her words are sometimes poignant. Early in 1865, when Louisa was trying to decide whether to visit the Dudleys in Middletown, Connecticut, Emily wrote, "Go, little girl, to Middletown. Life is so fast it will run away, notwithstanding our sweetest *whoa*" [II, 439]. Letters of 1866 and 1868 speak of some unspecified grief in the lives of the Norcrosses. In the latter year the Dudleys moved to Milwaukee. Emily wrote to her cousins,

Remember

> The longest day that God appoints
> Will finish with the sun.
> Anguish can travel to its stake,
> And then it must return.

[II, 459]

By 1870 Eliza Dudley's health was failing and the Norcrosses went to Wisconsin to care for her. Emily wrote them a Christmas greeting that year which was really a message of sympathy for Loo:

Untiring little Sisters.

What will I ever do for you, yet have done the most, for love is that one perfect labor nought can supersede. I suppose the pain is still there, for pain that is worthy does not go soon. The small can crush the great, however, only temporarily. In a few days we examine, muster our forces, and cast it away. . . . Love will not expire. There was never the instant when it was lifeless in the world, though the quicker deceit dies, the better for the truth, who is indeed our dear friend.

I am sure you will gain, even from this wormwood. The martyrs may not choose their food.

> God made no act without a cause,
> Nor heart without an aim,
> Our inference is premature,
> Our premises to blame.

[II, 484–85]

Emily's advice to Louisa, because of the simplicity of style, remains the least ambiguous evidence of her own attitude toward love. In the spring of 1871, as Eliza Dudley declined toward death, Emily wrote, "Of the 'thorn,' dear, give it to me, for I am strongest. Never carry what I carry, for though I think I bend, something straightens me" [II, 487]. Eliza died in June; sixteen months later John Dudley remarried. Emily wrote then to the stricken Louisa, "An ill heart, like a body, has its more comfortable days, and then its days of pain, its long relapse, when rallying requires more effort than to dissolve life, and death looks choiceless" [II, 500].

The same clarity, so unlike the gnomic style Emily used for her intellectual correspondents, sometimes resulted in prose art. Emily enjoyed riddles, but she could write well without them.

Sisters,

I hear robins a great way off, and wagons a great way off, and rivers a great way off, and all appear to be hurry-

ing somewhere undisclosed to me. Remoteness is the
founder of sweetness; could we see all we hope, or hear
the whole we fear told tranquil, like another tale, there
would be madness near. Each of us gives or takes
heaven in corporeal person, for each of us has the skill
of life. . . . It is not recorded of any rose that it failed
of its bee, though obtained in specific instances through
scarlet experience. The career of flowers differs from
ours only in inaudibleness. I feel more reverence as I
grow for these mute creatures whose suspense or transport may surpass my own.

[II, 504–05]

Emily's ardors, like the "career of flowers," are almost
inaudible during her middle years. The Reverend Charles
Wadsworth returned from California in 1869 and took
a new Philadelphia pulpit. Since no extant letters tell
Emily's reaction to the minister's return, one can only
assume that she was pleased. Her devotion to "Master"
seems to have changed gradually. Two poems written in
1871 are "Somehow myself survived the Night" and "I
should not dare to be so sad / So many Years again." [15]
No letters to Samuel Bowles survive to tell how Emily
felt toward him between 1864 and 1874; only one poem,
written about 1866, is known to have reached him:

Just Once – Oh Least Request –
Could Adamant refuse
So small a Grace –
So scanty put –
Such agonizing terms?
Would not a God of Flint
Be conscious of a sigh
As down his Heaven dropt remote –
"Just Once" – Sweet Deity? [16]

This poem seems to follow the general drift of the 1863 or
1864 poem, "If it had no pencil," and the 1865 stanza,

"Just to be rich." On the basis of these letter-poems, plus the 1863 letters from Bowles to Austin, Emily Dickinson and Samuel Bowles were neither seeing one another nor corresponding. First there had been Emily's refusal to see Bowles when he returned from Europe, then Bowles's requests, through Austin, for a letter, then Emily's poems asking Bowles to write.

Whether Emily and Bowles saw each other is unknown. There are no recorded meetings between April 1862 and June 1874. Presumably Bowles could have talked with Emily during Edward Dickinson's annual Commencement receptions. Certainly he was in Amherst at Commencement: in 1866 he became a trustee of Amherst College. Emily addressed a poem to him about 1870, but since it remained among her papers, Bowles either did not receive it, or left it in Austin's house at the end of his visit.

> He is alive, this morning —
> He is alive — and awake —
> Birds are resuming for Him —
> Blossoms — dress for his Sake.
> Bees — to their Loaves of Honey
> Add an amber Crumb
> Him — to regale — Me — Only —
> Motion, and am dumb.
>
>   Emily.

                                        [II, 472]

"Esther Wynn's Love-Letters," a story by "Saxe Holm," appeared in the December 1871 issue of *Scribner's Monthly Magazine*. The magazine had been founded by Dr. Holland in 1870; Emily Dickinson read it regularly. The story was an old woman's narrative about the discovery, when she was sixteen, of love letters hidden in a staircase fifty years before. The writer of these letters,

Esther Wynn, had loved a man she could not marry and had died in Jerusalem.

Although the time and setting of the story were remote,[17] and the staircase cache based on a Newport incident, Emily must have had little doubt that she was the model for Esther Wynn. The fictional letters were said to have enclosed pressed flowers, and poems like one which began,

> I wonder what the clover thinks?
> Intimate friend of Bob-o-links,
> Lover of Daisies slim and white,
> Waltzer with Butter-cups at night;
> Keeper of Inn for travelling Bees,
> Serving to them wine dregs and lees
> Left by the Royal Humming-birds. . . .[18]

Even the capitalization imitated Emily's. The "love-letters" themselves were less clearly Dickinsonian. The closest approximation of Emily's prose style sounded like this:

> FRIDAY EVENING.
> SWEETEST: – It is very light in my room to-night. The full moon and the thought of you! I see to write, but you would forbid me – you who would see only the moonlight and not the other.[19]

Esther Wynn also called her lover "my sweetest master"; the narrator said, "It was evident that at first the relation was more like one of pupil and master." [20]

The author who called herself "Saxe Holm" was Helen Fiske Hunt, known to the public as "H. H." Born in Amherst, exactly nine weeks older than Emily Dickinson, Mrs. Hunt had known her "Esther Wynn" as a child. Helen was orphaned in 1847 and never again lived in

Amherst for long, though she returned at Commencement for several years.[21] In July 1852 Austin wrote to Sue that he had seen Helen Fiske in Boston with her husband-to-be, Lieutenant Edward Hunt. To Austin, the thirty-year-old Hunt seemed "a large, ambling, long-faced, ungraceful, brass-buttoned individual of some forty or fifty years. . . ."[22]

Emily thought more highly of Hunt, in retrospect at least. In 1870 she told Higginson that "Major Hunt interested her more than any man she ever saw," and that he had said Carlo understood gravitation [II, 475]. Higginson asked about Hunt because he had known Helen Hunt only since 1866, when, as a widow recovering from the loss of husband and small son, she had come to his Newport boardinghouse. Mrs. Hunt had overcome her grief by writing; by 1871 she was a highly regarded poet. A few weeks before "Esther Wynn's Love-Letters" appeared, Emily wrote to Higginson, "Mrs. Hunt's Poems are stronger than any written by Women since Mrs Browning, with the exception of Mrs Lewes [George Eliot] – but truth like Ancestor's Brocades can stand alone – " [II, 491].

If Emily knew that Helen Hunt wrote the story, she said nothing about it. The next summer she was writing to Mrs. Hunt, though the letters have not been found.[23] The story, after all, did not really give Emily Dickinson away. Only her close friends could have recognized her in Esther Wynn, though superficially the poems were so much like hers that Mabel Loomis Todd, in 1886, thought them to be Emily's.[24] Had the identity of the model been obvious, Dr. Holland probably would not have published the story.

There is no reason to believe that Mrs. Hunt saw the letters Emily had written to "Master," though she knew Samuel Bowles. Her "pupil and master" were synonyms for "Scholar" and "Preceptor," names she had seen in the letters to Higginson. The poems Emily had sent Higginson—"There came a day at summer's full," for instance—told enough about her attitude toward love to suggest the rest. Besides, there was Amherst gossip. Helen's sister Ann, Mrs. Everett Banfield, whom Higginson visited the day he first met Emily [II, 473], could have supplied local talk about Emily if Helen Hunt had not heard it elsewhere.

None of Emily's letters before the publication of the story closely resemble Esther Wynn's; curiously, some of her later ones do. The fictional poet writes,

> Dear, did I ever before ask you to forego your wish for mine? Did I ever before withhold anything from you, my darling? Ah love, you know—oh how well you know, that always . . . my soul was forever restlessly asking, seeking, longing, for one more joy, delight, rapture to give you! [25]

About 1878 Emily wrote to Judge Lord,

> Dont you know you are happiest while I withhold and not confer – dont you know that "No" is the wildest word we consign to Language?
> You do, for you know all things – [top of page cut away]. It is anguish I long conceal from you to let you leave me, hungry. . . .
>
> [II, 617]

A trial phrase (crossed out) in an 1880 letter-draft to Lord also echoes the same passage: "Seems to withhold Darling" [III, 664]. Emily told Lord in 1883, "I feel like wasting my Cheek on your Hand tonight – " [III, 786]; Esther Wynn had written, "I would rather at this moment, dear, lay my cheek on your hand. . . ." [26] These similarities may mean that Mrs. Hunt's phrasing became Emily's through repeated reading, or perhaps only that love letters tend to be alike.

The marriage of Helen Hunt to William S. Jackson in 1875 elicited a cryptic congratulation from Emily Dickinson, and a more frequent correspondence between the two women followed. In August 1876 Mrs. Jackson sent Emily a circular for Roberts Brothers' forthcoming "No-Name" books—prose and poetry which would be published anonymously. The circular announced the first book, *Mercy Philbrick's Choice* (by Mrs. Jackson), and added, "It is intended to include in the Series a volume of anonymous poems from famous hands, to be written especially for it." [27] Emily sent the circular to Higginson. She had told Mrs. Jackson, she said, that she was "incapable." But Mrs. Jackson "was so sweetly noble, I would regret to estrange her, and if you would be willing to give me a note saying you disapproved it, and thought me unfit, she would believe you – " [II, 563].

Higginson's answer was no help: he thought Emily had been asked to write prose. Meanwhile Mrs. Jackson had written again, recalling the interview at which she gave Emily the circular and apologizing for accusing Emily of living away from the sunlight, "though really you looked so white and moth-like! Your hand felt like such a wisp in mine that you frightened me. I felt like a great ox talking to a white moth. . . ." Mrs. Jackson begged again. "You say you find great pleasure in reading my verses. Let somebody somewhere whom you do not know have the same pleasure in reading yours . . ." [II, 565].

Emily wrote to Higginson; it was not stories Mrs. Jackson had requested. "But may I tell her just the same that you dont prefer it? Thank you, if I may, for it seems almost sordid to refuse from myself again" [II, 566]. Emily was so upset that she neglected to use the special rhetoric of her other letters to Higginson. Mrs. Jackson must have realized that Emily was not being coy about publication. Without saying anything further, she submitted "Success is counted sweetest" to her publisher, and renewed her request for Emily's permission only when the book was almost ready to appear. On October 24, 1878, when *A Masque of Poets* was in press, she and her husband visited the Dickinson homestead. Emily again refused to submit any of her poems for publication, but relented within a few days, after a desperate letter from Helen Jackson which asked, "Can you refuse the only thing I perhaps shall ever ask at your hands?" [II, 625.]

So it was that "Success"—a poem written almost twenty years before, about 1859, and sent to Higginson during the distraught summer of 1862—came to be published in a widely read anthology.[28] Reviewers attributed the poem to Emerson: Emily had to balance this compliment against the five editorial changes in the twelve-line poem. Higginson, when he received *A Masque of Poets,* did his "scholar" the service of writing her name above the poem, correcting two of the edited lines, and noting, "altered probably by Mrs. Helen Hunt." [29]

After the publication of "Success," Helen Hunt Jackson and Emily Dickinson continued to correspond, though Emily never again answered any questions about publication. However shy and mothlike she seemed to Mrs. Jackson, she had set a granite will against intrusions on her privacy. Mrs. Jackson, who thought herself a great ox, was a good deal shyer than the "Success" episode suggests. She wrote for a living, but hid behind a series of pseudonyms or published anonymously; to the end of her life she denied writing the Saxe Holm stories.[30] One curious side effect of this denial was the fairly widespread rumor that Emily herself had written the stories. In July 1878 the *Springfield Union* asked, "Is Saxe Holm in Amherst? We claim the Yankee prerogative of 'guessing' that she does, and further, that she answers in private life to the honored name of Dickinson." The Amherst *Record* elaborated on the story, naming the supposed Saxe Holm as "Miss Emily Dickinson," "who has for many years secluded herself from society for the purpose of indulging in literary tastes and pursuits." The *Springfield Republican*, now run by Samuel Bowles the younger, replied, "we happen to *know* that no person by the name of Dickinson is in any way responsible for the Saxe Holm stories." [31]

Though Emily considered publication "the Auction / Of the mind of man," she grudgingly admitted its justification for those who earned a living by it:

Poverty – be justifying
For so foul a thing
Possibly – but We – would rather
From Our Garret go
White – Unto the White Creator –
Than invest – Our Snow – [32]

This, of course, was a private opinion, not to be imposed on others. Emily was eager to read the writings of her friends and never chided them for publishing. It was more in wonder than reproach that she asked Helen Hunt Jackson, "How can you print a piece of your soul?" [33]

Until early 1871 life at the Dickinson homestead was not disturbed by the fear of death in the immediate family. Then Edward Dickinson suffered an illness of several weeks' length. Emily wrote to the Norcrosses,

The terror of the winter has made a little creature of me, who thought myself so bold.

Father was very sick. I presumed he would die, and the sight of his lonesome face all day was harder than personal trouble. He is growing better, though physically reluctantly. I hope I am mistaken, but I think his physical life don't want to live any longer. You know he never played, and the straightest engine has its leaning hour.

[II, 486]

Though Mr. Dickinson recovered, fear for his life continued to disturb his daughter. Her love and reverence for her father had, if anything, grown as she matured. She could think objectively about him, as the letter to the Norcrosses shows, but she was still the dutiful daughter, childlike in her wish to please her father. Life without him was difficult to imagine.

Tensions between the two Dickinson houses fluctuated. In 1866 the second child of Austin and Sue, Martha, was born—an additional care to keep Sue from the homestead. A neighbor noted at the time that almost a week after the birth of Martha, Vinnie—always cool to Sue—had not yet gone to see mother and baby.[34] Emily was seldom at Austin's house now, so her letters to Sue—most of them epigrammatic notes—were often substitutes for conversation. When Sue was on vacation, Emily's letters to her resembled those to Mrs. Holland in their mixture of domestic narrative and aphorism.

Emily disliked partings. Year after year something interfered with proper farewells when Sue left for a vacation. In August 1866 Emily wrote, "I kissed my hand to the early train but forgot to open the Blind . . ." [II, 454]. An 1873 excuse is more to the point: "Without the annual parting I thought to shun the Loneliness that parting ratifies. How artfully in vain!" [II, 512.] When Sue was away Emily wrote letters like the following, which leads toward a poem by stating its theme in half a dozen prose variations, each with a separate imagery. Much of the prose is metrical.

To miss you, Sue, is power.

The stimulus of Loss makes most Possession mean.

To live lasts always, but to love is firmer than to live. No Heart that broke but further went than Immortality.

The Trees keep House for you all Day and the Grass looks chastened.

A silent Hen frequents the place with superstitious Chickens – and still Forenoons a Rooster knocks at your outer Door.

To look that way is Romance. The Novel "out," pathetic worth attaches to the Shelf.

Nothing has gone but Summer, or no one that you knew.

The Forests are at Home – the Mountains intimate with Night and arrogant at Noon, and lonesome Fluency abroad, like suspending Music.

> Of so divine a Loss
> We enter but the Gain,
> Indemnity for Loneliness
> That such a Bliss had been.

> [ii, 489]

At home, Sue caused continual friction between the houses. Either Austin or Vinnie was usually at odds with her. The specific acts which caused dissension during these years are lost; an account by a contemporary tells what kind some of them were. To John W. Burgess, Sue was "a really brilliant and highly cultivated woman of great taste and refinement, perhaps a little too aggressive, a little too sharp in wit and repartee, and a little too ambitious for social prestige. . . . Her imagination was exceedingly vivid, sometimes so vivid that it got away with her. . . ." [35] Emily, withdrawn from social events, had less chance than her brother and sister to be hurt. The rumors Sue spread about Emily's private affairs, however, may have gotten back to Emily by way of Vinnie. As one of the few who had access to the mysterious recluse, Sue could drop "confidential" tidbits about Emily and be believed. The various biographies which have proclaimed Emily's "one great love" to be this man or that have relied heavily on some of the preposterous stories circulated by Susan Dickinson. Sometimes there was a true incident which could be distorted. Dr. Wadsworth had actually come to see Emily, for instance. But Vinnie had not run to Austin's house saying that the minister wanted to take Emily away,[36] because Vinnie had been in Boston at the time. On record is Sue's description to Mabel Loomis Todd of Emily "in the arms of a man," but neither Sue nor her daughter ever admitted that Emily had been in love with Judge Lord, the man in question. Aside from gossip, Sue committed other acts, like the "theft" of "The Snake," which did not endear her to Emily. Even so, their friendship was never broken for long. Emily was always capable of forgiveness. One note in the handwriting of 1868 says, "Just say one word, 'Emily has not grieved me' Sign your name to that and I will wait for the rest." But another note of about the same time says, "Susan's Idolater keeps a Shrine for Susan" [II, 512].

Colonel Higginson visited Emily Dickinson for the second time on December 3, 1873. Their correspondence had lapsed; earlier in the year Emily had written two short notes as reminders. When Higginson came, his call was incidental to a lecture at Amherst College. His account of the meeting to his sister sounds lukewarm. Emily is "my eccentric poetess. . . . She says, 'there is one thing to be grateful for – that one is one's self & not somebody else' but Mary thinks this is singularly out of place in E. D.'s case." Higginson described Emily's entrance—in white, bearing a flower—and added, "I'm afraid that Mary's other remark 'Oh why do the insane so cling to you?' still holds"

[II, 518–19]. Although Emily kept asking her preceptor (by now also addressed as "Master" in her letters) to visit again, he did not return until the day of her funeral.

In November 1873 Edward Dickinson was elected to the Massachusetts legislature. He was now seventy, and the exertion of politics affected his health. Three months after his election Emily wrote to Loo and Fanny Norcross, "Father is ill at home. I think it is the 'Legislature' reacting on an otherwise obliging constitution" [II, 521]. By spring, however, Mr. Dickinson was attending to his legislative duties, giving Austin advice on cases their law office was handling, worrying about his grandson Ned's latest bout with epilepsy, and finding time to go to Boston functions like the ones he described in a letter of May 28, 1874:

> Dear Austin,
> Your letter was rec⁴ this morning—glad to hear that Ned seemed to be better, yesterday afternoon—hope he is still improving.
> Last evening I attended the meetings of the Young Men's Christian Association—heard Pres' Eliot of Harvard College, Phillips Brooks, & Edw. E. Hale—& was much pleased with their speeches.
> This evening, I expect to go to Faneuil Hall, to attend the annual supper of the Congregational Club.
> I suppose the Legislature will adjourn to-morrow noon, till Monday next, on account of "Decoration Day" and I expect I shall be home next Friday evening.
> I saw Louisa & Fanny, this noon, Joel's wife has gone to Philadelphia.
> The day has been beautiful, & there are many people here, attending the Anniversaries. To-day is the great day for all kinds of societies.
>   Your aff. father
>   E. Dickinson [37]

While Edward Dickinson busied himself with the political and social events of Boston, his daughter was living
according to the pattern of inward royalty she had chosen.
Emily was now forty-three. For several years her life had
been stable. The sameness of her existence is clearest in a
May letter to Mrs. Holland: the events which interest
Emily are the ones which she had described to Mrs. Holland exactly eight years before.

> Vinnie says Maggie is "Cleaning House." I should
> not have suspected it, but the Bible directs that the
> "Left Hand" circumvent the Right!
> We are to have another "Circus," and again the Pro-
> cession from Algiers will pass the Chamber-Window.
> The Minor Toys of the Year are alike, but the
> Major – are different.

[ii, 524]

This life might have gone on indefinitely. But on June 16,
1874, Edward Dickinson was stricken in Boston. Austin
brought the news to his mother and sisters while they
were at supper. "He had a despatch in his hand, and I
saw by his face we were all lost, though I didn't know
how," Emily wrote afterward to the Norcrosses. "He said
that father was very sick, and he and Vinnie must go.
The train had already gone. While horses were dressing,
news came that he was dead" [II, 526].

A friend is a solemnity and after the great
intrusion of Death, each one that remains
has a spectral pricelessness besides the
mortal worth.

—Emily Dickinson

7

Sacred Friendships

Emily Dickinson could never be certain of the heaven in
which her father and Dr. Wadsworth believed. As an
artist she could project various heavens in her poetry, but
they had for her the reality of art, not the assurance of
faith. To the end of her life Emily wavered between hope
and doubt about an attainable paradise the other side of
death. When someone she loved died, her sense of loss
was immense. The insistent theme of death in her poems
gained its meaning from her reverence for life. "So few
that live – have life," she wrote to Samuel Bowles in 1862,
"it seems of quick importance – not one of those – escape
by Death" [II, 418]. Twenty-two years later, Emily wrote
to Mrs. Holland, "Forgive the Tears that fell for few, but
that few too many, for was not each a World?" [III, 816.]
Unsure of the traditional heaven, Emily tried to bring
her "Lost" back to a kind of life by seeing them through

the eyes of others. It became her habit, after each loss, to correspond with someone who shared her bereavement. As she explained to Wadsworth's friend James Clark, "The sharing a sorrow never lessens, but when a Balm departs, the Plants that nearest grew have a grieved significance, and you cherished my friend" [III, 742].

The clear pattern of these friendships, which Emily Dickinson considered sacred, is evident only at rare moments until the correspondence with Maria Whitney after the death of Samuel Bowles. But it must have begun quite early. When Emily wrote to Edward Everett Hale in 1854 to ask if Ben Newton "was willing to die," she was seeking the same sort of assurance she would need after every bereavement. Hale was not a close friend of Newton; no correspondence followed.

For twenty years after Ben's death none of Emily's closest relatives or friends died. The letters to the Reverend Edward Dwight after Mrs. Dwight died are not quite in the "sacred" category; except for the heavily edited letters to the Norcrosses, there is nothing to show Emily's reaction to the death of Eliza Coleman Dudley.

The sudden death of Edward Dickinson left Emily stunned. She remained upstairs during his funeral. The only friend she was able to see at the time was—rather surprisingly—Samuel Bowles [II, 528]. In her sorrow she turned again to the man she had so long avoided. Afterwards she wrote to him, "The last day I saw you was the newest and oldest of my life. Resurrection can come but once – first – to the same House. Thank you for leading us by it" [II, 527].

It was Judge Lord, however, to whom Emily almost certainly turned for her sacred correspondence. None of her letters to Lord before 1878 survive, but there are several reasons to suppose she relied on him after her father's death. The last letter Edward Dickinson wrote to Austin mentioned an invitation to visit the judge. That alone would have given him a special place in Emily's affections. As her father's closest friend, however, Lord had lifelong claims. If Emily followed the pattern of her other shared griefs, her missing letters to Otis P. Lord must have mingled eulogy with questions about the sides of her father's nature which she could not have seen at home. That Emily did correspond with Lord is evident in a letter the judge wrote to Vinnie in March 1877: "I still have thought of you and Emily, whose last note gave me a good deal of uneasiness, for knowing how entirely unselfish she is, and how unwilling to disclose any ailment, I fear that she has been more ill, than she has told me. I hope you will tell me particularly about her. . . ." [1]

Otis Phillips Lord was an imposing figure. According to the Massachusetts Supreme Court tribute to him after his death, "There was something grand, almost heroic, in the quality and proportions of his character." [2] The judge's outspokenness gained him enemies, but even those who were not fond of him were impressed. Susan Dickinson, who disapproved of Emily's close friendship with Lord, described him as "a perfect figurehead for the Supreme Court, from his stiff stock to his toes, . . . his individuality was so bristling, his conviction that he alone was the embodiment of the law, as given on Sinai, so entire, his suspicion of all but himself, so deeply founded in the rock bed of old conservative Whig tenacities. . . ." [3]

Judge Lord's annual visits to Amherst, customary for many years, continued after Edward Dickinson died. Early in 1876 Emily wrote to Colonel Higginson that Lord had been with her for a week the previous October [II, 548]. A year later she reported that the judge had visited again, and wrote to her aunt Catharine Sweetser about the special character her long friendship with Otis Lord had assumed: "When I found it beyond my power to see you, I designed to write you, immediately, but the Lords came as you went, and Judge Lord was my father's closest friend, so I shared my moments with them till they left us . . ." [II, 567]. Lord's distinction is evident; after all, Aunt Catharine was Edward Dickinson's sister.

The letters Emily wrote about her father to her other correspondents do not strictly resemble her "sacred" letters, but they help to show how she slowly turned the sharpness of her grief into prose art. At first, in her letters to the Norcrosses and Higginson, she was narrative. To Higginson she wrote,

> The last afternoon that my Father lived, though with no premonition – I preferred to be with him, and invented an absence for Mother, Vinnie being asleep. He seemed peculiarly pleased as I stayed oftenest with myself, and remarked as the Afternoon withdrew, he "would like it to not end."
>
> His pleasure almost embarrassed me and my Brother coming – I suggested they walk. Next morning I woke him for the train – and saw him no more.
>
> His Heart was pure and terrible and I think no other like it exists.
>
> [II, 528]

By January 1875 Emily was capable of capturing more subtle sensations of bereavement. She wrote to Mrs. Holland an elegiac letter—an early example of a form which would bring her prose art to its peak—in terms of cold and winter:

> This austere Afternoon is more becoming to a Patriot than to one whose Friend is it's sole Land.
>
> No event of Wind or Bird breaks the Spell of Steel.
>
> Nature squanders Rigor – now – where she squandered Love.

Chastening – it may be – the Lass that she receiveth.
My House is a House of Snow – true – sadly – of few.
Mother is asleep in the Library – Vinnie – in the Dining Room – Father – in the Masked Bed – in the Marl House.

> How soft his Prison is –
> How sweet those sullen Bars –
> No Despot – but the King of Down
> Invented that Repose!

When I think of his firm Light – quenched so causelessly, it fritters the worth of much that shines. "Dust unto the Dust" indeed – but the final clause of that marvelous sentence – who has rendered it?
"I say unto you," Father would read at Prayers, with a militant Accent that would startle one.
Forgive me if I linger on the first Mystery of the House.
It's specific Mystery – each Heart had before – but within this World. Father's was the first Act distinctly of the Spirit.

[II, 526–27]

When Samuel Bowles returned to Springfield after the funeral of Edward Dickinson, he wrote at once to Emily. Her reply, even in her grief, shows she was eager to resume her friendship with him. In fact she wanted to think there had never been any strain in the relationship. "I should think that you would have few Letters," she wrote, "for your own are so noble that they make men afraid – and sweet as your Approbation is – it is had in fear – lest your depth convict us. . . . Come always, dear friend, but refrain from going. You spoke of not liking to be forgotten. Could you, tho' you would? Treason never knew you" [II, 526–27]. Thereafter Emily wrote to Bowles at least two or three times a year. Sometimes she spoke only of her father, or thanked Bowles for sending flowers on the anniversaries of Edward Dickinson's death. She also wrote at times about Bowles himself. Emily still felt she must define his effect on her, as she had tried to define it in so many letters of the early sixties. The tone of desperation and fear which had disturbed Bowles then was absent now, though it is clear that Emily was still concerned about Bowles's health. In 1875—probably in the spring—Emily wrote,

> It was so delicious to see you — a Peach before the time, it makes all seasons possible and Zones — a caprice.
>
> We who arraign the "Arabian Nights" for their under statement, escape the stale sagacity of supposing them sham.
>
> We miss your vivid Face and the besetting Accents, you bring from your Numidian Haunts.
>
> Your coming welds anew that strange trinket of Life, which each of us wear and none of us own, and the phosphorescence of your's startles us for it's permanence. Please rest the Life so many own, for Gems abscond —
>
> In your own beautiful words, for the Voice is the Palace of all of us, "Near but remote,"
>
> Emily.
>
> If we die, will you come for us, as you do for Father?
> "Not born" yourself, "to die," you must reverse us all.

[II, 540]

The imagery in this letter of jewels and exotic splendor is much like that of Emily's poetry during the war years. Another familiar motif, the godlike quality of the man Emily had once addressed as "Sweet Deity," appears in an 1877 letter to him: "You have the most triumphant Face out of Paradise — probably because you are there constantly instead of ultimately" [II, 574].

In the summer of 1877 Bowles came to Amherst. There were other visitors in the Dickinson homestead when he arrived, and Emily, who by this time seldom received more than one friend at a time, refused to see him. Bowles shouted up the stairs, "Emily, you damned rascal! No more of this nonsense! I've traveled all the way from Springfield to see you! Come down at once!" [4]

Emily came down. The direct command must have delighted her. Her conversation that afternoon, according to others who heard it, was brilliant. Afterwards she wrote to Bowles,

> I went to the Room as soon as you left, to confirm your presence — recalling the Psalmist's Sonnet to God, beginning
>
> I have no Life but this —
> To lead it here —
> Nor any Death — but lest
> Dispelled from there —
> Nor tie to Earths to come,
> Nor Action new
> Except through this Extent
> The love of you.
>
> It is strange that the most intangible thing is the most adhesive.
>
> Your "Rascal"
>
> I washed the Adjective.

[II, 589]

In the same joyful letter Emily told Bowles she wanted to give him a book when he came again. She never had the opportunity. By September Samuel Bowles was so weakened by illness that he remarked to his daughter, "I can hardly brush my hair without sitting down." [5] In October he was bedridden; on December 1 he suffered a cerebral hemorrhage. As the year ended Bowles was still alive, but his doctor had written to Sue, "Just how long he may last it is impossible to predict—not very long however." [6] Emily wrote to Mrs. Holland and Dr. Wadsworth about her newest griefs:

> Mrs Lord – so often with us – has fled – as you know – Dear Mr Bowles is hesitating – God help him decide on the Mortal Side!
> This is Night – now – but we are not dreaming. Hold fast to your Home, for the Darling's stealthy momentum makes each moment – Fear –
> I enclose a Note, which if you would lift as far as Philadelphia, if it did not tire your Arms – would please me so much.
> Would the Doctor be willing to address it? Ask him, with my love.
>
> [II, 596]

On January 16, 1878, Samuel Bowles died. Emily wrote at once to Mrs. Bowles, "To remember our own Mr Bowles is all we can do. With grief it is done, so warmly and long, it can never be new" [II, 599]. Three days later she turned to her "safest friend," Colonel Higginson, for comfort:

> Dear friend,
> I felt it shelter to speak to you.
> My Brother and Sister are with Mr Bowles, who is buried this afternoon.
> The last song that I heard – that was since the Birds – was "He leadeth me – he leadeth me – yea, though I walk." Then the voices stooped – the arch was so low –
>
> [II, 599]

The death of Samuel Bowles was Emily Dickinson's second bereavement in four years. Still, there was not the shock of sudden death this time. Emily had had nearly twenty years to prepare her mind for the loss. Soon she was trying to help Mary Bowles:

> I hasten to you, Mary, because no moment must be lost when a heart is breaking, for though it broke so long, each time is nearer than the last, if it broke truly. To be willing that I should speak to you was so generous, dear.
> Sorrow almost resents love, it is so inflamed.
> I am glad if the broken words helped you. I had not hoped so much, I felt so faint in uttering them, thinking of your great pain. Love makes us "heavenly" without our trying in the least. 'Tis easier than a Saviour – it does not stay on high and call us to its distance; its low Come unto me" begins in every place It makes but one mistake, it tells us it is "rest" – perhaps its toil is rest, but what we have not known we shall know again, that divine "again" for which we are all breathless.
> I am glad you "work." Work is a bleak redeemer, but it does redeem; it tires the flesh so that can't tease the spirit.
> Dear "Mr. Sam" is very near, these midwinter days. When purples come on Pelham, in the afternoon we say "Mr. Bowles's colors." I spoke to him once of his Gem chapter [Revelation 21], and the beautiful eyes rose till they were out of reach of mine, in some hallowed fathom.

> Not that he goes – we love him more
> Who led us while he stayed.
> Beyond earth's trafficking frontier,
> For what he moved, he made.

> [II, 601–02]

Although Emily comforted Mrs. Bowles, she was more concerned about Maria Whitney. Mary Bowles had her children for consolation: Miss Whitney, who, like Emily, had loved Bowles beyond sentimentality, had only the memory of her love. It is not known when Emily Dickinson became aware that Bowles responded to Miss Whitney's love. Perhaps she had drawn her conclusions from the fact that Bowles was always inventing opportunities to be near "Cousin Maria" (she was related to Mrs. Bowles), even when Miss Whitney went to California or Europe. As early as 1864 Emily had sent Maria Whitney the following poem:

> How well I knew her not
> Whom not to know has been
> A Bounty in prospective, now
> Next door to mine the pain.[7]

The occasion for the poem may have been the death of Miss Whitney's sister, but the meaning can be applied as well to the relationship between these two friends of Samuel Bowles during his illnesses and after his death.

Maria Whitney was the intellectual woman *par excellence*. The letters Bowles wrote to her (or such of them as she allowed his biographer to print in 1885) were forever answering her questions or comments on religion, philosophy, and national affairs. At the time of Bowles's death she was teaching French and German at Smith College. She was, in short, everything that Mary Bowles was not. Her idealism, as the letters Bowles wrote to her reveal it, probably kept her "affair" with him platonic, in the best nineteenth-century sense.

Emily Dickinson's letters to Maria Whitney are incomplete. The autograph letters are missing, and Miss Whitney deleted many passages from the transcripts Mabel Loomis Todd made in preparation for *Letters* (1894).[8] Two transcripts of complete letters survive to suggest what was removed from the correspondence: references to

Mrs. Bowles and to Samuel Bowles's love for Miss Whitney. In one, for instance, Miss Whitney allowed Mrs. Todd to print, "Your name is taken as tenderly as the names of our birds, or the flower, for some mysterious cause, sundered from its dew . . . ," [9] but refused permission to publish the words that followed: "Hoarded Mr Samuel – not one bleat of his Lamb – but is known to us – " [III, 662]. The second transcript is of a letter Miss Whitney suppressed completely. It was written late in 1878, a few days after Helen Hunt Jackson visited Emily. The Jacksons had also seen Mrs. Bowles in Springfield.

> They found her, they said, a stricken woman, though not so ruthless as they feared. That of ties remaining, she spoke with peculiar love of a Miss Whitney of Northampton, whom she would soon visit, and almost thought of accompanying them as far as yourself.
>
> To know that long fidelity in ungracious soil was not wholly squandered, might be sweet to you.
>
> [II, 573]

The final sentence is a clue to the relationship between Mrs. Bowles and Miss Whitney.

The letters to Miss Whitney, maimed as they are, confirm the special character of Emily Dickinson's friendship with Bowles. Even in death Samuel Bowles was described in the imagery which had filled Emily's love poems years before: darkness, light, the Orient, and deity. Letters of 1878–82 contain the following passages:

> I have thought of you often since the darkness, – though we cannot assist another's night. I have hoped you were saved. That he has received Immortality who so often conferred it, invests it with a more sudden charm. . . .
>
> [II, 602]

> I dreamed Saturday night of precious Mr. Bowles. One glance of his would light a world.[10]

I trust you may have the dearest summer possible to loss –

One sweet sweet more – One liquid more – of that Arabian presence! . . .

In a brief memoir of Parepa, in which she was likened to a Rose – "thornless until she died," some bereaved one added – to miss him is his only stab, but that – he never gave.

A word from you would be sacred.

[III, 662]

The death of Judge Lord's wife (on Emily's forty-seventh birthday) was overshadowed by the final illness of Samuel Bowles. The following summer Lord visited Amherst as usual, though he now stayed at the Amherst House rather than the Dickinson homestead. Probably Emily welcomed him as the friend to whom she could speak most freely about her father. Suddenly all was different: in the summer of 1878 Emily knew she was in love with Otis Lord, and Lord discovered how much he loved Emily.

There was no immaturity on either side of this new fulfillment. Lord was sixty-eight years old. His marriage had been a happy one. Emily was nearly forty-eight, long past her desperate search for a master, far beyond infatuation. Though she was now describing Samuel Bowles as one "for whom we moan while consciousness remains" [II, 620], she would not suppress a new love for the sake of a remembered one. The poems in which Emily Dickinson celebrated her 1878 "day at summer's full" are moving speeches, not cries of pain.

We talked with each other about each other
Though neither of us spoke –
We were listening to the seconds Races
And the Hoofs of the Clock –
Pausing in Front of our Palsied Faces

Time compassion took –
Arks of Reprieve he offered to us –
Ararats – we took – [11]

No doubt Emily's virtual worship of her father was reflected in her love for his best friend. Psychological interpretations of Emily Dickinson's life and art depend heavily on the "father-image" in her loves: the series of scholar-schoolmaster relationships tends to confirm them. As a note of caution, however, it should be pointed out that while Emily called Judge Lord "Papa" at times, she did not regard herself as his daughter. In April 1882 she told Lord that her recent illness had had one "grace"; "It kept the faint Mama from sleep, so she could dream of Papa awake – an innocence of fondness" [III, 727].

Emily's letters to Otis Lord survive in partial drafts. The actual correspondence is lost. What remains tells a great deal about Emily Dickinson. For one thing, there is now a tangible, factual love (which can be verified as real and mutual by external evidence): a yardstick for measuring Emily's other intense friendships. These painfully personal letters help to dispel the generations of nonsense which have followed publication of the poems. The ingenious theories that explained Emily Dickinson's poetry and seclusion in terms of a single unshared love relied on rumor and romantic supposition. Since 1954, when Millicent Todd Bingham published the letters to Lord, such theories have been untenable. Whatever "Master"—or a number of masters—may have meant to Emily, she loved Otis Phillips Lord in her later years. Moreover, marriage was possible this time.

Emily did not marry Lord. She persisted in writing poetry; she continued to dress in white. She remained within her father's house and still was unwilling to meet in person most of those who came to call. If the pattern of her life had depended upon satisfaction in love, some outward change should have appeared. None did.

The letters to Judge Lord begin in 1878 with the first surprise and joy of mutual love:

> My lovely Salem smiles at me. I seek his Face so often – but I have done with guises.
>
> I confess that I love him – I rejoice that I love him – I thank the maker of Heaven and Earth – that gave him me to love – the exultation floods me. I cannot find my channel – the Creek turns Sea – at thought of thee –
>
> [II, 614–15]

The imagery is that of Emily's earlier love. Flood and sea persist in her poetry and prose, but "Arks of Reprieve" replace the spar on which the castaway drifts with "hands – beseeching – thrown."

Much in love as she was, Emily would not abandon the deliberate life she had chosen. By 1878 she was as complete a recluse as she would ever be. There had been no Commencement receptions—her last contact with groups of people—since her father's death. Her physical world was bounded by the walls and hedges of home. That, she felt, was as wide a horizon as she could compass without losing something of her search for the essential. She had told Higginson that she was grateful to be herself and not someone else: if she left the existence she had elected, she would be leaving the individual "royalty" she had won at such great cost. One 1878 letter to Judge Lord tries to make this clear to him: "It is anguish I long conceal from you to let you leave me, hungry, but you ask the divine Crust and that would doom the Bread" [II, 617].

Emily understood what she was refusing. Her frankness about sexual possibilities justifies by itself the title of the book in which the letters to Lord were first published: "A Revelation." About 1880 she wrote to the judge,

It is strange that I miss you at night so much when I
was never with you — but the punctual love invokes you
soon as my eyes are shut — and I wake warm with the
want sleep had almost filled — I dreamed last week that
you had died — and one had carved a statue of you and
I was asked to unvail it — and I said what I had not
done in Life I would not in death when your loved eyes
could not forgive — . . . .

Lest I had been too frank was often my fear — How
could I long to give who never saw your natures Face —

[III, 664–65]

Passages like this, considering Emily's character and
that of Judge Lord, are fairly good indications that the
judge proposed marriage to Emily. She wore a ring he
gave her until her death, another hint of betrothal. But
marriage, even a journey beyond the homestead, was impossible. Until November 1882 Emily might have offered
the excuse—a true one—that the care of her mother, invalid since 1875, required her constant presence at home.
A month after Mrs. Dickinson's death, however, Emily
was still refusing an invitation to visit the judge in
Salem:

> You said with loved timidity in asking me to your dear
> Home, you would "try not to make it unpleasant." So
> delicate a diffidence, how beautiful to see! I do not think
> a Girl extant, has so divine a modesty.
>
> You even call me to your Breast with apology: Of
> what must my poor Heart be made?
>
> That the one for whom Modesty is felt, himself
> should feel it sweetest and ask his own with such a
> grace, is beloved reproach. The tender Priest of Hope
> need not allure his Offering — 'tis on his Altar ere he
> asks.

Even so, Emily liked to think of marriage. In the same
year, 1882, Lord called his diminutive friend "Jumbo."

She replied, "Emily 'Jumbo'! Sweetest name, but I know a sweeter – Emily Jumbo Lord. Have I your approval?" [III, 747.]

The words Emily Dickinson chose when she wrote to Otis Lord were often simple, seldom literary. "Sweet" became a favorite word and spread into her other correspondences. For Lord's amusement Emily made a point of using the legal language which had always surrounded the Dickinsons. In 1878 she described a conversation with her nephew Ned in which the boy had quoted Austin: law in Massachusetts "would amount to something" if there were another judge like Lord. "I told him I thought it probable – though recalling that I had never tried any case in your presence but my own, and that, with your sweet assistance – I was murmurless." A lawyer's daughter could appreciate accounts of trials: "We were much amused at the Juror's 'cough' you thought not pulmonary, and when you were waiting at your Hotel for the Kidder Verdict, and the Jury decided to go to sleep, I thought them the loveliest Jury I had ever met" [III, 727].

Judge Lord had a sense of humor to match Emily's. The friendship of the two before the death of Edward Dickinson seems to have consisted, in large part, of an exchange of jokes. Various examples of "the Judge Lord brand of humor" appear in the writings of Emily's niece Martha, though Martha did not always understand, even half a century later, that Lord had been joking. She wrote, for instance, "While I was a little girl [Aunt Emily] had always revelled in my hats with 'dare-devil bows,' and some 'stratified stockings' which were red with white stripes—much in vogue among my playmates—and which had once caused the pompous Judge Lord to enquire if I was 'intended for a tonsorial advertisement. . . .' " [12] Sue described Judge Lord "at his best," reciting with mock solemnity the hymn which begins,

My thoughts on awful subjects roll;
Damnation and the dead . . .

to the great amusement of the Dickinsons.[13]

Love which was returned was a joy to Emily, but one event after another tempered her pleasure. When Judge Lord came to Amherst he brought his wife's nieces, Abby and Mary Farley, with him. Years later Abby described Emily to a friend, unintentionally revealing herself, rather than Emily, by the words she chose. "Little hussy—didn't I know her? I should say I did. Loose morals. She was crazy about men. Even tried to get Judge Lord. Insane, too." [14] Abby's attitude at the time of the love affair survives in a letter she wrote to Ned Dickinson in April 1883: "A letter has just arrived from your neighbor containing sweet flowers, for 'dear Otis' I suppose. What a lot of humbug there is in this world. . . . Uncle Lord is writing in the next room a letter for the 'Mansion' such a sweet one—I suppose." [15]

The Farleys were close friends of Susan Dickinson, and enlisted her support. Mabel Loomis Todd, who arrived in Amherst in 1881, recorded Sue's reaction upon hearing that Vinnie had invited the Todds to the homestead:

> Sue said at that, "You will not allow your husband to go there, I hope!" "Why not?" I asked innocently. "Because they have not, either of them, any idea of morality," she replied, with a certain satisfaction in her tone. . . . "I went in there one day, and in the drawing room I found Emily reclining in the arms of a man. What can you say to that?" [16]

Perhaps it is unfair, so long after the events, to suggest a reason for the Farleys' opposition to Emily Dickinson's final love. One fact is plain: if Emily married Lord, the nieces of his dead wife Elizabeth Farley Lord would be unlikely to inherit much of his estate. Abby Farley was Otis Lord's chief beneficiary [III, 942].

Sue's opposition was more subtle. By the late eighteen seventies there were few ties between Sue and the Dickinsons. The whole family adored her youngest child, Gilbert; on the other hand, the death of Edward Dickinson had deprived Sue of an ally. During his lifetime tensions among the others had remained out of sight. Now, Vinnie and Sue no longer spoke to each other, and Austin, so long unhappy with a wife incapable of loving him, was close to estrangement. In October 1884 Sue wrote to her daughter Martha, "We laughed over your letter last night till I lost off my glasses. Even Papa broke down and for a moment forgot, that he does not allow himself to applaud his family." [17] Emily tried to remain faithful to her girlhood friend, now her "pseudo Sister," but loyalty to Austin was still a firmer bond. She wrote indirectly about the tensions of the "other house" to a few close friends, but usually did so only when she felt that Austin needed special attention.

While he lived, Samuel Bowles helped sustain Austin's spirit. He was not entirely happy in his own marriage, as his letters to Austin indicate as early as 1862, though his problem was difference of temperament, not lack of love. The two men held a strength of friendship against the disappointment they shared. Later the Reverend and Mrs. Jonathan L. Jenkins became Austin's mainstays. The Jenkinses moved to Pittsfield early in 1877; soon after, Emily wrote to Mrs. Jenkins, "Austin brought the note and waited like a hungry Boy for his crumb of words. Be sure to speak his name next time, he looks so solitary" [II, 581]. After Samuel Bowles died, Emily told Mr. and Mrs. Henry Hills, "I am glad you care so much for Austin – He will need you more!" [II, 600].

Austin never fluctuated in his devotion to his sisters,

whom he visited almost every day. Little acts which pleased them are typified by one which Emily described to Mrs. Holland about 1879: "Austin and Sue have just returned from the Belchertown Cattle Show – Austin brought me a Balloon and Vinnie a Watermelon. . . . Wasn't it primitive?" [II, 648.]

Emily's attempts to remain on good terms with Sue continued to alternate between success and failure. In one note of about 1878 she told Sue, "I must wait a few Days before seeing you – You are too momentous. But remember it is idolatry, not indifference." When no excuse seemed plausible she wrote, "I can defeat the rest, but you defeat me, Susan" [II, 631]. One of the reconciliations appears in a letter of about 1881 to Dr. Holland, who had, answered Emily's question, "How did you snare Howells?" (*A Fearful Responsibility* was appearing serially in *Scribner's Monthly*) with a short note: "Case of bribery – money did it" [III, 702]. Emily wrote to Holland, "Your small Note was as merry as Honey, and enthralled us all – I sent it over to Sue, who took Ned's Arm and came across – and we talked of Mr Samuel and you, and vital times when you two bore the Republican, and came as near sighing – all of us – as would be often wise – I should say next door – Sue said she was homesick for those 'better Days,' hallowed be their name" [III, 716].

Susan Dickinson had made herself the social leader of Amherst. It was her habit to "collect" rare personalities. Emily, though unseen by Sue's guests, was the prize of the collection. Sue regarded her sister-in-law as a strange blossom, almost a personal possession, whom she alone had the right to exhibit. (It was this attitude which especially outraged Vinnie.) But Sue's description of Emily, who so hated publicity, "in the arms of a man" was extreme disloyalty. Her pretended concern for the safety of young Professor Todd in the presence of Emily and Vinnie—let alone her claim that neither had any idea of morality—was not only insulting; it was slanderous. In view of such acts, it is reasonable to doubt Sue's claims of fondness for Emily.

To offset the fact of Emily's love for Judge Lord, Susan Dickinson continued to circulate stories about heartbroken attachments to nebulous young clergymen long dead. She also involved family friends. Mabel Loomis Todd wrote in her diary in 1882, "It is hinted that Dr. Holland loved her very much & she him, but that her father who was a stern old lawyer & politician saw nothing particularly promising or remarkable in the shy, half-educated boy, & would not listen to her marrying him." [18] (This story is easily disposed of; Holland married his wife when Emily was fourteen, long before he met the Dickinsons.) At one time or another Sue named most of the family's friends as "the man," with two notable exceptions: Samuel Bowles and Otis Lord. (In the same spirit, her daughter Martha, who claimed to have learned of Emily's "true love" at Vinnie's deathbed, never named Judge Lord as a candidate. The fact that Vinnie "was bitter in her denunciations" of Sue and Martha, at the time she allegedly confided Emily's secrets to the latter,[19] is almost beside the point.)

Sue needed Emily's support in the family war—"Vesuvius at home," Emily called it. Paradoxically, her opposition to Judge Lord, who might have taken Emily out of the family sphere, only widened the distance between the sisters-in-law. Meanwhile other events kept Emily within her chosen path of seclusion. Each of her bereavements was a strain which demanded a straiter discipline. Her father and Samuel Bowles were gone; in October 1881 J. G. Holland died. Emily may have established a "sacred" correspondence with his *Scribner's Monthly* col-

league, Roswell Smith. In 1894 Mabel Loomis Todd
wrote to an editor of the magazine (since November 1881
called *The Century*), "Emily Dickinson's sister tells me
that for some years before her death she was accustomed
to send off many letters and packages addressed to 'Roswell Smith, Century Company.'" [20] None of the correspondence has ever been found. Six months after Holland
died, the Reverend Charles Wadsworth was dead; a
month later, the threat of another death gave Emily a
new fear.

On May 1, 1882, Judge Lord suffered a stroke. Two
weeks later Emily wrote to him,

> . . . I enclose the Note I was fast writing, when the
> fear that your life had ceased, came, fresh, yet dim,
> like the horrid Monsters fled from in a Dream.
>
> Happy with my letter, without a film of fear, Vinnie
> came in from a word with Austin, passing to the Train.
> "Emily, did you see anything in the Paper that con-
> cerned us?" "Why no, Vinnie, what"? "Mr Lord is very
> sick." I grasped at a passing Chair. My sight slipped
> and I thought I was freezing. While my last smile was
> ending, I heard the Doorbell ring and a strange voice
> said "I thought first of you." Meanwhile Tom [Kelley,
> a hired man,] had come, and I ran to his Blue Jacket
> and let my Heart break there – that was the warmest
> place. "He will be better. Dont cry Miss Emily. I could
> not see you cry."
>
> Then Vinnie came out and said "Prof. Chickering
> thought we would like him to telegraph." He "would
> do it for us."
>
> "Would I write a Telegram?" I asked the Wires how
> you did, and attached my name.
>
> The Professor took it, and Abby's brave – refreshing
> reply I shall always remember. . . .
>
> [III, 730–31]

The note Emily had been writing when news of Lord's illness came was the one she had begun on April 30, the day before. In this love letter to Otis Lord appears her first reference to the death of Charles Wadsworth on April 1:

> I am told it is only a pair of Sundays since you went from me. I feel it many years. Today is April's last – it has been an April of meaning to me. I have been in your Bosom. My Philadelphia has passed from Earth, and the Ralph Waldo Emerson – whose name my Father's Law Student taught me, has touched the secret Spring. Which Earth are we in?
> *Heaven*, a Sunday or two ago – but that also has ceased –
>
> [III, 727]

The epithet "My Philadelphia" is a sign of Wadsworth's importance to Emily Dickinson and an indication that she had talked to Lord ("My lovely Salem") about him. The context—Wadsworth's death sandwiched between other events in the "April of meaning"—shows that in 1882 the clergyman was not the center of Emily's existence, if he had ever been.

Almost everything known about the friendship between Emily Dickinson and the Reverend Charles Wadsworth is derived from the series of letters she wrote to his friends James and Charles Clark. During his 1860 visit the minister had said he was thinking of visiting James Clark in Northampton [III, 738]. When Wadsworth died Emily chose Clark as her sacred correspondent.

It is necessary to recall, in evaluating Emily's letters to the friends of her "Lost," that each correspondence has a single center. In June 1883, for instance, she was writing of Wadsworth to Charles Clark, "I felt it almost a bliss of sorrow that the name so long in Heaven on earth, should be on earth in Heaven. Do you know if either of his sons have his mysterious face or his momentous nature?" [III, 779.] In the same month she wrote to Maria Whitney, "It is Commencement now. Pathos is very busy. The past is not a package one can lay away. I see my father's eyes, and those of Mr. Bowles – those isolated comets. If the future is mighty as the past, what may vista be?" [III, 780.] Aside from what she felt about the dead, Emily still loved Judge Lord.

These various loyalties did not conflict: each friendship, each love was individual. Emily wrote to Lord (in the May 1 part of the letter which mentions Wadsworth's death), "The trespass of my rustic Love upon your Realms of Ermine, only a Sovreign could forgive – I never knelt to other – " Perhaps Emily paused in writing. It was not quite true that she had never "knelt to other" than Lord. Twenty years before she had been "low at the knee" of another man whom she had called "My Sovreign." She continued, "The Spirit never twice alike, but every time another – that other more divine. Oh, had I found it sooner! Yet Tenderness has not a Date – it comes – and overwhelms. The time before it was – was naught, so why establish it?" [III, 728.]

When Emily Dickinson began to write to James Clark in the summer of 1882, she knew very little about the Reverend Charles Wadsworth. It is easy to see why, if all the minister's letters to her were as vague as the one which has survived. "In an intimacy of many years with the beloved Clergyman," she told Clark, "I have never before spoken with one who knew him, and his Life was so shy and his tastes so unknown, that grief for him seems almost unshared" [III, 737]. She went on to describe Wadsworth's second (final) visit with her in the summer of 1880. This account of the interview (with some additional phrases from an 1886 description of the same event to Charles Clark) is so clear a narrative that its brevity is regrettable.

> I saw him two years since for the last time, though how unsuspected! He rang one summer evening to my glad surprise – I was with my lilies and heliotropes. Said my sister to me, "The gentleman with the deep voice wants to see you, Emily," hearing him ask of the servant.
>
> "Where did you come from?" I said, for he spoke like an apparition. "Why did you not tell me you were coming, so I could have it to hope for?"
>
> "Because I did not know it myself. I stepped from my pulpit to the train," was his quiet reply, and when I asked, "How long," "Twenty years," said he with inscrutable roguery.
>
> [III, 738, 901]

Emily did not tell James Clark that Wadsworth had come to Amherst only twice. Rather, she worded her letters to suggest more frequent interviews. After describing the 1880 visit, she continued, "He once remarked to me in talking, 'I am liable at any time to die,' but I thought it no omen. He spoke on a previous visit of calling upon you, or perhaps remaining a brief time at your Home in Northampton" [III, 738]. Clark, as he read about events "two years since," "once," and "on a previous visit" would be unlikely to realize that only two meetings were described.[21] Had Clark known that the "intimacy of many years" was conducted almost entirely by mail, he might have been less willing to share his memories of Wadsworth.

The questions Emily asked about Charles Wadsworth were nearly those of a stranger. "I thought it possible you might tell me if our lost one had Brother or Sister," she wrote, adding—perhaps for reassurance—that the minister had been in mourning for his mother when he had visited in 1860. She continued, "I felt too that perhaps you . . . might know if his Children were near him at last, or if they grieved to lose that most sacred Life. Do you know do they resemble him?" [III, 742].

James Clark answered Emily's questions, adding information about Wadsworth's disagreement with his two older children. This was confidential, of course, and Emily replied, "Thank you . . . for the monition, tho' to disclose a grief of his I could not surmise – " [III, 745]. By now, in her third letter to Clark, Emily had firmly established her sacred friendship. The letter is elegiac:

He was a Dusk Gem, born of troubled Waters, astray in any Crest below. Heaven might give him Peace, it could not give him Grandeur, for that he carried with himself to whatever scene –

Obtaining but his own extent
In whatsoever Realm –
'Twas Christ's own personal Expanse
That bore him from the Tomb.

[III, 744–45]

The last sentence quoted above must have pleased Emily: in the same year, writing to Samuel Bowles the younger [111] about his father and uncle, she said, "Heaven may give them rank, it could not give them grandeur, for that they carried with themselves" [III, 735]. The poem (with "our" substituted for "his") she also sent to Higginson. However personal Emily's grief might be for one friend or another, she was primarily an artist when words were involved.

Clark called on Emily late in 1882 or early in 1883. Emily had met no strangers since Helen Hunt Jackson had brought her husband to the homestead in 1878; her interview with Clark, whom she had known only a few months, is further evidence of her great desire to learn more about Dr. Wadsworth. Other talks were prevented by Clark's illness soon after his visit. During the spring of 1883 Emily began to write to his brother, Charles Clark. "Would it be possible you would excuse me," she asked him in April, "if I once more inquire for the Health of the Brother whom Association has made sacred?" [III, 772.] James Clark died in June. Emily continued to write to Charles, whom she now regarded as doubly sacred for his associations with both his brother and "the beloved Clergyman":

> I never met your brother but once. An unforgotten once. To have seen him but once more, would have been almost like an interview with my "Heavenly Father," whom he loved and knew. . . . I am eager to know all you may tell me of those final days. We asked for him every Morning, in Heart, but feared to disturb you. . . . Though Strangers, please accept us for the two great sakes.
>
> [III, 778]

The image of Wadsworth in the letters Emily wrote to the Clark brothers is at times that of remote deity, at other times that of the man who twice visited Amherst. The minister had not mentioned his home life, except during his visits; he had written letters of spiritual advice or sent copies of his sermons. Emily was accustomed to attribute special powers to absent friends like Higginson or Helen Hunt Jackson, but she knew their personal lives through their letters to her. Wadsworth remained unknown and therefore awesome. Emily's long friendship with him was the spiritual intimacy, in Calvinist rather than Roman Catholic terms, of penitent and unseen confessor. When Wadsworth was dead, Emily tried to discover the man of daily affairs, although she did not relinquish her image of the Christlike preceptor. As a result, the clergyman became in her letters a strange figure who seems holy at one moment, banal at another. In one 1882 letter to James Clark, Emily wrote,

> The Griefs of which you speak were unknown to me, though I knew him as a "Man of sorrow," and once when he seemed almost overpowered by a spasm of gloom, I said "You are troubled." Shivering as he spoke, "My Life is full of dark secrets," he said. He never spoke of his Home, but of a Child – "Willie," whom, forgive me the arrogance, he told me was like me – though I, not knowing "Willie," was benighted still. . . . I do not yet fathom that he has died – and hope I may not till he assists me in another World – "Hallowed be it's Name!"
>
> [III, 745]

Emily mentioned the death of Wadsworth to Judge Lord, Higginson, Mrs. Holland, and presumably the Norcrosses. Only the Clarks, as sacred friends, received detailed accounts of her friendship with the minister, but messages to Higginson and Mrs. Holland are illuminating. The two scholarly biographers who presented Wadsworth as "Master" saw in the minister's impending departure for California a primary reason for Emily's April 15, 1862 letter to Higginson.[23] Yet Emily did not feel it "shelter" to write to Colonel Higginson immediately after Wadsworth died, as she had on the day of Bowles's funeral: she waited until summer, then wrote simply, "My closest earthly friend died in April –" [III, 737]. The loss of two preceptors within a month undoubtedly was part of Emily's reason for writing to Higginson in 1862, but when she first wrote to him, only one of them, Bowles, had "left the land."

As the first anniversary of Wadsworth's death ap-

proached, Emily wrote to Mrs. Holland, who had forwarded letters to Wadsworth, "All other Surprise is at
last monotonous, but the Death of the Loved is all moments – *now* – Love has but one Date – 'The first of
April . . .' " [III, 760]. These are the words which offer
the most concrete evidence that Emily Dickinson loved
Dr. Wadsworth. For lack of further proof, it is impossible
to tell which kind of love she meant, or at what period
she first felt it. The kind she felt toward Judge Lord, to
whom she was still writing love letters, would not have
April 1 as its "one date," but as Emily had told Lord, the
spirit was never twice alike.

Wadsworth's high rank among Emily's masters is in-
disputable. Vinnie and Austin, though they told Mrs.
Todd that they did not think Emily had been in love with
the minister, asked her to omit most references to Wadsworth when she published Emily's letters. In 1931, when
she published in full the letters to the Clarks, Mrs. Todd
explained, "At that time (1894) the letters and sections
omitted seemed too personal for publication. That the
preacher was peculiarly dear to Emily was reason enough
to conceal his identity from the public." [24]

It is possible that Emily Dickinson turned to her
"heavenly father" with a devotion which stood above her
other ardors because of its very remoteness. One poem of
1882 may be a clue:

> Image of Light, Adieu –
> Thanks for the interview
> So long – so short –
> Preceptor of the whole –
> Coeval Cardinal –
> Impart – Depart – [25]

As "Preceptor of the whole" the Reverend Charles Wadsworth would indeed be Emily's closest earthly friend: the

man she had consulted when other schoolmasters of her
art or intellect or emotions could not help her, the man
she had steadfastly revered for his strength of character
and faith.

Emily was bereaved for the second time within a year
when her mother died in November 1882. Mrs. Dickinson had suffered a paralyzing stroke on the first anniversary of her husband's death. Three years later, in 1878,
she broke a hip, and remained bedridden the rest of her
life. The constant care she required brought her daughters closer to her than before. "We were never intimate
Mother and Children while she was our Mother," Emily
wrote to Mrs. Holland, "but Mines in the same Ground
meet by tunneling and when she became our Child, the
Affection came –" [III, 754].

Mrs. Dickinson's function in the family was, as Vinnie
said, to love. The manifestations of her love seem to have
been ineffectual. Austin told Mabel Loomis Todd that his
mother's chief claim to attention had been her attempts
to make guests comfortable by anticipating their needs.
Once, when Emily was deep in an intellectual conversation, her mother kept interrupting to make sure that the
guest needed nothing more. At a high point in the discussion she bustled in and asked, "Aren't your feet cold?
Wouldn't you like to come in the kitchen and warm
them?" As Austin recalled to Mrs. Todd, "Emily gave up
in despair at that. 'Wouldn't you like to have the Declaration of Independence read, or the Lord's Prayer repeated,'
and she went on with a long list of unspeakably funny
things to be done." [26] On another occasion as the whole
family sat at dinner, Mrs. Dickinson tried to make conversation. "The mercury stands at seventy-eight," she
volunteered. "Should you have thought it so warm, Edward – or warmer?" In a loud whisper Emily commented
to the others, "Providence ought to be above it." [27]

Her mother, Emily told Higginson in 1862, did not care for thought. Emily came to pity this lack when Mrs. Dickinson, as an invalid, was often restless. "Mother misses power to ramble to her Neighbors – and the stale inflations of the minor News," she wrote to Mrs. Holland. "I wish the Sky and she had been better friends, for that is 'sociability' that is fine and deathless" [II, 593]. Emily realized, however, that her mother chatted "about nothing momentous, but things vital to her" [II, 604].

With pity came gentle deceptions. Mrs. Dickinson's mind wandered; sometimes she asked for her husband, forgetting that he was dead. After the Reverend Jonathan L. Jenkins moved from Amherst, Emily wrote to him, "Mother asked me last Sabbath 'why Father did'nt come from Church,' and 'if Mr Jenkins preached?' I told her he did and that Father had lingered to speak with him" [II, 618]. When Mrs. Dickinson was frightened by her own illness, Emily took care "to tell her 'Health will come tomorrow,' and make the counterfeit look real . . ." [III, 675].

Until Mrs. Dickinson was paralyzed she appeared rarely in Emily's letters, and even then chiefly as a source of fun. In 1863, for instance, Emily described to Loo and Fanny Norcross her mother's trouble with a new false tooth. "She kept to her bed, Sunday, with a face that would take a premium at any cattle-show in the land" [II, 428]. The new tenderness toward an invalid revealed itself in frequent references to her. Emily no longer found her mother's illnesses funny. She appreciated at last the love which had been the center of Mrs. Dickinson's life. In 1876 Emily wrote to Mrs. Higginson, "I have now no Father, and scarcely a Mother, for her Will followed my Father, and only an idle Heart is left, listless for his sake" [II, 555].

There was no sacred correspondence after Mrs. Dickinson died, simply because no one knew her as well as her children. To Maria Whitney, however, Emily sent a memorial poem, "To the bright east she flies," and to the Norcrosses she wrote a prose elegy about the mother who at last had come to be more than a dutiful presence in the homestead:

> She was scarcely the aunt you knew. The great mission of pain had been ratified – cultivated to tenderness by persistent sorrow, so that a larger mother died than had she died before. There was no earthly parting. She slipped from our fingers like a flake gathered by the wind, and is now part of the drift called "the infinite."
> We dont know where she is, though so many tell us.
> I believe we shall in some manner be cherished by our Maker – that the one who gave us this remarkable earth has the power still further to surprise that which he has caused. Beyond, all is silence . . . Mother was very beautiful when she had died. Seraphs are solemn artists. The illumination that comes but once paused upon her features, and it seemed like hiding a picture to lay her in the grave; but the grass that received my Father will suffice his guest, the one he asked at the altar to visit him all his life.
> I cannot tell how Eternity seems. It sweeps around me like a sea while I do my work.[28]

The Physician says I have "Nervous
prostration." Possibly I have – I do not
know the Names of Sickness. The Crisis
of the Sorrow of so many years is all that
tires me –

—*Emily Dickinson*

8

The Weight of Grief

Although Emily Dickinson secluded herself from the
everyday life of Amherst, she was always interested in it.
Even in her last years she made friends—on her own terms
—with people whose vitality impressed her. Her friendship with Mabel Loomis Todd, who became her posthumous editor, is a case in point.

Professor and Mrs. Todd arrived in Amherst in September 1881. Though they were a full generation younger
than the Dickinsons (Mrs. Todd was only five years
older than Austin's son Ned), a close friendship began
at once. David Todd's dignity, reticence, and unobtrusive
way of being helpful—repairing the homestead clocks, for
example—appealed to the Dickinsons. Vinnie declared the
young astronomer "*gold* in character." [1] Mabel Loomis
Todd, on the other hand, charmed them with her artistry
and vivacity. She sang and played the piano with profes-

sional skill. She also wrote fiction and painted flowers on wood or brass. Her mind was quick and her beauty striking. Mrs. Todd was equally impressed with the Dickinsons. She described Austin as "a truly regal man, tall, slender and magnificent in bearing," and Sue as "well dressed with an India shawl over her shoulders which became her dark beauty." [2] Within a year Mrs. Todd was writing of Austin, "I most extravagantly admire him. He is almost in every particular my ideal man." [3]

As a member of Sue's circle in 1882 and early 1883 Mrs. Todd took part in the many activities of the group: sports, teas, and theatricals. For instance, she played the leading role in a dramatic version of Frances Hodgson Burnett's novel, "A Fair Barbarian." When summer came, Sue and her coterie spent a week in the cool hills east of Amherst, styling themselves "The Shutesbury School of Philosophy" and sometimes entertaining the local public. In July 1882 "Mrs. Todd of Washington" sang for the group and "about 30 townspeople of Shutesbury. . . ." [4]

"Soon after our arrival," Mrs. Todd wrote, "I began to hear about a remarkable sister of Austin's who never went out and saw no one who called." [5] She noted that Emily was called "the myth." It was not long before Vinnie invited the Todds to the homestead, though neither of them came face to face with the mysterious Miss Emily. Mrs. Todd became accustomed to playing the piano and singing in the homestead parlor while Emily remained half-hidden, "her dress a spot of white in the dim hall." [6] At this distance the two became friends. "I did not need to see her," Mrs. Todd wrote afterward, "for her personality was vibrant in her voice—its vaguely surprised note dominant." [7] At the end of each recital Emily sent in a poem, with sherry, cake, or a flower, on a silver tray. A few weeks after the two became acquainted, Mrs. Todd visited her parents in Washington, and Emily wrote to her, "The parting of those that never met, shall it be delusion, or rather, an unfolding snare whose fruitage is later?" [III, 716.]

Mrs. Todd made a painting of Indian pipes for Emily in the autumn of 1882. Emily thanked her in prose as delicate as the white plants:

> Dear Friend,
>
> That without suspecting it you should send me the preferred flower of life, seems almost supernatural, and the sweet glee that I felt at meeting it, I could confide to none. I still cherish the clutch with which I bore it from the ground when a wondering Child, an unearthly booty, and maturity only enhances mystery, never decreases it. To duplicate the Vision is almost more amazing, for God's unique capacity is too surprising to surprise.
>
> I know not how to thank you. We do not thank the Rainbow, although it's trophy is a snare.
>
> To give delight is hallowed – perhaps the toil of Angels, whose avocations are concealed –
>
> I trust you are well, and the quaint little Girl with the deep Eyes, every day more fathomless.
>
> > With joy,
> > E. Dickinson.
>
> > > [III, 740]

Emily kept the painting in her bedroom the rest of her life. In 1890 it was reproduced on the cover of *Poems by Emily Dickinson*. Emily sent Mrs. Todd one of her finest poems in October 1882, saying,

> I cannot make an Indian Pipe, but please accept a Humming Bird.
>
> A Rout of Evanescence
> With a revolving Wheel –

A Resonance of Emerald –
A Rush of Cochineal –
And every Blossom on the Bush
Adjusts it's tumbled Head –
The mail from Tunis probably,
An easy Morning's Ride –

E. Dickinson.

[III, 740]

Poems like this convinced Mrs. Todd of Emily's genius, and she recorded in her journals much about the poet which would otherwise have been lost. Her later persistence in publishing the poems, collecting hundreds of Emily's letters, and writing down the recollections of Austin and Lavinia Dickinson has made Mrs. Todd a primary source of Dickinson scholarship.

Friends like Mrs. Todd did not meet Emily directly, but it should not be thought that Emily secluded herself from everyone. Rather, she made an unusual distinction between formal and informal visitors. It was part of her love of paradox—so evident in her poetry—not merely to live at an angle to the usual social rules, but to reverse them completely. Thus Maggie Maher, the "warm and wild and mighty" Irishwoman in the homestead, had definite instructions about front-door callers: "the Servant Conscientiously says at the Door We are invariably out –" [III, 926]. The excuse must have been irritating or amusing to those who knew Emily never left the house. At the back door, paradoxically, few were considered strangers: Emily was willing to talk to tramps or gypsies or the Indian women who sold baskets from door to door. In August 1880 she wrote to Colonel Higginson,

I was touchingly reminded of your little Louisa this Morning by an Indian Woman with gay Baskets and a dazzling Baby, at the Kitchen Door – Her little Boy "once died," she said, Death to her dispelling him – I asked her what the Baby liked, and she said "to step." The Prairie before the Door was gay with Flowers of Hay, and I led her in – She argued with the Birds – she leaned on Clover Walls and they fell, and dropped her – With jargon sweeter than a Bell, she grappled Buttercups – and they sank together, the Buttercups the heaviest – What sweetest use of Days!

[III, 668]

The Dickinson servants had complete access to Emily. Maggie, of course, was in the house: she came to be as devoted as Vinnie to the "protection" of Emily from invasions of privacy. The men who worked in the barn or fields also showed unusual tenderness for the recluse. When news of Judge Lord's illness came in May 1882, Professor Chickering was kept at the front door while Emily cried in the arms of the handyman Tom Kelley. It was to fulfill Emily's wishes that her coffin, borne on the shoulders of the family's hired men, was carried out of the homestead by the back door, and through the barn— another paradox.

Children too came to the kitchen door and were allowed in Emily's presence in the green-walled kitchen. Playmates of Austin's children saw her, as did Millicent Todd, though their parents were denied the privilege. In March 1883, when Mrs. Todd and her daughter were in Washington, Emily wrote two drafts of a letter which seems not to have been mailed. The references to the friend's absence and small daughter (as well as the oblique mention of painting, similar to the earlier "I cannot make an Indian Pipe") make it almost certain that the letter was to Mrs. Todd. One draft is devoted to the child:

I dream of your little Girl three successive Nights – I hope nothing affronts her –

To see her is a Picture –
To hear her is a Tune –
To know her, a disparagement of every other Boon –
To know her not, Affliction –
To own her for a Friend
A warmth as near as if the Sun
Were shining in your Hand –

Lest she miss her "Squirrels," I send her little Playmates I met in Yesterday's Storm – the lovely first that
came –

Forever honored be the Tree
Whose Apple winter-worn –
Enticed to Breakfast from the sky
Two Gabriels Yester Morn.

They registered in Nature's Book
As Robins, Sire and Son –
But Angels have that modest way
To screen them from renown –

[III, 766–67]

The other draft, on the back of the same sheet, is less
intimate. It begins, "I cannot tint in carbon nor embroider
Brass, but send you a homespun rustic picture I certainly
saw in the terrific storm. Please excuse my needlework – "
A space is left for "Forever honored be the Tree"; then
Emily adds a note about the "rustic picture" of robins: "If
you have any doubts as to its Authenticity, I sent Oats to
the same Guests by the man at the Barn . . ." [III, 915–
16]. Emily's contact with the mother was vicarious; with
the child it was direct.

Emily Dickinson considered children her confederates
—conspirators with her against the pleasantries of adult
society. At any rate, she gave the children that impression.
Upstairs in the homestead (her niece Martha recalled),

Emily would listen to the departure of Vinnie's guests
and whisper, "hear them kiss! – the traitors!" [8] Sometimes
she wrote to the children she knew best. In one note to
twelve-year-old MacGregor Jenkins she said, "Please never
grow up, which is 'far better' – Please never 'improve' –
you are perfect now" [III, 704]. The cult of childhood is
one of the few elements of romanticism which Emily retained to the end of her life. The childlike quality resulted at times in art of the sort which Traherne and
Blake had produced before her; when she did not control
it carefully, the result was a childish bathos.

Children were impressed by Emily. As MacGregor
Jenkins recalled in 1891,

> one summer morning, . . . Miss Emily called me. She
> was standing on a rug spread for her on the grass, busy
> with the potted plants which were all about her . . .
> a beautiful woman dressed in white, with soft, fiery,
> brown eyes and a mass of auburn hair. . . . She talked
> to me of her flowers, of those she loved best, of her fear
> lest the bad weather harm them; then, cutting a few
> choice buds, she bade me take them, with her love, to my
> mother. . . . To have seen "Miss Emily" was an event,
> and I ran home with a feeling of great importance to
> carry her message.[9]

The children closest to Emily Dickinson were, of
course, Ned, Mattie, and Gilbert Dickinson. Toward
Ned, Emily felt a special tenderness. The boy suffered
attacks of epilepsy and his illness was the constant concern of the whole family. The last letters Edward Dickinson wrote to Austin show how much Ned's illness worried
his father and grandfather. According to Mattie, Emily
was so frightened by Ned's condition in the summer of
1883 that one evening she left the homestead, crossed the

lawn to Austin's house, and whispered through a window, "Is he better? – Oh, is he better?" [10]

Ned shared his aunt's love of books and her skepticism toward orthodox religion. Emily sent him irreverent poems like "The Bible is an antique Volume"; in prose she lightly scolded him for stealing a pie, or discussed such neighborhood personalities as Dennis Scannell, a Dickinson handyman:

> Dennis was happy yesterday, and it made him graceful – I saw him waltzing with the Cow – and suspected his status, but he afterward started for your Home in a frame that was unmistakable –
>
> You told me he had'nt tasted Liquor since his Wife's decease – then she must have been living at six o'clock last Evening –
>
> I fear for the rectitude of the Barn –
>
> [II, 641]

As Ned matured he realized how unusual his aunt was, and sometimes quoted her conversations to his family. In the Dickinson Collection at Harvard is a note in Sue's handwriting, dated March 7, 1883: "Emily speaking to Ned of someone who was a good scholar, but uninteresting said, 'She has the facts but not the *phosphorescence* of books –'" [11]

Emily saw less of her niece Martha than of Ned. In 1884, when she received a picture of seventeen-year-old Mattie, Emily wrote to Sue, "I was surprised, but Why? is she not of the lineage of the Spirit? I knew she was beautiful – I knew she was royal, but that she was hallowed, how could I surmise, who had scarcely seen her since her deep Eyes were brought in your Arms to her Grandfather's Thanksgiving?" [III, 813.] Martha's "lineage of the Spirit" came from Sue, not Austin. In the rift between Austin and Sue, Martha sided with her mother. Disagreements between father and daughter became frequent. Only one appears in Emily's letters, an early incident which Emily thoroughly enjoyed. In February 1877 Austin and ten-year-old Mattie visited Dr. Holland, vacationing in Northampton. Afterward Emily wrote to Mrs. Holland, "Austin said he was much ashamed of Mattie – and she was much ashamed of him, she imparted to us. They are a weird couple" [II, 576].

In later years Mattie married a Russian and became the *grande dame* Madame Bianchi, as formidable a hostess in Amherst as her mother had been, and often as scintillating. Her fondness for embroidering the truth, one of Sue's traits, has been the despair of Dickinson biographers for many years.[12] As a young girl, however, she seemed like an idealized embodiment of Emily's younger self, even in "royalty." When Mattie sent her aunt a photograph in November 1882, Emily wrote,

> That's the Little Girl I always meant to be, but was'nt – The very Hat I always meant to wear, but did'nt and the attitude toward the Universe, so precisely my own, that I feel very much, as if I were returning Elisha's Horses, or the Vision of John at Patmos –
>
> [III, 751]

Austin was forty-six and Sue forty-four when their third child, Thomas Gilbert, was born in 1875. The baby seemed an answer to unspoken prayer. Ned, now fourteen, was often bedridden with epilepsy; Gilbert was a healthy child and an assurance that the Dickinson name would continue. For the present, Gilbert strengthened dissolving family ties. Sue had become almost a stranger: Vinnie was her enemy most of the time, Emily could remain a friend only with difficulty, and Austin was embittered by Sue's extravagance and lack of love. Love for Gilbert was a force which united them all.

The growth of the little boy, seen through Emily's eyes, is evidence that Emily did not "reject the world": only irrelevant parts of it. At times it is difficult to remember that her descriptions of Gilbert are the words of a recluse.

20 June 1877 ·
Vinnie rode last Twilight – with Austin and the Baby, but the latter cried for the Moon, which saddened their Trip. He is an ardent Jockey, for so old a man, and his piercing cries of "Go Cadgie," when they leave him behind, rend the neighborhood.

[II, 584–85]

early 1878
"Home – Sweet Home" – Austin's Baby sings – "there is no place like Home – 'tis too – over to Aunt Vinnie's."

[II, 604]

early July 1879
Austin's Baby says when surprised by statements – "There's – *sumthn* – else – there's *Bumbul* – Beese."

[II, 633]

about 1880 (to Sue)
Memories of Little Boys that live –
"Weren't you chasing Pussy," said Vinnie to Gilbert?
"No – she was chasing herself" –
"But was'nt she running pretty fast"? "Well, some slow and some fast" said the beguiling Villain – Pussy's Nemesis quailed –
Talk of "hoary Reprobates"!
Your Urchin is more antique in wiles than the Egyptian Sphinx –

[III, 673]

In time Gilbert became one of Emily's correspondents. Emily Dickinson affected childishness in some of her letters to the Norcrosses: reading them, one is embarrassed for Emily and for the cousins who apparently responded in kind. Emily's letters to actual children, though somewhat like those to the cousins, seem more spontaneous. In 1881, at the age of fifty, Emily wrote to Loo and Fanny Norcross, "Mother heard Fanny telling Vinnie about her graham bread. She would like to taste it. Will Fanny please tell Emily how, and not too inconvenient? Every particular, for Emily is dull, and she will pay in gratitude, which, though not canned like quinces, is fragrantest of all we know" [III, 715]. In the same year Emily wrote to Gilbert, "Gilbert asked a little Plant of Aunt Emily, once, to carry to his Teacher – but Aunt Emily was asleep – so Maggie gave him one instead – Aunt Emily waked up now, and brought this little Plant all the way from her Crib for Gilbert to carry to his Teacher – Good Night – Aunt Emily's asleep again – " [III, 701].

If Gilbert had lived to maturity, the bitterness which became the Dickinsons' way of life might have been held at a distance. By 1883, it is true, Austin was so often at the homestead that he seemed never to have "passed to a wedded Home" [III, 765]. But Gilbert, "God's little Blond Blessing," was the delight of the whole family. His sister illustrates how true a Dickinson he was by recounting his plans for the proceeds of an "animal show": "We're going to give half to the *college*," Gilbert said, "and half to the cat!" [13] Gilbert was the rare child who could impress his elders without being priggish. "Twice when I had Red Flowers out," Emily recalled in 1884, "Gilbert knocked, raised his sweet Hat, and asked if he might touch them – Yes, and take them too, I said, but Chivalry forbade him – Besides, he gathered Hearts, not Flowers – " [III, 842].

Various descriptions of this likable child survive—Gilbert playing so often at the church that his father called it "Gib's church," Gilbert calling Mrs. Holland's new son-in-law "Mr. Bridegroom," Gilbert perched atop a wagonload of chairs and cushions on the way to Shutesbury. Then suddenly, on October 5, 1883, Gilbert was dead. He had caught typhoid fever while playing in a mudhole with his friend Kendall Emerson. Before the numbness of reaction conquered Emily she wrote to Sue an elegiac letter of great power and beauty—perhaps the finest letter she ever wrote—in which life, not death, was dominant:

> The Vision of Immortal Life has been fulfilled –
> How simply at the last the Fathom comes! The Passenger and not the Sea, we find surprises us –
> Gilbert rejoiced in Secrets –
> His Life was panting with them – With what menace of Light he cried "Dont tell, Aunt Emily"! Now my ascended Playmate must instruct *me*. Show us, prattling Preceptor, but the way to thee!
> He knew no niggard moment – His Life was full of Boon – The Playthings of the Dervish were not so wild as his –
> No crescent was this Creature – he traveled from the Full –
> Such soar, but never set –
> I see him in the Star, and meet his sweet velocity in everything that flies – His Life was like the Bugle, which winds itself away, his Elegy an echo – his Requiem ecstasy –
> Dawn and Meridian in one.
> Wherefore would he wait, wronged only of Night, which he left for us –
> Without a speculation, our little Ajax spans the whole –

> Pass to thy Rendezvous of Light,
> Pangless except for us –
> Who slowly ford the Mystery
> Which thou hast leaped across!

[III, 799]

The physical effects of loss came quickly to Emily. Nine days after Gilbert's death a neighbor, Mrs. John Jameson, wrote to her son, "Miss Emily Dickinson . . . went over to Austin's with Maggie the night Gilbert died, the first time she had been in the house for 15 years—and the odor of the disinfectants used, sickened her so that she was obliged to go home about 3 AM—and vomited—went to bed and has been feeble ever since, with a terrible pain in the back of her head—" [14] In January 1884 Emily told Charles Clark she had been very ill since early October. To Mrs. Holland she confessed the sorrow she had hidden when she wrote to Sue. "Chill, then stupor, then the letting go" had already prostrated her; Emily herself, not Gilbert, was the subject of a letter to Mrs. Holland in which grief was dramatized in a series of variations on "names":

> Sweet Sister.
>   Was that what I used to call you?
>   I hardly recollect, all seems so different –
>   I hesitate which word to take, as I can take but few, and each must be the chiefest, but recall that Earth's most graphic transaction is placed within a syllable, nay, even a gaze –
>   The Physician says I have "Nervous prostration."
>   Possibly I have – I do not know the Names of Sickness. The Crisis of the sorrow of so many years is all that tires me – As Emily Brontë to her Maker, I write to my Lost "Every Existence would exist in thee – " . . .
>   "Open the Door, open the Door, they are waiting for me," was Gilbert's sweet command in delirium. *Who*

were waiting for him, all we possess we would give to know – Anguish at last opened it, and he ran to the little Grave at his Grandparents' feet – All this and more, though *is* there more? More than Love and Death? Then tell me it's name!

[III, 802–03]

Christmas in 1883 was especially difficult for the Dickinsons. Emily wrote the first of three annual messages to Gilbert's playmate Kendall Emerson: "Christmas in Bethlehem means most of all, this Year, but Santa Claus still asks the way to Gilbert's little friends – Is Heaven an unfamiliar road?" [III, 804.] In a minor way, Kendall thus became a "sacred" friend: the question, however rhetorical in this case, was typical of such friendships.

The emptiness which all the family felt had not drawn Austin and Sue together. Mrs. Todd noted in her journal a month after Gilbert's death, "Mr. D. nearly died too. Gilbert was his idol, and the only thing in his house which truly loved him, or in which he took any pleasure." [15] Austin found his marriage even more hopeless than before and turned to his sisters and friends for support. He was already greatly dependent on Professor and Mrs. Todd, especially on Mrs. Todd. Emily and Vinnie were aware that Sue no longer invited the Todds to her home, but they were glad Austin had found a warmth which Sue denied him. Earlier they had written to Mr. and Mrs. Hills and the Jenkinses to ask for special consideration of Austin; at Christmas time, 1883, Vinnie wrote to Mrs. Todd, who was out of town, "Austin is oppressed by these 'glad days' & I hardly know how I shall cheer him so many weeks without you to help him. Write to him often." [16]

Emily Dickinson never recovered completely from her shock at Gilbert's death. Her losses had a cumulative effect, like a slow poison. In the autumn of 1884 she wrote, "I have not been strong for the last year. The Dyings have been too deep for me, and before I could raise my Heart from one, another has come . . ." [III, 843].

Few poems date from these last years, but the prose elegies are many—often so rhythmic that only a shading of tone keeps them from being poetry. The sacred correspondences continued, though they tended now to be less exclusive. When Judge Lord died in March 1884, only five months after Gilbert, Emily told Maria Whitney and Charles Clark about her new loss. This death, after so many others, seemed almost anticlimactic to Emily. She wrote, "When I tell my sweet Mrs. Holland that I have lost another friend, she will not wonder I do not write, but that I raise my Heart to a drooping syllable – " [III, 816]. To the Norcrosses Emily wrote, "I hardly dare to know that I have lost another friend, but anguish finds it out" [III, 817].

Emily had forewarning of Judge Lord's death. He had been at the point of death several times during the preceding year. She told her Aunt Catharine that she had hoped the persuasions of the spring, added to her own, might delay the event, but she had prepared herself for it in verse:

> Still own thee – still thou art
> What surgeons call alive –
> Though slipping – slipping I perceive
> To thy reportless Grave –
>
> Which question shall I clutch –
> What answer wrest from thee
> Before thou dost exude away
> In the recallless sea?

When Lord was dead, Emily wrote,

'Tis not the swaying frame we miss,
It is the steadfast Heart,
That had it beat a thousand years,
With Love alone had bent,
It's fervor the electric Oar,
That bore it through the Tomb,
Ourselves, denied the privilege,
Consolelessly presume — 17

For her sacred correspondent, Emily turned to Benjamin Kimball of Boston, kinsman, close friend, and executor of the estate of Otis Lord. The letters to Kimball followed what by now had become a standard pattern. The first begins, "To take the hand of my friend's friend, even apparitionally, is a hallowed pleasure" [III, 860]. The tone of the second is reminiscent of the letters to the Clarks and Maria Whitney, though the words are new. As usual, Emily had asked for a description of her "lost" from another viewpoint:

> Had I known I asked the impossible, should I perhaps have asked it, but Abyss is it's own Apology.
>
> I once asked him what I should do for him when he was not here, referring half unconsciously to the great Expanse — in a tone italic of both Worlds "Remember Me," he said. I have kept his Commandment. But you are a Psychologist, I, only a Scholar who has lost her Preceptor.
>
> . . . Your noble and tender words of him were exceedingly precious — I shall cherish them.
>
> . . . Abstinence from Melody was what made him die. Calvary and May wrestled in his Nature.
>
> Neither fearing Extinction, nor prizing Redemption, he believed alone. Victory was his Rendezvous —
>
> I hope it took him home. . . .
>
> > Sacredly,
> > E. Dickinson

New griefs did not lessen Emily's memories of her other masters. In 1884 George S. Merriam was writing a biography of Samuel Bowles and had consulted Sue and Austin. Sue turned to Emily, who replied,

> I felt it no betrayal, Dear — Go to my Mine as to your Own, only more unsparingly —
> I can scarcely believe that the Wondrous Book is at last to be written, and it seems a Memoir of the Sun, when the Noon is gone —
> You remember his swift way of wringing and flinging away a Theme, and others picking it up and gazing bewildered after him, and the prance that crossed his Eye as such times was unrepeatable —
>
> [III, 828]

To what extent Sue made use of Emily's "Mine" (her letters from Bowles, and books he had given her) is unclear. Merriam had copies of the letters Bowles had written in the summer of 1877 because they had been dictated to an assistant.[18] One of the letters, to a "woman friend," had accompanied a gift of *"Warrington" Pen-Portraits:* a memoir of W. S. Robinson, who for many years had been a *Springfield Republican* contributor. Apparently Merriam had no copy of the memoir, and wanted to see the description of a "vision" the dying Robinson had experienced. Emily's letter to Sue continues, "I wish I could find the Warrington Words, but during my weeks of faintness, my Treasures were misplaced, and I cannot find them – I think Mr Robinson had been left alone, and felt the opinions while the others were gone – " [III, 828].

The letter from Samuel Bowles to his "woman friend" tells little but his great weariness; it was written in midsummer, 1877, probably soon after his last visit to the Dickinsons.

It was very sweet to see you at last. I hope I may oftener come face to face with you. I have little strength or time for writing and so testifying to my remembrance, and you are very good to like me so much and to say such sweet and encouraging things to me. I think I may be depended on to the extent of my power and as long as I stay. And it helps me to stay to know that there are those who want me and depend on me, even in the distant unpractical way that is after all the best intercourse of most of us, and certainly all that is left to us.

I spoke to you of "Warrington's" revelations of immortality at the close. They were greatly impressive to me. Here is the record. You may like to read it, even from an enemy.[19]

"Warrington" would count as an enemy because he had spoken very unkindly of the Bell-Everett party's nomination of Edward Dickinson for lieutenant governor in 1860,[20] and because he had included Judge Lord in a group of lawyers who, "though men of learning and shrewdness, were not men of genius; . . . not men of whom anecdotes are told; men who say things worth repeating and remembering; poetical things." [21] The sentence in Bowles's letter, beginning "It helps me to stay . . . ," echoes Emily's letter of the same summer to Bowles: "It is strange that the most intangible thing is the most adhesive." Another expression is used verbatim in an 1885 letter to the Norcrosses; Emily uses it, as Bowles had used it, in reference to a gift. "A friend sent me *Called Back*. It is a haunting story, and as loved Mr. Bowles used to say, 'greatly impressive to me' " [III, 856].[22]

Emily could not bring herself to talk with Bowles's family. In 1881 she thought she might be able to: she wrote to Mrs. Bowles, " 'Would you see us, would Vinnie?' Oh, my doubting Mary! Were you and your brave son in my father's house, it would require more prowess than mine to resist seeing you" [III, 708]. The next year, however, she wrote to Samuel Bowles the younger, who was visiting Austin and Sue, "My Mother and Sister hoped to see you, and I, to have heard the voice in the House, that recalls the strange Music of your Father's – " [III, 735]. The son reminded Emily of the father so much that when she wrote to congratulate him on his engagement in 1883 she used the imagery she had associated with "Mr. Samuel," including a quotation from Revelation 21, "his Gem chapter."

> There is more than one "deluge," though but one is recorded, and the duplicate of the "Dove," hallows your own Heart. I had feared that the Angel with the Sword would dissuade you from Eden, but rejoice that it only ushered you. "Every several Gate is of one Pearl."

> > Morning is due to all –
> > To some – the Night –
> > To an imperial few –
> > The Auroral Light.

> > > > [III, 796]

Bowles forwarded the letter to his fiancée, Elizabeth Hoar, with the comment, "This is from the friend whom I have never seen."

Maria Whitney tried to see Emily Dickinson in the spring of 1883. Emily sent down a note, and later apologized by mail. But her sacred correspondence with Miss Whitney continued. Two years after the abortive visit Emily was still speaking of Samuel Bowles to "his Lamb." "I was much quickened toward you and all Celestial things," she wrote in 1885, "to read that the Life of our loved Mr Bowles would be with us in Autumn . . ." [III, 862].

As Emily withdrew from the conversations of ordinary society, dialogue became more frequent in her letters. During the years when she wrote poems in vast numbers, epigrams became her usual form of speech and prose; afterward, she began to place her aphorisms in a broader narrative context. Terseness still seemed appropriate to most occasions, but now and then a dramatic event evoked a style closer to fiction than to the essay.

Not action but reaction was the basis of Emily's narratives—naturally so, because Emily had no active part in any event outside her home. She could tell the Norcrosses how she received the news of her father's death, or describe conversations with Ned or Gilbert, or give her first reaction to Judge Lord's illness. This was the extent of society. The accounts of her meetings with Wadsworth quote the minister, but speak at greater length of her own response.

Perhaps the best of the narrative letters is the one Emily wrote to Louisa and Fanny Norcross after an 1879 fire destroyed much of the Amherst business center. The drama in this letter is centered not on the fire but on Emily's mind at the time of it. Only concern for her mother, and the devoted reassurances of Maggie Maher and Vinnie, interrupt the steady inward focus.

> We were waked by the ticking of the bells, — the bells tick in Amherst for a fire, to tell the firemen.
>
> I sprang to the window, and each side of the curtain saw that awful sun. The moon was shining high at the time, and the birds singing like trumpets.
>
> Vinnie came soft as a moccasin. "Don't be afraid, Emily, it is only the fourth of July."
>
> I did not tell that I saw it, for I thought if she felt it best to deceive, it must be that it was.
>
> She took hold of my hand and led me into mother's room. Mother had not waked, and Maggie was sitting

by her. Vinnie left us a moment, and I whispered to Maggie, and asked her what it was.

"Only Stebbins's barn, Emily"; but I knew that the right and left of the village was on the arm of Stebbins's barn. I could hear buildings falling, and oil exploding, and people walking and talking gayly, and cannon soft as velvet from parishes that did not know that we were burning up.

And so much lighter than day was it, that I saw a caterpillar measure a leaf far down in the orchard; and Vinnie kept saying bravely, "It's only the fourth of July."

It seemed like a theatre, or a night in London, or perhaps like chaos. The innocent dew falling "as if it thought no evil," . . . and sweet frogs prattling in the pools as if there were no earth.

At seven people came to tell us that the fire was stopped, stopped by throwing sound houses in as one fills a well.

Mother never waked, and we were all grateful; we knew she would never buy needle and thread at Mr. Cutler's store, and if it were Pompeii nobody could tell her. . . .

Vinnie's "only the fourth of July" I shall always remember. I think she will tell us so when we die, to keep us from being afraid.

[II, 643–44]

Emily Dickinson's prose about nature, like her narratives, was generally subjective. Rather a large part of her posthumous fame depends on the widespread opinion that she was a "nature poet," yet she wrote little in the genre of objective nature description. Reading her account of the 1879 fire, one need not suppose that Emily sat at the window training a telescope on an actual caterpillar in the Dickinson orchard. Her famous hummingbird in "A Route of Evanescence" was not the bird itself but its speed and the color and movement of flowers tumbled by its flight. In 1876 she wrote to Higginson, "Nature is a Haunted House – but Art – a House that tries to be haunted" [II, 554]. Words could capture some of the qualities nature already possessed, but they were not to be mistaken for the original. Moreover, nature gained its meaning from the mind which experienced it:

> To hear an Oriole sing
> May be a common thing –
> Or only a divine.
>
> It is not of the Bird
> Who sings the same, unheard,
> As unto Crowd –
>
> The Fashion of the Ear
> Attireth that it hear
> In Dun, or fair –
>
> So whether it be Rune,
> Or whether it be none
> Is of within.
>
> The "Tune is in the Tree – "
> The Skeptic – showeth me –
> "No Sir! In Thee!" [23]

Nature, then, was more a point of departure than a goal in Emily's references to it. When she thanked Mrs. Todd for the painting of "the preferred flower of life," Emily recalled particularly "the clutch with which I bore it from the ground when a wondering Child. . . ." Perhaps the most objective nature description in her prose was a letter of thanks for witch hazel, written to the Norcrosses in 1876. Here, as elsewhere, the mind's reaction and recollection were at least as important as the plant:

Oh that beloved witch-hazel which would not reach me
till parts of the stems were a gentle brown, though one
loved stalk as hearty as if just placed in the mail by
the woods. It looked like tinsel fringe combined with
staider fringes, witch and witching too, to my joyful
mind.

I had never seen it but once before, and it haunted
me like childhood's Indian pipe, or ecstatic puff-balls,
or that mysterious apple that sometimes comes on river-
pinks; and is there not a dim suggestion of a dandelion,
if her hair were ravelled and she grew on a twig instead
of a tube, – though this is timidly submitted.

[II, 568]

Ordinarily Emily did not concentrate even this much
on nature. She used it for scene-setting, or humor, or
commentary on human actions and thoughts. Among the
prose fragments in the "scrapbasket" she kept during the
last ten years of her life are several about aspects of nature.
None of these jottings is known to have been employed
in letters: they can be regarded simply as prose.

Flowers are so enticing I fear that they are sins – like
gambling or apostasy.

[III, 923]

I saw two Bushes fight just now – The wind was to
blame – but to see them differ was pretty as a Lawsuit

[III, 924]

Science is very near us – I found a megatherium on my
strawberry

The consciousness of subsiding power is too startling to
be admitted by men – but comprehended by the Meadow, over which the Flood has quivered, when the
waters return to their kindred, and the tillage is left
alone –

[III, 927]

The Grass is the Ground's Hair, and it is singed with heat — . . . (and it curls like a Girl's in the damp wind)

The Leaves are very gay — but we know they are elderly — 'Tis pathos to dissimulate, in their departing case —

[III, 928]

We must travel abreast with Nature if we want to know her, but where shall be obtained the Horse —

[III, 929] 24

Like nature, humor is a constant in the letters of Emily Dickinson, appearing sometimes for its own sake, more often in another context. The death of one friend after another exhausted Emily in her last years, but her sense of humor seldom failed. As she described her terror at the news of Judge Lord's stroke, she noted, "I grasped at a passing Chair." Among the poems she sent to Sue in the bleak days after Gilbert died is one which turns the tragedy into a childhood china-cabinet mishap:

Climbing to reach the costly Hearts
To which he gave the worth,
He broke them, fearing punishment
He ran away from Earth —

[II, 800]

In the summer of 1884, when she was seriously ill and mourning Gilbert and Judge Lord, Emily answered a letter from Mrs. Holland's son Theodore with light formality:

Dear Sir.
    Your request to "remain sincerely" mine demands investigation, and if after synopsis of your career all should seem correct, I am tersely your's —

I shall try to wear the unmerited honor with becoming volume —

Commend me to your kindred, for whom although a Stranger, I entertain esteem —

[III, 833]

If there were any doubt about the matter, letters like this should be proof that Emily Dickinson was never soured by her years of seclusion and grief. Even the difficult refusal to see her friends, especially when she had thought an interview might be possible, could be treated with a certain humor. She wrote to kindly, stuttering Professor Joseph K. Chickering, who unsuccessfully tried several times to see her,

We shun it ere it comes,
Afraid of Joy,
Then sue it to delay
And lest it fly,
Beguile it more and more —
May not this be
Old Suitor Heaven,
Like our dismay at thee?

[III, 758]

There are 248 surviving letters from the last three and a half years of Emily's life, in spite of her failing health— far more than from any earlier period. Gauging by the intact correspondence with Higginson and Sue (with an allowance for the letters to Sue after Gilbert died), Emily was writing no more than usual. It is simply that fewer of her late letters had been destroyed when her posthumous fame began.

Emily Dickinson's published notes of 1883–86 were sent to fifty-five recipients, of whom twenty-one received poems. Other letters (those to Roswell Smith and William H. Dickinson, for instance) are lost. It is plain that Emily kept in touch with the world she refused to meet in person. Many of the letters, of course, were occasional: wedding congratulations, condolences, or thank-you notes. Of the neighbors only a few, like Mrs. J. Howard Sweetser (who summered in Amherst), Mrs. Henry Hills, and Mrs. Edward Tuckerman can be counted as regular correspondents.

There are few dull lines in the late letters. In so routine a matter as declining a wedding invitation, Emily was an artist. In May 1884 she wrote to Judge and Mrs. E. R. Hoar, whose daughter was about to marry Samuel Bowles the younger, "I should hardly dare risk the Inclemencies of Eden at this perilous Season – With proud congratulations that the shortest route to India has been supremely found. Honoringly, E. Dickinson – " [III, 823]. To Eugenia Hall, before her marriage, Emily wrote, "Will the sweet Cousin who is about to make the Etruscan Experiment, accept a smile which will last a Life, if ripened in the Sun?" [III, 892.] Her short letters to "Sweet Nellie," Mrs. J. Howard Sweetser, usually dealt with food or flowers, but Emily could turn a simple note of thanks into a message like this. "To have woven Wine so delightfully, one must almost have been a Drunkard one's-self – but that is the stealthy franchise of the demurest Lips. Drunkards of Summer are quite as frequent as Drunkards of Wine, and the Bee that comes Home sober is the Butt of the Clover" [III, 784–85].

According to Martha Dickinson Bianchi, "mere acquaintances, strangers even," sent Emily Dickinson gifts for the sole purpose of receiving her letters of thanks.[25] Likely as it is that Mrs. Bianchi was deflating some Amherst enemy who had letters from Emily, the statement is credible. A letter from "Miss Emily" was an event in many a household. For a major poet this was

negligible fame, but for a recluse renown enough. As
early as 1862 a distant cousin, Eudocia Flynt, wrote in her
diary, "Had a letter from Emily Dickinson!!!!" [II, 414.]

As always, Emily wrote her letters to match the capacities of the recipients. A fellow artist could evoke her most
condensed prose. In April 1884, when the statue of John
Harvard was unveiled in Cambridge, Emily wrote to
Daniel Chester French,

> We learn with delight of the recent acquisition to
> your fame, and hasten to congratulate you on an honor
> so reverently won.
> Success is dust, but an aim forever touched with dew.
> God keep you fundamental!

> Circumference, thou Bride of Awe –
> Possessing, thou shalt be
> Possessed by every hallowed Knight
> That dares to covet thee.[26]

Another who received cryptic messages was Mabel Loomis
Todd. Emily wrote in March 1885 to thank her for a yellow jug painted with red trumpet-vine blossoms. "Nature
forgot – The Circus reminded her – Thanks for the Ethi-
opian Face. The Orient is in the West. 'You knew, Oh
Egypt' said the entangled Antony – " [III, 870]. When
Mrs. Todd's parents visited Amherst in 1884, Emily began to correspond with them. It was to the Loomises that
she wrote the revealing line, "In all the circumference of
Expression, those guileless words of Adam and Eve never
were surpassed, 'I was afraid and hid Myself' " [III, 847].

From October 1883 until her death Emily was seldom
well for long. She found a little humor—to the extent of a
play on words—in her illness: in September 1884 she
wrote to Helen Hunt Jackson, who was recuperating from
a broken leg, "I, too, took my summer in a Chair, though

from 'Nervous prostration,' not fracture, but take my Nerve by the Bridle now, and am again abroad – " [III, 840]. To Loo and Fanny Norcross Emily described her illness in plainer words and greater detail:

> Eight Saturday noons ago I was making a loaf of cake with Maggie, when I saw a great darkness opening and knew no more until late at night. I woke to find Austin and Vinnie and a strange physician bending over me, and supposed I was dying, or had died, all was so kind and hallowed. I had fainted and lain unconscious for the first time in my life. Then I grew very sick and gave the others much alarm, but am now staying. The doctor calls it "revenge of the nerves"; but who but death had wronged them?
>
> . . . The little boy we laid away never fluctuates, and his dim society is companion still. But it is growing damp and I must go in. Memory's fog is rising.
>
> [III, 826–27]

The "great darkness" came on June 14, a day before the tenth anniversary of Edward Dickinson's death. Emily had "another bad turn," Austin recorded, on October 12: a year and a week after Gilbert died.[27]

The course of Emily's sickness, seldom as she mentioned it, can be traced in the length of her letters. When she was bedridden she usually wrote short notes—many of them thanking the neighbors or "the Susan who never forgets to be subtle" for their kindness to her. When she was "abroad" (within the homestead, of course) her letters were longer. The handwriting of the letters after June 1884 also reveals illness in its extreme slant, irregularity (perhaps the result of writing while propped up in bed) and loose formation of capitals.[28]

By the summer of 1885 Emily realized how weak she was. She wrote to thank Judge Lord's friend Benjamin

Kimball for offering her his legal advice. She would keep his promise in solemn reserve, she said, but "Even to ask a legal question might so startle me that my Voice would pass to another World before it could be uttered" [III, 881].

The same summer Emily suffered the last of her bereavements. On August 6 the *Republican* reported that Helen Hunt Jackson was dying in San Francisco. Emily wrote at once to Colonel Higginson, enclosing the news item.

> I was unspeakably shocked to see this in the Morning Paper –
> She wrote to me in Spring that she could not walk, but not that she would die – I was sure you would know. Please say it is not so.
> What a hazard a Letter is!
> When I think of the Hearts it has scuttled and sunk, I almost fear to lift my Hand to so much as a Superscription.
>
> [III, 884]

Mrs. Jackson died of cancer on August 12. Emily wrote to the publisher Thomas Niles for details of the death, and at the same time asked young Samuel Bowles to forward a letter to William Jackson, whose address she did not know. Higginson, however, seems to have been the sacred correspondent. Two of Emily's last letters, written in April 1886, follow the familiar elegiac pattern. Higginson had sent Emily his sonnet "To the Memory of H. H."; Emily wrote to him,

> The beautiful Sonnet confirms me – Thank you for confiding it –
>
> The immortality she gave
> We borrowed at her Grave –

The Weight of Grief

For just one Plaudit famishing,
The Might of Human Love —

The sweet Acclamation of Death divulges it — There
is no Trumpet like the Tomb —

Of Glory not a Beam is left
But her Eternal House —
The Asterisk is for the Dead,
The Living, for the Stars —

Did you not give her to me?

Your Scholar.

[III, 904]

Other friendships which had become "hallowed" continued as Emily declined toward her own death. In April
1886 she was still trying to learn more about Dr. Wadsworth from Charles Clark: "Do you as time steals on,
know anything of the 'Willie' whom Mr Wadsworth so
loved — and of whom he said with a smile 'should he find
a gold Watch in the street he would not pick it up, so
unsullied was he,' and did his Daughter regret her flight
from her loved Father, or the son who left the Religion
so precious to him?" [III, 900.] The last part of the question was based not on Wadsworth's words to Emily but
on the "griefs" James Clark had disclosed to her in 1882.
Clark replied, and Emily wrote to him, "I am glad his
Willie is faithful, of whom he said 'the Frogs were his
little friends' and I told him they were my Dogs, the last
smile that he gave me. . . . Excuse me for the Voice, this
moment immortal" [III, 901].

One of Emily's last letters to Maria Whitney, probably
written in the spring of 1885, affirmed again her love for
Samuel Bowles, a love which Miss Whitney shared: "I
fear we shall care very little for the technical resurrection,

when to behold the one face that to us comprised it is too much for us, and I dare not think of the voraciousness of that only gaze and its only return" [III, 862]. These words call to mind one of the great 1862 love poems, "I cannot live with You – ," in which Emily says she could not be in heaven with her master because his face "Would put out Jesus' – " nor serve God

> Because You saturated Sight –
> And I had no more Eyes
> For sordid excellence
> As Paradise [29]

"The crisis of the sorrow of so many years," complicated by Bright's disease, was killing Emily. In April 1886 she told Colonel Higginson that she was able to roam in her room after a winter of illness; to her mortally ill Aunt Elisabeth—who, as a nineteen-year-old afraid of bogeys under the bed, had appeared in Emily's earliest known letter, back in 1842—Emily wrote, "the Crocuses are so martial and the Daffodils to the second Joint, let us join hands and recover" [III, 902]. But sickness returned. On May 13 Emily became unconscious, and after two days of "that terrible breathing," as Austin put it in his diary,[30] she was dead. On May 19 her small white coffin was borne out the back door of the homestead and across the fields to the village cemetery. In her hands, at the last, Vinnie placed two heliotropes, "to take to Judge Lord."

Properly a study of Emily Dickinson's life as revealed in her prose should end with the last of it: a message to Loo and Fanny Norcross written just before Emily slipped into her final coma.

> Little Cousins,
> Called back –
> > > Emily.

[III, 906]

There is little to say in the face of such finality. Emily was deliberate even in her dying. But she left her "letter to the world," nearly eighteen hundred poems, unpublished. Probably she never considered publication of her prose at all.

On November 12, 1890, the day *Poems by Emily Dickinson* appeared, Colonel Higginson wrote to his co-editor, Mabel Loomis Todd, "We *must* have another volume by and by & this must include prose from her letters, often quite as marvellous as her poetry." [31] On December 1 Austin brought Mrs. Todd a package of Emily's letters to Samuel Bowles. After she read them, Mrs. Todd agreed with Higginson: "Some of Emily's letters *must* be published." [32] Four years later she saw to it that they were.

Notes

INTRODUCTION

1 *The Letters of Emily Dickinson*, edited by Thomas H. Johnson and Theodora Ward (Cambridge, 1958), II, 570. References to this edition (hereafter called *Letters*) will be indicated in the text by volume and page number only, in brackets.

2 *The Poems of Emily Dickinson*, edited by Thomas H. Johnson (Cambridge, 1955), II, 734 35. This edition will hereafter be referred to as *Poems*.

3 "Packet" does not accurately describe the booklet grouping into which Emily Dickinson gathered hundreds of poems. Each booklet is made up of several sheets of paper, lightly sewn together along the left margin. I use the word "packet" because it is used throughout *Poems*. Emily Dickinson's word for the booklets is not known; Lavinia Dickinson called them "volumes," Millicent Todd Bingham, "fascicles."

4 In *Letters* the name is given as Louise; Miss Norcross signed letters thus in her later years. The Dickinsons, however, knew her as Louisa. Letters of Edward Dickinson which speak of "Louisa" are printed in Millicent Todd Bingham's *Emily Dickinson's Home*

(New York, 1955), pp. 464, 469. Mabel Loomis Todd, who discussed Loo with Austin and Lavinia Dickinson, and even with Frances Norcross, used only the name Louisa. See *Letters of Emily Dickinson*, edited by Mabel Loomis Todd (New York, 1931), pp. 214–15. (This edition will be referred to as *Letters* (1931).

5 Bingham, *Emily Dickinson's Home*, p. 413.

6 Paxton Hibben, *Henry Ward Beecher: An American Portrait* (New York, 1942), pp. 57–58.

7 Millicent Todd Bingham, *Ancestors' Brocades: the Literary Debut of Emily Dickinson* (New York, 1945), pp. 26–27.

8 Bingham, *Ancestors' Brocades*, p. 152.

9 George F. Whicher, *This Was a Poet: a Critical Biography of Emily Dickinson* (New York, 1938), p. 147.

10 *Poems*, I, 73.

11 *Poems*, II, 673. The catalogue of manuscripts in the Millicent Todd Bingham Collection, in the Amherst College Library, lists Bowles as the recipient of this poem: in 1891, when Mabel Loomis Todd was copying poems sent to Bowles, she headed her transcript of this poem, "Bowles."

12 *Poems*, I, 356–57.

13 *Poems*, I, 374.

14 *Poems*, I, 142.

15 Bingham, *Ancestors' Brocades*, p. 8.

16 *Macbeth*, II, iii, 99.

17 See Whicher, *This Was a Poet*, p. 232.

18 *Poems*, I, 162.

CHAPTER I

1 *Celebration of the Two Hundredth Anniversary of the Settlement of Hadley, Massachusetts* (Northampton, 1859), p. 77.

2 Bingham, *Ancestors' Brocades*, p. 310.

3 The Dickinsons lived in the eastern half of the homestead until April 1840, though the owner was David Mack, Jr.

4 Bingham, *Ancestors' Brocades*, Plate I.

5 Bingham, *Emily Dickinson's Home*, Plate IX. There are many other copies of the daguerreotype, all taken from a photograph made in the eighteen nineties. This one, however, is from a

1954 photograph of the daguerreotype, and the details are very clear.

6 *Letters of Emily Dickinson*, edited by Mabel Loomis Todd (Boston, 1894), I, 130; *Letters* (1931), p. 130. The 1894 edition will be referred to as *Letters* (1894).

7 Mrs. John Jameson, MS letter to John F. Jameson, dated May 16, 1886, in the Library of Congress. Published by Jay Leyda, *The Years and Hours of Emily Dickinson* (New Haven, 1960), II, 471.

8 Leyda, *The Years and Hours of Emily Dickinson*, I, 226.

9 Leyda, *The Years and Hours of Emily Dickinson*, I, 41.

10 Leyda, *The Years and Hours of Emily Dickinson*, I, 328.

11 Bingham, *Ancestors' Brocades*, p. 233.

12 Bingham, *Emily Dickinson's Home*, p. 286.

13 Bingham, *Emily Dickinson's Home*, p. 233.

14 Bingham, *Emily Dickinson's Home*, p. 387.

15 Bingham, *Emily Dickinson's Home*, pp. 358–59.

16 Martha Dickinson Bianchi, *Emily Dickinson Face to Face* (Boston, 1932), p. 54.

17 The misdating began with Sue. In March 1853, when both Sue and Emily were twenty-two, Emily sent Sue "On this wondrous sea." Mrs. Bianchi wrote on the manuscript, "The first verse Aunt Emily sent to Mamma—(She *thought* when both were sixteen or so.)" Sue's later transcript of the poem survives; on it she wrote "1848." See *Poems*, I, 6–7.

18 Bingham, *Ancestors' Brocades*, p. 401.

19 Whicher, *This Was a Poet*, p. 34.

20 Bingham, *Emily Dickinson's Home*, p. 54.

21 Bingham, *Ancestors' Brocades*, p. 373.

22 Bingham, *Emily Dickinson's Home*, pp. 161–62, 187–88, 240–42.

23 Bingham, *Emily Dickinson's Home*, p. 282.

24 Bianchi, *Emily Dickinson Face to Face*, p. 118.

25 Susan Gilbert (Dickinson), MS. letter to Frank Gilbert, dated January 6, 1854, in the Harvard College Library. Published in Leyda, *The Years and Hours of Emily Dickinson*, I, 293.

26 Bingham, *Emily Dickinson's Home*, pp. 74–75.

27 Edward Hitchcock, *The Power of Christian Benevolence Illustrated in the Life and Labors of Mary Lyon* (New York, 1858), pp. 210–11.

28 Fidelia Fisk, *Recollections of Mary Lyon* (Boston, 1866), p. 329.

29 Hitchcock, *The Power of Christian Benevolence*, pp. 374–75.

30 *Poems*, I, 284.

31 George S. Merriam, *The Life and Times of Samuel Bowles* (New York, 1885), I, 339.

32 Bingham, *Ancestors' Brocades*, p. 98.

33 *Poems*, III, 876.

34 *Poems*, III, 899.

CHAPTER 2

1 *Letters* (1931), p. 128.

2 Bingham, *Emily Dickinson's Home*, pp. 176–80.

3 Fisk, *Recollections of Mary Lyon*, p. 197.

4 *Poems*, I, 294.

5 William S. Tyler, *A History of Amherst College* (New York, 1895), p. 280.

6 This sentence from a letter by the Reverend H. N. Barnum is quoted in Bingham, *Emily Dickinson's Home*, p. 94.

7 Whicher, *This Was a Poet*, pp. 73–75.

8 Bingham, *Emily Dickinson's Home*, p. 96.

9 Hitchcock, *The Power of Christian Benevolence*, p. 156.

10 *Letters* (1894), I, 130; *Letters* (1931), p. 130.

11 Rhymes and near-rhymes in this passage may indicate a poem, or parts of two poems, written as prose.

12 Bingham, *Emily Dickinson's Home*, p. 399.

13 Bingham, *Emily Dickinson's Home*, p. 375.

14 Thomas H. Johnson, *Emily Dickinson: An Interpretive Biography* (Cambridge, 1955), p. 22.

15 Bingham, *Emily Dickinson's Home*, p. 401.

16 Merriam, *Life and Times of Samuel Bowles*, I, 63–64.

17 *Emily Dickinson's Letters to Dr. and Mrs. Josiah Gilbert Holland*, edited by their granddaughter Theodora Van Wagenen Ward (Cambridge, 1951), p. 19.

18 *Letters* (1894), I, 129–30; *Letters* (1931), pp. 128–29.

19 Johnson, *Emily Dickinson*, p. 172.

20 J. G. Holland, *Every-Day Topics, Second Series* (New York, 1882), p. 86, quoted in Harry H. Peckham, *Josiah Gilbert Holland in Relation to His Times* (Philadelphia, 1940), p. 73.

21 Leyda, *The Years and Hours of Emily Dickinson*, II, 10.

22 *Letters* (1894), I, 131; *Letters* (1931), p. 131.

23 Whicher, *This Was a Poet*, p. 220.

24 Ik Marvel [Donald G. Mitchell], *Reveries of a Bachelor: or, a Book of the Heart* (New York, 1851), pp. 53–54.

25 *The Writings of Ralph Waldo Emerson*, Concord Edition (Boston, 1904), VI, 279.

26 *The Writings of Henry David Thoreau*, Riverside Edition (Boston, 1893), II, 184.

CHAPTER 3

1 The dates given for poems are those in *Poems*, except when other documentation raises a doubt. The editor of *Poems* writes (I, lxii), "Except in instances where direct evidence in letters can be used to date a poem—and they are relatively few—all assigned dates are tentative and will always remain so."

2 I am grateful to Millicent Todd Bingham for raising the question of the disparity between Emily's account and the actual Washington weather, and for supplying me with weather data of February 1855, which come from the Report of the Surgeon General, Hydrographic Office.

3 Martha Dickinson Bianchi, *The Life and Letters of Emily Dickinson* (Boston, 1924), pp. 48–49.

4 Bingham, *Emily Dickinson's Home*, p. 375.

5 The Reverend Charles Wadsworth, "The Bright Side" (Philadelphia, 1877), pp. 11–12.

6 *Poems*, I, 238.

7 A facsimile of the autograph letter is printed in Bingham, *Emily Dickinson's Home*, pp. 370–71. Jay Leyda dates this letter mid-December? 1877—presumably on the basis of hand-writing and stationery. *The Years and Hours of Emily Dickinson*, II, 283.

8 Bingham, *Emily Dickinson's Home*, p. 372.

9 *Poems*, I, 139.

10 *Poems*, I, 227–28.

11 Malcolm Cowley, "Walt Whitman's Buried Masterpiece," *Saturday Review*, XLII (October 31, 1959), 12.

12 *Poems*, III, 866.

13 Merriam, *Life and Times of Samuel Bowles*, I, 217.

14 Bianchi, *Emily Dickinson Face to Face*, p. 281. In view of Sue's general inaccuracy about dates, this statement (uncorroborated elsewhere) may or may not be true.

15 Mabel Loomis Todd's 1891 transcript of the poem is headed "To Mr. Bowles."

16 Leyda, *The Years and Hours of Emily Dickinson*, I, 367.

17 Bianchi, *Emily Dickinson Face to Face*, p. 157.

18 *Poems*, I, 84. Mabel Loomis Todd's 1891 transcript of this poem is headed "Mr. Bowles." I am grateful to Theodora Ward for first informing me that this and several other poems were sent to Bowles.

19 *Poems*, I, 69.

20 I am indebted to Richard B. Sewall for the mid-March dating of Wadsworth's visit. Whicher, in *This Was a Poet* (p. 104), wrote, "The meeting probably occurred in late February or early March 1860, when Lavinia was visiting the Norcross cousins in Boston." In Johnson's *Emily Dickinson* (p. 76) the date is given as "early in 1860." Jay Leyda, in *The Years and Hours of Emily Dickinson* (II, 7), dates the meeting "Mid-March? [1860]."

CHAPTER 4

1 *Poems*, I, 142–43.

2 *Poems*, I, 215.

3 *Poems*, I, 168.

4 *Poems*, II, 531.

5 Mabel Loomis Todd's 1891 transcript of this poem is headed, "To Mr. Bowles."

6 Merriam, *Life and Times of Samuel Bowles*, I, 216–17.

7 Samuel Bowles, MS letter to William Austin Dickinson, undated, in the Harvard College Library. Published in Leyda, *The Years and Hours of Emily Dickinson*, II, 71. Leyda suggests a mid-December date for the letter.

8 Merriam places Bowles's attack of sciatica after a sleigh-ride from Amherst (mentioned in this letter) "in the early spring of

1861." The editors of *Letters* suggest a date in February 1861, soon after Bowles's birthday on February 9. See Merriam, *Life and Times of Samuel Bowles*, I, 310.

9 *Poems*, I, 90.

10 *Poems*, I, 113.

11 *Poems*, I, 188.

12 *Poems*, I, 170.

13 Leyda, *The Years and Hours of Emily Dickinson*, II, 38.

14 Samuel Bowles, MS letter to William Austin Dickinson, undated, in the Harvard College Library.

15 Merriam, *Life and Times of Samuel Bowles*, I, 316.

16 Bingham, *Emily Dickinson's Home*, p. 421.

17 For the sake of clarity I have omitted brackets around parts of words reconstructed by the editors of *Letters*.

18 *Poems*, II, 673. Mabel Loomis Todd's 1891 transcript of the poem is headed, "Bowles." The catalogue of the Millicent Todd Bingham Collection at Amherst College dates the poem October? 1863; Jay Leyda, *The Years and Hours of Emily Dickinson* suggests a date of July 2? 1863; *Poems* dates it "about 1864."

19 Millicent Todd Bingham, *Emily Dickinson: A Revelation* (New York, 1954), p. 8.

20 *Poems*, I, 203. The catalogue of the Millicent Todd Bingham Collection at Amherst College lists Bowles as the recipient of this poem.

21 *Poems*, I, 356.

22 Merriam, *Life and Times of Samuel Bowles*, I, 315.

23 It is possible that Emily was asking Bowles to forward a letter to Dr. Wadsworth. In that case her opening lines could be read thus: "Are you willing to forward the enclosed letter? I am so much in need of guidance. To offer *you* the same kind of guidance, it might some Sabbath come *my* turn . . ." The occasion for a letter to Wadsworth might well be the news of his call to San Francisco.

24 The letter to Benjamin Kimball in which the word appears was first published in Mrs. Bingham's *Emily Dickinson: A Revelation*, p. 69, sixteen years after Whicher's biography.

25 Samuel Bowles, MS letter to William Austin Dickinson, [March? 1863], in the Harvard College Library.

26 Samuel Bowles, MS letter to William Austin Dickinson, undated, in the Harvard College Library. Published in Leyda, *The Years and Hours of Emily Dickinson*, II, 75.

27 *Poems*, I, 330.

28 Merriam, *Life and Times of Samuel Bowles*, I, 340.

29 Samuel Bowles, MS letter to William Austin Dickinson, dated April 9, 1862, in the Harvard College Library. Published in Leyda, *The Years and Hours of Emily Dickinson*, II, 52.

CHAPTER 5

1 *Springfield Daily Republican*, March 29, 1862, p. 3.

2 Higginson's actual words had been, "Such being the majesty of the art you seek to practice, you can at least take time and deliberation before dishonoring it."

3 T. W. Higginson, "Letter to a Young Contributor," *Atlantic Monthly*, IX (April 1862), 402, 407.

4 T. W. Higginson, "Emily Dickinson's Letters," *Atlantic Monthly*, LXVIII (October 1891), 444.

5 Jay Leyda, *The Years and Hours of Emily Dickinson*, II, 55.

6 Mabel Loomis Todd recorded Austin Dickinson's reaction to the letters Higginson printed in his 1891 *Atlantic Monthly* article: "He says Emily definitely posed in those letters. . . . He did tell me when we had the proof of Mr. Higginson's article here, in the summer, that publishing those letters would be against his taste, because he thought they put Emily in a false position . . ." (Bingham, *Ancestors' Brocades*, p. 167).

7 *Poems*, I, 229.

8 Johnson, *Emily Dickinson*, p. 117.

9 In this case, Emily was telling the whole truth. No picture of her had been made since the daguerreotype of about 1847. It is known that she was considered plain, that she imitated the hair style of Elizabeth Barrett Browning, that her hair remained auburn until her death, and that she looked more like Austin than like Vinnie. The "portrait" which appears in books by Martha Dickinson Bianchi and in many anthologies is a retouching of the daguerreotype and was made some years after Emily Dickinson's death. It can be recognized at once by the exaggerated white ruff at the neck.

10 Jay Leyda suggests a date of February? 1861 for this letter. *The Years and Hours of Emily Dickinson*, II, 24.

11 Merriam, *Life and Times of Samuel Bowles*, I, 379.

12 *Poems*, II, 381–82.

13 "Surry" is presumably Henry Howard, earl of Surrey, beheaded in 1547 and perhaps one of Emily's "Martyr Poets."

14 Bingham, *Ancestors' Brocades,* p. 322.

15 *Poems,* I, 284.

16 *Poems,* II, 568.

17 The editors of *Letters* state, "no date can be surely assigned." They have placed the letter directly after "Title Divine — is Mine!" on the theory that it is the "Verse" referred to. In *Poems* (II, 598), the date is given as "about 1863."

18 Merriam, *Life and Times of Samuel Bowles,* I, 338–39.

19 Samuel Bowles, MS letter to William Austin Dickinson, early 1863 (?) in the Harvard College Library. Published in part in Johnson, *Emily Dickinson,* p. 79; published complete, with "vows" suggested for the illegible word, in Leyda, *The Years and Hours of Emily Dickinson,* II, 76.

20 Samuel Bowles, MS. letter to William Austin Dickinson, April 18, 1863? in the Harvard College Library. Published, except for the word "chronic" in Leyda, *The Years and Hours of Emily Dickinson,* II, 77.

21 Samuel Bowles, MS. letter to William Austin Dickinson, April 25, 1863? in the Harvard College Library. Published, except for the word "belongs," in Leyda, *The Years and Hours of Emily Dickinson,* II, 71. Leyda suggests a date of mid-December? 1862.

22 Bingham, *Ancestors' Brocades,* p. 238.

23 *Poems,* II, 632.

24 *Poems,* II, 632.

25 The catalogue of the Millicent Todd Bingham Collection at Amherst College Library suggest date of Spring? 1861 for this letter. Nothing in the letter is inconsistent with such a date.

26 Mabel Loomis Todd's transcript of this poem is headed "Sent to Mr. Bowles."

27 Samuel Bowles, *Across the Continent* (Springfield, 1865), p. 329.

28 "Sailing" was printed as "failing" in *Letters* (1894), I, 177. The autograph letter is missing. See Theodora Ward, *Emily Dickinson's Letters to Dr. and Mrs. Josiah G. Holland,* pp. 70–71; and *Letters,* II, 445.

29 *Poems,* II, 607.

Notes

CHAPTER 6

1 Bingham, *Emily Dickinson's Home,* pp. 413–14.

2 William Dean Howells, "The Editor's Study," *Harper's Magazine,* LXXXII (January 1891), 318. Quoted in Bingham, *Ancestors' Brocades,* p. 96.

3 *Poems by Emily Dickinson,* Second Series, edited by two of her friends, T. W. Higginson and Mabel Loomis Todd (Boston, 1891), Preface. Reprinted in Bingham, *Ancestors' Brocades,* pp. 417–19.

4 *Poems,* III, 978.

5 *Poems,* II, 679.

6 Leyda, *The Years and Hours of Emily Dickinson,* II, 272–273.

7 Leyda, *The Years and Hours of Emily Dickinson,* II, 253.

8 John L. Spicer, "The Poems of Emily Dickinson," *Boston Public Library Quarterly,* VIII (July 1956), 142. Mr. Spicer points out that the editor of *Poems* mistakenly gave the *Daily Republican* (correct) version of the poem as the one sent to Higginson.

9 *Poems by Emily Dickinson,* edited by two of her friends, Mabel Loomis Todd and T. W. Higginson (Boston, 1890), Preface. Reprinted in Bingham, *Ancestors' Brocades,* pp. 416–17.

10 Bianchi, *Emily Dickinson Face to Face,* p. 25.

11 *Poems,* II, 665.

12 *Poems,* II, 510.

13 The conversation not only sounds like one of Emily's letters; parts of it have been published as such by Martha Dickinson Bianchi in *Life and Letters of Emily Dickinson,* pp. 275–76. Mrs. Bianchi treated the conversation as a letter of August 1870 to Higginson. The deliberate error was repeated (with Mrs. Bianchi's endorsement) in *A Treasury of the World's Great Letters,* edited by M. Lincoln Schuster (New York, 1940), pp. 366–67.

14 Bingham, *Ancestors' Brocades,* p. 248.

15 *Poems,* III, 832–33.

16 *Poems,* II, 761–62.

17 There are a few anachronisms. Esther Wynn, supposedly writing in the seventeen seventies or before, describes playing Beethoven's music.

18 Saxe Holm [Helen Hunt], "Esther Wynn's Love-Letters," *Scribner's Monthly Magazine*, III (December 1871), 171.

19 Saxe Holm, "Esther Wynn's Love-Letters," p. 170.

20 Saxe Holm, "Esther Wynn's Love-Letters," p. 168.

21 Ruth Odell, *Helen Hunt Jackson (H. H.)*, (New York, 1939), p. 48.

22 Bianchi, *Emily Dickinson Face to Face*, p. 17.

23 The poem, "Because He loves Her," was written on a slit-open envelope addressed "Mrs. Helen Hunt. Bethleem."; in 1872 Mrs. Hunt summered in Bethlehem, N.H. See *Poems*, III, 855, and Johnson, *Emily Dickinson*, p. 160.

24 Bingham, *Ancestors' Brocades*, p. 84.

25 Saxe Holm, "Esther Wynn's Love-Letters," p. 173.

26 Saxe Holm, "Esther Wynn's Love-Letters," p. 173.

27 Copies of the circular were pasted inside the front cover of *Mercy Philbrick's Choice*.

28 See Johnson, *Emily Dickinson*, pp. 164–71, for a longer account of Helen Hunt Jackson's part in the publication of "Success."

29 Whicher, *This Was a Poet*, p. 131.

30 Odell, *Helen Hunt Jackson*, p. 137.

31 Leyda, *The Years and Hours of Emily Dickinson*, II, 297.

32 *Poems*, II, 544.

33 Bingham, *Ancestors' Brocades*, p. 166.

34 Leyda, *The Years and Hours of Emily Dickinson*, II, 119.

35 John W. Burgess, *Reminiscences of an American Scholar* (New York, 1934), p. 60. Quoted in Whicher, *This Was a Poet*, p. 34. Burgess was a student at Amherst College, 1864–67.

36 Bianchi, *Life and Letters of Emily Dickinson*, p. 47.

37 Bingham, *Emily Dickinson's Home*, pp. 468–69.

CHAPTER 7

1 Theodora Ward, "The Finest Secret," *Harvard Library Bulletin*, XIV (Winter, 1960), 97.

2 Bingham, *Emily Dickinson: A Revelation*, p. 46.

3 Susan Gilbert Dickinson, MS. "Annals of the Evergreens," in the Harvard College Library.

4 See note in *Letters*, II, 589–90. Another version of the incident, attributed to Lavinia Dickinson, appears in Bianchi, *Emily Dickinson Face to Face*, pp. 62–63.

5 Merriam, *Life and Times of Samuel Bowles*, II, 427.

6 David P. Smith, M.D., MS. letter to Susan Gilbert Dickinson, dated December 29, 1877, in the Harvard College Library. Published in Leyda, *The Years and Hours of Emily Dickinson*, II, 284.

7 *Poems*, II, 634.

8 Bingham, *Ancestors' Brocades*, p. 257.

9 *Letters* (1894), II, 337.

10 *Letters* (1894), II, 349–50; *Letters* (1931), p. 337. Miss Whitney is not identified as the recipient of these sentences (which do not appear in the 1958 *Letters*), but there is no reason to doubt that she was. The sentences are dated "about 1882."

11 *Poems*, III, 1019.

12 Bianchi, *Emily Dickinson Face to Face*, p. 33.

13 Susan Gilbert Dickinson, MS. "Annals of the Evergreens," in the Harvard College Library.

14 Bingham, *Emily Dickinson: A Revelation*, p. 23.

15 Abby Farley, MS. letter to Edward Dickinson, dated April 8, 1883, in the Harvard College Library. Published in Leyda, *The Years and Hours of Emily Dickinson*, II, 396.

16 Bingham, *Emily Dickinson: A Revelation*, p. 59.

17 Leyda, *The Years and Hours of Emily Dickinson*, II, 434.

18 Leyda, *The Years and Hours of Emily Dickinson*, II, 377.

19 Bingham, *Ancestors' Brocades*, p. 373. The quoted phrase is that of Vinnie's close friend Mary Lee Hall. Martha Dickinson Bianchi stated in *Emily Dickinson Face to Face*, p. 52, that Lavinia "committed without reserve the trust of her sister Emily's life to her niece. . . ." However, a friend of the niece, Robert H. Paterson, recalls a conversation on the subject with Mrs. Bianchi, quite different from her published statement. As Mr. Paterson remembers them, these were the words of Martha Dickinson Bianchi in December 1936:

"After other people were finding a man the publisher approached me and told me I had to choose—that as the heir and last member of the family my word would stop the whole business. I therefore chose the Philadelphia clergyman.

"You ask me whether I believe this is true or not? I don't know. Of course you must understand that I could never agree with my Aunt Emily's point of view or anything she stood for."

20 Bingham, *Ancestors' Brocades,* p. 279.

21 Because of such wording, it may seem difficult to separate accounts of the two meetings. Careful reading and a few facts resolve the problem. "Once," followed by "on a previous visit," places Wadsworth's talk of death in the 1880 visit, and his mention of Clark in the 1860 interview. William Wadsworth ("Willie") was born in 1868: all references to him are of 1880. Wadsworth's mother died on October 1, 1859. The minister was still in mourning when he first came to Amherst.

22 Emily's friend Samuel Bowles was the third of the name in direct line, his son the fourth.

23 Whicher, *This Was a Poet,* p. 108; Johnson, *Emily Dickinson,* p. 120.

24 *Letters* (1931), p. 343.

25 *Poems,* III, 1072.

26 Bingham, *Ancestors' Brocades,* pp. 8–9. Another version of this anecdote, identifying the caller as Mrs. Holland, appears in the preface to Martha Dickinson Bianchi's *The Single Hound* (Boston, 1914).

27 Bianchi, *Emily Dickinson Face to Face,* p. 24.

28 Leyda, *The Years and Hours of Emily Dickinson,* II, 386. The text derives from a transcript by Mabel Loomis Todd and differs from the printed text in *Letters* at several points.

CHAPTER 8

1 Bingham, *Ancestors' Brocades,* p. 9.

2 Bingham, *Ancestors' Brocades,* p. 6.

3 Leyda, *The Years and Hours of Emily Dickinson,* II, 377.

4 Millicent Todd Bingham, *Mabel Loomis Todd: Her Contributions to the Town of Amherst* (privately printed, 1935), p. 5. A photograph described as "Cast of 'The Fair Barbarian,' about 1882" in *Letters,* III, facing p. 779, is actually a picture of the Shutesbury group, taken in the Amherst studio of J. L. Lovell on August 7, 1882.

5 Bingham, *Ancestors' Brocades,* p. 6.

6 *Letters* (1894), II, 433; *Letters* (1931), p. 423.

7 *Letters* (1931), p. 419.

8 Bianchi, *Emily Dickinson Face to Face,* p. 10.

9 Leyda, *The Years and Hours of Emily Dickinson,* II, 240.

Notes

10 Bianchi, *Emily Dickinson Face to Face*, pp. 66–67.

11 For no apparent reason, Martha Dickinson Bianchi altered this note when she published it in *Emily Dickinson Face to Face*, p. 169: "Sometimes [Ned] made a note of what she said. Among these is one dated March 7, 1883: 'Aunt Emily, speaking of someone who was a good scholar but uninteresting, said, "She has the facts but not the phosphorescence of learning" '—to Emily the most abhorrent of qualifications!"

12 See Whicher, *This Was a Poet*, pp. 311, 315.

13 Bianchi, *Emily Dickinson Face to Face*, p. 172.

14 Leyda, *The Years and Hours of Emily Dickinson*, II, 406.

15 Leyda, *The Years and Hours of Emily Dickinson*, II, 411.

16 Bingham, *Ancestors' Brocades*, p. 10.

17 *Poems*, III, 1120, 1100.

18 Merriam, *Life and Times of Samuel Bowles*, II, 419n.

19 Merriam, *Life and Times of Samuel Bowles*, II, 426.

20 *"Warrington" Pen-Portraits: A Collection of Personal and Political Reminiscences, from 1848 to 1876, from the Writings of William S. Robinson*. Edited by Mrs. W. S. Robinson (Boston and New York, 1877), pp. 287–88. See also Leyda, *The Years and Hours of Emily Dickinson*, II, 17.

21 Robinson, *"Warrington" Pen-Portraits*, p. 457.

22 This passage is the only direct reference to Bowles in all the letters to Louisa and Frances Norcross, who allowed nothing "too personal" to appear in print.

23 *Poems*, II, 404.

24 With the exception of the words in parentheses, I have omitted from these prose fragments Emily Dickinson's alternate phrasing, and words which she crossed out.

25 Bianchi, *Emily Dickinson Face to Face*, pp. 37–38.

26 Leyda, *The Years and Hours of Emily Dickinson*, II, 422. The text derives from a transcript by Mrs. William P. Cresson. The capitalization in the poem suggests that this is a more accurate transcript than the one, also by Mrs. Cresson, which appears in *Letters*, III, 822.

27 Bingham, *Emily Dickinson: A Revelation*, p. 66.

28 *Poems*, I, lviii–lix.

29 *Poems*, II, 492–93.

30 Leyda, *The Years and Hours of Emily Dickinson*, II, 471.

31 Bingham, *Ancestors' Brocades*, p. 72.

32 Bingham, *Ancestors' Brocades*, p. 84.

Index

Adams, Sydney, 62
Allen, Charles, 113, 115
Amherst Academy, 51–53, 77–78
Amherst College, 10, 30–31, 35, 57, 64, 89, 101, 103, 125, 159, 163, 164–165, 171, 173, 180, 196, 205
Amherst Collegiate Magazine, 66
Amherst Record, 177
Atlantic Monthly, 130, 131, 132, 134, 135

Banfield, Ann Fiske (Mrs. Everett Banfield), 174
Bangs, Mrs., 152
Banks, Governor Nathaniel P., 101, 102
Banks, Mrs., 101, 102
Beecher, the Rev. Henry Ward, 12, 13, 37

Bianchi, Martha Dickinson (niece), 37, 81, 96, 178, 180, 198, 200, 202, 219–222, 224, 226, 239, 248, 253, 255, 256, 257, 258, 259
Bible, 23, 46, 48, 71, 136, 140, 221, 232
Bingham, Millicent Todd, 28, 48, 55, 83, 116, 195, 216, 218–219, 246–247, 248, 250, 251, 252, 254, 255, 256, 257, 258, 259
Bliss, the Rev. Daniel, 34
Bismarck, Otto von, 110
Blake, William, 220
Boltwood, Mrs. Lucius, 13
Bowles, Charles, 115, 123
Bowles, Mary (Mrs. Samuel Bowles), 24, 89, 90–93, 98, 99–100, 114–116, 123, 124–125, 127, 128, 149, 190–193, 231–232

Bowles, Samuel, 12, 13, 14, 16, 19–22, 24, 47, 48, 49, 56, 64, 67–68, 69, 72, 83, 84, 87, 89, 90–93, 96, 98, 99–100, 101–102, 104, 106–109, 113–128, 129, 130, 132, 133, 134, 139–149, 152, 153–156, 160, 161, 162, 163, 170–171, 173–174, 183, 184, 187–194, 200, 201, 202, 205, 209, 230–232, 243–244, 245, 251

Bowles, Samuel (the younger), 24, 177, 207, 232, 239, 242

Brontë, Charlotte, 131

Brontë, Emily, 226

Brooks, Phillips, 181

Browne, Sir Thomas, 136

Browning, Elizabeth Barrett, 136, 173, 253

Browning, Robert, 136

Burgess, John W., 179

Burnett, Frances Hodgson, 215

Byron, George Gordon, Lord, 118

Calvinism, 46, 50, 60, 208

Carter, Mr., 40

Channing, Ellery, 13

Channing, William Ellery, 13

Chapman, Judge Reuben, 94

Chickering, Joseph K., 87, 203, 218, 238

Civil War, 89, 116, 125–126, 133, 144, 149, 155, 159

Clark, Charles, 81, 82, 116, 204–205, 206, 208, 209, 210, 226, 228, 229, 243

Clark, James, 81, 100, 116, 184, 204, 205, 207–209, 210, 229, 243

Coleman, Eliza. *See* Dudley, Eliza Coleman

Concord Monitor, 75

Cowley, Malcolm, 88

Crowell, Mary Warner, 19

Denniston, Dr. E. E., 113, 132

Dickens, Charles, 113

Dickinson, Austin. *See* Dickinson, William Austin

Dickinson, Edward (father), 13, 25, 27–28, 30, 31–35, 41, 43, 44, 47, 49, 61, 68, 70, 71, 80, 89, 91, 101, 102, 111, 137, 151, 158, 159, 165, 171, 177–178, 181–182, 183–186, 187, 188, 194, 195, 196, 198, 200, 202, 205, 211, 212, 213, 220, 231, 233, 241, 246

Dickinson, Edward (nephew), 110, 111, 143, 181, 198, 199, 201, 214, 220–222, 233

Dickinson, Mrs. Edward (mother), 26–28, 30–31, 33, 34, 41, 43, 44, 71, 87, 91, 137, 150, 158, 159, 164, 186, 187, 197, 211–213, 224, 232, 233–234

Dickinson, Elisabeth (aunt), 26–28, 151, 244

Dickinson, Emily:
"ecstatic moments," 87–88, 95, 161
girlhood and schooling, 23, 25–29, 51–53; *see also* Amherst Academy; Mount Holyoke Female Seminary
illnesses, 44, 53–55, 225–228, 240–241, 244–245
legend of, 12, 24, 62
love poems, 16, 17, 20–21, 48–49, 81, 86–89, 99, 104–108, 116, 118, 119, 120, 121, 126, 138–139, 141, 153, 154, 155, 156, 160, 170, 174, 180, 244
marriage poems, 22, 40, 121
religious thought, 9, 43, 45–50, 57–60, 63, 76, 81, 82, 98, 100, 108, 114–115, 137, 183, 221
romanticism, 38–39, 76, 78, 220

seclusion from world, 5, 6,
12, 13, 30, 60, 67, 81,
87–88, 91, 94, 134, 138,
144–145, 147, 153, 158–
182, 189, 195–197, 202,
217–218, 223, 232–233,
238, 240
sentimentalism, 38, 40, 72–
76, 85, 94
wit, 16, 26, 31–32, 45, 48–
49, 52–53, 94, 102, 148,
164, 198, 211, 236–238,
240
Dickinson, Gilbert. *See* Dickinson, Thomas Gilbert
Dickinson, Lavinia (sister),
13, 15, 23, 26–28, 29–30,
31, 32–33, 34, 35, 36, 37,
38, 41, 44, 45, 58, 59, 67,
68, 70, 80, 81, 87, 90, 93,
94, 95, 96–97, 100, 111,
125, 127, 137, 140, 144–
145, 150, 152, 153, 155,
158, 159, 162, 164, 178–
180, 182, 185, 186, 187,
190, 199, 200–201, 202,
203, 206, 210, 211, 214,
215, 217, 218, 220, 222–
224, 227, 231, 232, 233–
234, 241, 244, 246, 247,
253, 257
Dickinson, Loring (uncle), 61
Dickinson, Lovina, 40
Dickinson, Martha. *See* Bianchi, Martha Dickinson
Dickinson, Samuel Fowler
(grandfather), 35
Dickinson, Susan Gilbert
(Mrs. William Austin
Dickinson), 11, 16, 29,
30, 32, 36–43, 63–64, 70,
72–73, 74, 79, 80, 89, 90,
91, 94, 96, 102, 108,
110–112, 124, 126, 132,
133, 134, 135, 143, 148–
149, 155, 162, 163, 165,
178–180, 185, 190, 198–
202, 215, 221–223, 225–
227, 230, 232, 237, 238,
241, 248

Dickinson, Thomas Gilbert
(nephew), 84, 152, 200,
222–228, 233, 237, 238,
241
Dickinson, William Austin
(brother), 13, 26–28, 29–
30, 31, 32, 33, 34, 35, 36,
37–38, 40–43, 44, 47, 48,
52, 58, 62, 64, 67, 69–
70, 75, 81, 89, 90, 94, 95,
96, 108, 111, 112, 113,
118–119, 124, 125–126,
127, 128, 137, 139, 141,
144–145, 147–149, 154,
155, 158, 159, 165–166,
171, 173, 178, 179, 181,
182, 184–185, 186, 190,
198, 200–201, 203, 210,
211, 215, 217, 218, 220–
227, 230, 232, 241, 244,
245, 247, 253
Dickinson, William H.
(cousin), 34, 90, 238–239
Dudley, Eliza Coleman, 66,
80, 103, 168–169, 184
Dudley, the Rev. John, 103,
168–169
Dwight, Mrs. Edward, 17, 123,
133, 184
Dwight, the Rev. Edward, 17,
90, 119, 123, 184

Eliot, George, 173
Emerson, Kendall, 225, 227
Emerson, Ralph Waldo, 3, 12–
13, 37, 61, 72, 74–75, 97,
204
Emmons, Henry Vaughan, 10–
11, 64–67, 70, 89, 122

Farley, Abby, 199–200, 203
Farley, Mary, 199
Fay, Mrs. Samuel (aunt), 35,
36
Fields, James T., 131
Fiske, Ann. *See* Banfield, Ann
Fiske
Fiske, Helen. *See* Jackson,
Helen Hunt
Flynt, Eudocia (cousin), 240

Ford, Emily Fowler, 13–14,
  29, 53, 60, 71, 90
Fowler, Professor, 30–31
Fowler, Emily. *See* Ford,
  Emily Fowler
French, Daniel Chester, 14,
  240
Fry, Mrs., 101

Gilbert, Frank, 42
Gilbert, Martha, 40–41
Gilbert, Susan. *See* Dickinson,
  Susan Gilbert
Gould, George, 62
Graves, John (cousin), 11, 64,
  65, 66–67, 89
Graves, Louise, 66

Hale, Edward Everett, 78, 181,
  184
Hall, Eugenia (cousin), 239
Harrington, Brainerat, 34
Harvard, John, 240
Haven, Mrs. Joseph, 11, 90,
  91, 93
Hawthorne, Nathaniel, 75
Higginson, Louisa, 217
Higginson, Mary Thacher
  (Mrs. Thomas Went-
  worth Higginson, second
  wife), 22, 166, 180, 212
Higginson, Colonel Thomas
  Wentworth, 3, 5, 11, 12,
  13, 14, 15, 16, 17, 19, 22,
  23, 25, 47, 49, 65, 69, 72,
  74, 78, 79, 82, 84, 87, 90,
  110, 119, 129–138, 142,
  143–144, 149, 152, 156,
  158, 159, 161, 162, 163,
  165–167, 173, 174, 175,
  176, 180–181, 185, 186,
  190, 196, 207, 208, 209,
  212, 217, 235, 238, 242,
  244, 245, 255
Higginson, Mrs. Thomas
  Wentworth (first wife),
  3, 13, 49
Hills, Henry, 200, 227
Hills, Mrs. Henry, 200, 227,
  239

Hitchcock, Edward, 45
Hoar, Judge E. R., 239
Hoar, Mrs. E. R., 239
Hoar, Elizabeth, 232, 239
Holland, Annie, 16, 69, 165
Holland, Elizabeth (Mrs.
  Josiah G. Holland), 12,
  15, 16, 64, 67–70, 72, 81,
  89, 94, 95, 96, 110, 141,
  155, 156, 160, 163–164,
  165, 178, 182, 183, 186,
  190, 201, 202, 209, 210,
  211, 212, 222, 225, 226,
  228, 237, 258
Holland, Josiah G., 13, 16,
  67–70, 72, 82, 89, 96,
  119, 133, 165, 171, 173,
  201, 202, 203, 222
Holland, Sophia, 56
Holland, Theodore, 69, 237
Howells, William Dean, 13,
  159–160, 201
Humphrey, Jane, 51, 59, 61,
  62, 63
Humphrey, Leonard, 77–78
Hunt, Lieut. Edward, 173
Hunt, Helen Fiske. *See* Jackson, Helen Hunt

Indicator (Amherst College),
  10

Jackson, Helen Hunt (Mrs.
  William S. Jackson), 5–6,
  7–9, 12–13, 14, 15, 22–
  23, 172–177, 193, 207,
  208, 240–241, 242–243
Jackson, William S., 22–23,
  175, 193, 242
James, William, 88
Jameson, Mrs. John, 30, 226
Jenkins, Mrs. Jonathan L.,
  200, 220, 227
Jenkins, the Rev. Jonathan L.,
  200, 212, 227
Jenkins, MacGregor, 220
Johnson, Thomas H., 72, 80
Jones, Mr., 26–27

Keats, John, 136

Kelley, Tom, 203, 218
Kimball, Benjamin, 84, 229,
    241–242, 252

Leland, the Rev. Martin, 32
Linnell, Tempe, 62
Lincoln, Abraham, 153
Loomis, Eben J., 8, 13, 240
Loomis, Mrs. Eben J., 240
Lord, Elizabeth Farley (Mrs.
    Otis Phillips Lord), 186,
    190, 194, 199,
Lord, Judge Otis Phillips, 9,
    12, 13, 14, 49, 81, 84, 90,
    123, 151–152, 160, 184–
    186, 194–204, 209, 210,
    218, 228–229, 231, 233,
    237, 241, 244
Lyon, Mary, 43, 45, 46, 48,
    50, 59

Mack, Deacon David, 75
Maher, Maggie, 166, 182, 217,
    218, 224, 233, 241
Marvel, Ik. *See* Mitchell,
    Donald G.
"Master," 16, 19–22, 47, 49,
    64, 81, 84, 85, 99, 103–
    107, 115, 119, 121–123,
    126, 138, 139, 140–141,
    146, 151, 156, 160, 166,
    170, 173, 195, 209, 244
Mather, Cotton, 46
Melville, Herman, 151
Merriam, George S., 68, 108,
    160, 189, 230, 251, 252,
    253, 254
Mitchell, Donald G., 73–74
Mount Holyoke Female Sem-
    inary, 43–46, 48, 55, 58,
    61

New England, 13, 23, 30, 46,
    54, 60, 61, 108, 155, 159,
    160, 167
Newman, Anna (cousin), 35–
    36, 111, 153
Newman, Clara (cousin), 35–
    36, 111

Newman, Mrs. Mark (aunt),
    35
Newton, Benjamin Franklin,
    56, 61–62, 64, 72, 74,
    78–79, 132, 133, 184, 204
Nightingale, Florence, 102
Niles, Thomas, 14, 242
Norcross, Emily (cousin), 44
Norcross, Frances (cousin),
    12, 14, 19, 69, 75–76,
    89–90, 98, 101, 103, 112,
    125, 142, 150–152, 155,
    165, 168–170, 177–178,
    181, 182, 184, 186, 209,
    212, 213, 224, 228, 231,
    233, 235–236, 241, 244,
    247
Norcross, Joel (uncle), 10, 53,
    61, 150
Norcross, Lavinia (aunt), 26,
    61, 93, 100, 150
Norcross, Louise, Louisa
    (cousin), 12, 14, 19, 89–
    90, 98, 101, 103, 112,
    125, 142, 150–152, 155,
    165, 167–170, 177–178,
    181, 182, 184, 186, 209,
    212, 213, 224, 228, 231,
    233, 235–236, 241, 244

Parker, Theodore, 72, 98
Phelps, Elizabeth Stuart, 14–
    15
Poe, Edgar Allan, 65, 72

Robinson, W. S., 230–231
Root, Abiah, 27, 28, 44, 45,
    46, 48, 51, 52, 53, 56, 58,
    59, 63, 67, 77
Ruskin, John, 136

Sanborn, Franklin B., 13, 75
Scannell, Dennis, 221
Scott, Kate, 90, 94–96, 122
Scribner's Monthly Magazine,
    13, 171, 201, 202–203
Shakespeare, William, 23, 71
Smith, Adam, 30–31
Smith, James, 34
Smith, Roswell, 203, 238

Smith, Thankful, 34
Southey, Robert, 131
Springfield Republican, 12, 67, 72, 75, 101, 108, 121, 124, 130, 134, 139, 155, 156, 162, 177, 230, 242
Springfield Union, 176–177
Stearns, Frazar, 125–126
Sweetser, Catharine (aunt), 13, 185–186, 228
Sweetser, Joseph (uncle), 91
Sweetser, Mrs. J. Howard, 36, 239
Sweetser, Mrs. Luke, 40

Tennyson, Alfred, Lord, 18
Thacher, Mary P. *See* Higginson, Mary Thacher
Thompson, Joseph P., 103
Thoreau, Henry David, 13, 48, 72, 75–76, 160, 161
Thurston, Mr., 34
Todd, David, 23, 199, 202, 214, 215, 227
Todd, Mabel Loomis (Mrs. David Todd), 5, 13, 15, 23, 25, 75, 81, 146, 150, 159–160, 167–168, 173, 180, 192–193, 199, 202, 203, 210, 211, 214–218, 227, 235, 240, 245, 247,

248, 251, 252, 253, 254, 255, 258
Todd, Millicent. *See* Bingham, Millicent Todd
Tuckerman, Mrs. Edward, 239

Wadsworth, the Rev. Charles, 12, 25, 79–84, 90, 100, 115, 116, 118, 121, 123, 125, 133, 139, 140, 152, 156, 170, 180, 183, 184, 190, 203–211, 233, 243, 252
Ward, Theodora Van Wagenen, 69, 80, 251, 254, 256
Washburn, Emily, 55
Washington Evening Star, 80
Webster, Noah, 14
Whicher, George F., 19, 73, 122–123, 247, 248, 249, 251, 252, 256, 259
Whitman, Miss, 28
Whitman, Walt, 13, 72, 88
Whitney, Maria, 13, 90, 102, 108, 139, 142, 147, 184, 191–194, 205, 213, 228, 229, 232, 243–244
Whitney, William Dwight, 13
The Woman's Journal, 14
Wood, Abby, 59